LEAVING SCONSET

Kathleen Witt Richen

ISBN: 1532705786
ISBN 13: 9781532705786

LEAVING SCONSET

I wrote this novel over ten years ago and it is actually my first. You may notice that some of the Nantucket landmark restaurants spoken of in the book have changed ownership during the intervening years. I find it's a walk down memory lane and for those of you familiar with my beloved home, I hope you enjoy remembering the times you spent at these restaurants.

I want to mention two literary ladies from Nantucket who are no longer with us. Mimi Beman, who owned Mitchell's Book Corner for decades encouraged me to publish Leaving Sconset and I'm happy to report to you, Mimi that it's on its way. Mary Miles edited the story for me and I believe it was one of her final efforts before passing away.

My dear friend and poetess Anne Foye has been a continual source of encouragement and inspiration and I want to thank her for this and for the precious gift of friendship. My children and their spouses and my grandchildren stand by me and I am inspired by their love and devotion. All of you bring so much depth and joy to me.

This book is for my husband Neville Richen, for gifts too numerous and precious to list. As he would say, One Love,

Kathy, 2016

CHAPTER ONE

Camilla stood on the back verandah of Sconset House watching the sun emerge from the mirror-smooth stretch of ocean. Below her cliff top restaurant the fine, cream-colored sand met a sea whose other shore was somewhere in Portugal. A late spring morning this warm and still was a good omen of the type of summer weather everyone on Nantucket and, in particular, Sconset had their fingers crossed hoping for. Everything was ready for the staff to arrive for the twentieth season of the now-famous restaurant. Camilla and her husband, Billy Smith, had dreamed of this success as they worked long, hard years, and now it was one of the finest on the east coast, on an island renowned for its abundance of superb restaurants.

"A perfect start," Camilla mused, then wondered uneasily at the sense of dread that churned in the pit of her stomach. It was as if something was missing, or misplaced, and she couldn't put her finger on what it was.

With a sigh, Camilla unclipped her long chestnut- brown hair and shook it free as she sank into one of the many Adirondack chairs overlooking the crystal blue Atlantic. Once again she went over her mental checklist in an attempt to dispel the ominous feeling that was threatening to ruin one of the days she looked forward to all year. Surf and Turf, the two cottages she and Billy maintained for their staff were aired out and dusted; the beds were made, the refrigerators were stocked and fresh flowers were arranged in vases on the bureau of each room. The telephones had been turned back on. Billy and chef Brandon Gates had written detailed descriptions of all the menu items and were busy preparing each dish for the traditional first meal, a chance for the staff to celebrate the new season and learn first-hand about the dishes they would be serving all summer. A list of the flight arrival times of all the staff members was in her pocket and she had the Explorer all fueled up for the numerous trips she would make to the airport and back. Everything was ready ...and yet, Camilla was anxious and uncertain. This was not like her at all and she did not know how to deal with it.

Grabbing at straws, Camilla decided her unease must have something to do with the imminent gallery opening for her paintings at her close friend Anne Hitchcock's gallery on Old South Wharf. Camilla wove her way through the large dining rooms to the phone at the maitre'd stand and phoned Anne. They arranged to meet for breakfast at Hutch's in the airport while Camilla waited for her first pick up, due in at ten. Not bothering to change from her comfy grey sweat pants and over-sized sweat shirt, she yelled to Billy in the kitchen that she was leaving early and bounded down the front stairs and over the clam shelled walk to the rose colored Explorer with "Sconset House" discreetly lettered in gold on the door. In a moment she was winding from Elbow Lane, whizzing around the rotary and gaining speed on the Milestone Rd.

She knew that her agitation was getting the best of her and eased her foot back on the accelerator, slowing her speed and taking a deep breath. The feeling was still there, but Camilla decided to master it. After all, if it was about a painting, that was something she could surely fix she told herself. Still, a nagging voice in the back of her mind was trying to tell her it was not about the paintings.

Anne, who lived fairly close to the airport, hailed her from a one of the treasured few tables along the bank of windows overlooking the runways. Anne was Camilla's oldest friend on Nantucket and had actually brought her there many years ago to room with her while they spent a season waitressing at the now defunct Opera House Restaurant. Camilla fell in love with the island that summer as Anne, who had summered on island with her family all her life, suspected she would. Camilla complimented her friend's ultra-short new haircut which caused her paprika colored curls to frame her round face perfectly.

"I ordered coffee, Cam," Anne, who had been off-island in New York for a month began and halted after taking a good look at her friend. "What's wrong with you? You look awful." Anne knew as well as anyone how important the restaurant and in particular, the staff was to Camilla. The young people who came back year after year were her family, the children Camilla and Billy were never able to have. Usually, Camilla was sparkling on the day the staff arrived. That was not the case today.

"Oh, Annie, I just don't know what's wrong. I feel like something really bad is about to happen and I want to stop it. And I'm so tired, I don't think I can. I..." stammered Camilla.

"Wait a minute girl," Anne interrupted. "You say you're tired?" Answering Camilla's slow nod with a long look into her eyes, Anne said, "Stand up."

Obeying, Camilla stood and self-consciously arranged her bulky clothes and disheveled hair. Without warning, her eyes filled with tears, which spilled over and began rolling down her cheeks. With a flush, she fell back into her seat and dabbed at her eyes with a napkin.

Taking her friend's free hand, Anne softly whispered, "It's okay, honey. Whatever it is, we'll get it taken care of." When Camilla had collected herself enough to look up with a sheepish grin, Anne continued. "You've lost a lot of weight, Cam. I bet you don't fit into any of your summer clothes. A shopping trip to Newbury Street is just what Dr. Anne recommends. And while we're there, you need to stop in to see Dr. Anderson for a complete physical. Okay?"

"A physical? I'm fine, Annie. I'm just losing it a little bit, that's all. I just..."

"You trust me to broker your paintings, don't you?" asked Anne. At Camilla's nod she continued, "So trust me now. Let Billy take over the restaurant stuff with the staff tomorrow and let's get up to Boston. Dr. Anderson is one of my Dad's golf cronies and I know he'll see you on a moment's notice. I'm serious, Camilla."

With a quick laugh, Camilla said, "I know you're serious when you call me Camilla. But, really, I'm fine. I've been over everything I need to do in my mind a hundred times and I decided that it must be my painting. Is it off this year?"

"Are you *crazy*?" Anne practically screamed. Camilla spent her entire winter each year painting what in some cases were museum quality oils. Art dealers from all over the world had approached her over the years to promote her work, but Camilla sold exclusively through Anne's little gallery in a converted fishing shack which was one of many such galleries in the artist colony on Old South Wharf on Nantucket's picturesque harbor. During the winter Billy traveled extensively with his best friend from college, Dave Collins. Dave was a photographer for *Let's Hike* magazine and every winter the two took off on at least three extended treks all over the world. While Dave shot pictures for the magazine, Billy took pictures for Camilla to paint. It was an arrangement that worked for Camilla and Billy.

"No, I really was afraid that maybe something was wrong with my work. I can't tell. You know how it is," Camilla replied.

"I know you never know, but I think that piece you did looking down from the mountain in Peru through the fog is one of your best ever. I've already been approached by the Guggenheim to let them exhibit it this summer."

"The Guggenheim? I don't think I've had anything there, have I?"

"No." Anne said. "Your work this year is exquisite. Your soul flows through the paint and onto the canvas, Camilla. The paintings are imbued with an essence only you can create. If you were to paint year round, you'd ..."

"Annie, you know I can't paint year round. The restaurant is very important to me. It's the only thing Billy and I do together," Camilla quickly interrupted.

"You and Billy are business partners, Camilla. I know you and he work terrifically well together, but what kind of marriage is that? You know I can't bear being away from John for more than a couple of days at a time. But you're perfectly happy being alone most of the winter. I think your art is the most satisfying thing in your life, Camilla, and you purposely deny yourself the pleasure of it to work in the restaurant. You could hire someone to take your place, Cam. But you can't hire anyone to paint the way you do."

"Stop," Camilla broke in, dabbing away at fresh tears. "You know I can't. I owe Billy, I owe him."

"Stop persecuting yourself because you couldn't have kids. You certainly tried everything. It just wasn't in the cards for you and Billy. Don't give away half of your life each year out of guilt, sweetheart," Anne implored.

"I understand what you're saying, Annie. Really, I do. But you just don't know, you really don't. No one does."

Anne looked at the suffering written all over her dearest friend's features and changed the subject. "So, are you looking forward to meeting the new girl you hired? What's her name, Janine or something?"

"Her name's Jasmine. She seems like a dream. I have her linked with Dotty Kelly for orientation."

"Good idea. Dotty'll show her the ropes right away," Anne said in agreement. The staff at Sconset House had been the same for the past five years, but over the winter Jenny Lewis had married and moved to California, so Camilla had had to find a replacement. Everyone knew that a job at Sconset House was the best summer gig on Nantucket. The Smiths made sure their staff was completely comfortable, giving them housing in their two cottages down on Low Beach and making sure they had everything they needed in order to give full attention to serving their faithful customers. After weeks of telephone interviews, Camilla had hired Jasmine Hunter, a painting restoration expert from the Metropolitan in New York. She had her summers free because her assistants were apprentices from Pratt Institute, so when they were on break, so was she.

Camilla had clicked with Jasmine and reassured her that she would fit in on Nantucket because for many generations, Nantucket had been a fully integrated community. Jasmine had been concerned because she was black. They both decided that Sconset House would be a perfect fit and now she was about to set foot on Nantucket for the first time at two p.m.

The conversation between Camilla and Annie drifted along through breakfast and by the time Anne had to run downtown to open the gallery, Camilla was feeling better and ready to whole heartedly greet Dave Johnson and Jessica Raymond, the first two staff members to arrive.

Anne Hitchcock allowed her concern for Camilla to resurface as soon as she entered her car for the ride into town. She had seen her friend distraught this way only once, and that was when she had first met Camilla and had invited her out to Nantucket for the summer so many years ago. Camilla was suffering over something then that she never spoke to Ann about. And now Camilla was distraught and looked terrible as well.

Ann's first task when she opened the gallery was to phone her tennis partner and friend, Dr. Mary Carver. When she told Mary about her visit with Camilla, Mary's first response was that maybe Camilla was finally beginning to yearn for something deeper than what she had with Billy. Ann told her she thought it was physical and wanted Mary to see for herself.

They planned to dine together with their husbands at the opening night preview of Sconset House, just two days away. Mary promised that if she suspected anything was seriously amiss with Camilla, she'd discreetly ask her to stop by the office for tests.

Feeling somewhat relieved, Anne stood in the center of her shanty gallery and allowed her eyes to roam from painting to painting. The majesty of Camilla's work touched her deeply. Again, she was in awe of this woman who simply delivered a year's worth of work to her door and trusted her implicitly to promote and sell it. Camilla's work had created wealth for both of them. She knew that Camilla did not need any income from Sconset House in order to live well. It wasn't money that kept her devoted to Billy, and she was pretty sure it wasn't love. Camilla was certainly fond of Billy and they seemed happy enough together, but the passion that flowed from Camilla into her work was nowhere to be seen when she was with Billy. Camilla's relationship with Billy had always been an enigma to her. "Why, Camilla, *why*?" she muttered out loud.

CHAPTER TWO

All day long Camilla picked up the members of her staff as they arrived at the airport. In each case, it was a long overdue homecoming. Her husband Billy had mixed feelings about his wife's strong connection to her staff, but in his heart he knew that these young people were filling a void in her life and he stood back quite a bit so that she was able to enjoy their company each season.

By four o'clock everyone had arrived and amid hugs, kisses, and shrieks of glee, Camilla left Surf and Turf to return to the restaurant and help with the final preparations for the first meal. As the day progressed, she had felt better and better. Her sense of dread retreated to the back of her mind where it rested for a moment. "Just a case of nerves," she told herself

The staff of Sconset House was the envy of all the veteran restaurant people on Nantucket, because they had no housekeeping chores and were given lovely accomodations overlooking the ocean. The

staff was loyal and professional, just what Camilla wanted. The most senior waiter was Jared Miles, from Manhattan. During the off-season Jared worked for a caterer in the city. It was a great job for him because he could choose when he wanted to work, which allowed him to create his line of women's hats. They were very exclusive and people had to deal directly with him to have one custom made. The waiting time for a *Hat by Jared* was a month or so during the winter. He always shipped his machine and a carton of materials to Nantucket so that he could work during the day on his long list of orders. Jared also brought along Prescott Taylor, his lover of many years.

Prescott was not able to arrive until the last week of July and had to depart on Labor Day. He was a drama critic for the *New York Times* and enjoyed every minute of his summer hiatus with Jared at Sconset House. He was also one of Camilla's closest friends. While in Sconset, he worked with Camilla at the maitre'd stand and was a distinguished and entertaining host. When Prescott arrived, he and Jared moved into Crow's Nest, the guest quarters on the second story of the restaurant and Jared left his room at Surf set up as a workshop. The arrangement was perfect.

Dave Johnson was an All-American boy. He hailed from Ohio where he had been a football star at Ohio State. Despite his parents' wishes that he settle down to a "legitimate" career, Dave loved working as a waiter. After all, he made good money and had his days free to hang out to his heart's content on the various beaches of Nantucket. In the winter, he did the same thing in Key West. Needless to say, this tall sandy-haired guy had an adoring circle of female companions whom he enjoyed completely. Over the past few years, a young lady now and then had her feathers ruffled by him had to be handled by Camilla, but other than that, Dave was an enthusiastic and important member of the staff.

Jeffrey Tompkins was a different type altogether. No one was quite certain just how old he was, and Camilla never divulged private details, but he was old enough to have two grown children in their late twenties who came out to visit their dad on and off during the summer. Jeffrey had lost his wife to cancer six years ago could not bear to vacation in their old favorite Martha's Vineyard. So he chose Nantucket for his first widowed vacation and rented a cottage near Surf and Turf. His winter job was in the banquet department of the Plaza Hotel and as a professional waiter he found himself enjoying the high standard of food and service at Sconset House. He and Camilla had spent several lovely afternoons on the verandah sipping iced tea and trading business anecdotes, and before he left that first year, he had made arrangements to waiter the following season for Sconset House. Working, he found, made the summer go more easily. Jeffrey was somewhat withdrawn (except when his children arrived) but was a father figure on the staff. And the New York crowd loved him. Seasoned guests would often lean over and confide to their new-comer friends that "He's from the Plaza, you know."

The final male Sconset staff member was Brian Folger, a Nantucket native. Brian grew up on the waitstaff at almost every restaurant downtown during his high school and college days. When he returned to build houses during the off-season with his father some years ago, he had re-built the verandah for Camilla and Billy. He and Billy became pals and met for drinks at the Atlantic Café on those long winter evenings when Billy was home between treks. Five years ago, a waiter had begun to succumb to AIDS halfway through the season and a frantic Camilla asked Billy to have Brian come in to pinch hit. Brian said that that was the day he came home to his second family, meaning Sconset House. Brian spent a lot of time with Camilla during her lonely winter spells. The years that Billy was away during holidays Brian had invited her to share Thanksgiving and Christmas with his family. He was the closest thing to a son that Billy and Camilla had and they loved him as if he were their own. Even though Brian owned his own home out in Madaket, he opted to let his two sisters enjoy it with their families during the summer so he could move into Surf each season and be a true member of the team.

The four men of Sconset House were balanced by four women. Dottie Kelly was the spirit of the clan. She was one of those petite women with enough energy to power a rocket. "Slow down, Dottie!" was the only criticism she ever received from Camilla. Dottie had been divorced six years ago and allowed her ten-year-old daughter to summer with family in her hometown Camden, Maine. She bought a house up there a few years ago and began making pottery during the winter. Getting ready to stock the shop shelves for summer with her now-famous sets of bowls, plates and mugs kept her pretty busy all winter, and the chance to move around and mingle with folks at Sconset House made her life complete. Although she vowed to never marry again, her pledge didn't mean that she wouldn't date, and she probably had the busiest social life in Sconset. Camilla was looking forward to Dottie's delivery of a new set of special strawberry shortcake bowls she'd designed and made for Sconset House last winter and she hoped Dottie's bubbly spirit would make the new waitress, Jasmine, feel at home right away.

Jessica Raymond brought elegance and grace to Sconset House. No one knew too much about her except that she wrote free-lance for several magazines and lived on the upper west side. While Jessica kept her personal life to herself, when it came to the other staff members she always had support and words of wisdom to offer those in need. She was the one sought out when the stress of high season threatened to fray nerves and set off disputes. Her long legs gave her the appearance of gliding through the dining room and her smooth, efficient service produced a long list of devoted customers. Many a night the reservation list would note next to a name "requests Jessica."

Maeve O'Connor had washed up on Nantucket's shores from Ireland about ten years ago. She was at the leading edge of a large group of young Irish men and women who found that Nantucket felt enough like home to relocate there. The financial rewards far outweighed the possibilities for the well educated Irish back home, which led to a large, tight-knit Irish community on-island. Maeve had obtained a green card some years ago, which allowed her the opportunity to travel home to Ireland and re-enter the States without worry. Down to earth and hard working, Maeve was the backbone of the staff. And yet her lilting accent and subtle sense of fun lent the appearance of a more light-hearted spirit. Over the years she had studied painting with Camilla and then went on to study at the Museum School of the Museum of Fine Arts in Boston, Camilla's old alma mater. For the last three years she had painted in Ireland and had her work represented by a fine gallery in Dublin. She was known there as Camilla's protégé.

Camilla let out a sigh of relief that everyone was in their place. Jasmine was on Dottie's arm saying her first hellos and gleaning personal bits about everyone that Dottie was whispering in her ear. Camilla, who had only spoken to Jasmine on the phone, was dazzled by her beauty. Long, wavy locks were gathered in a smooth French twist which accented her slightly slanted almond-shaped eyes. Tall and slim, she possessed an elegance and calm smile that would serve her well at Sconset House. She reminded Camilla of someone, but she couldn't put her finger on who it was.

Dinner was announced for six sharp and the staff was preparing to don their best outfits for what had evolved into a formal event. Traditionally, Billy presided over the evening in a tux. Everyone loved dressing up, since the season's uniforms, which would be distributed tonight, would become the new outfit for the foreseeable future. Rumor had it that the black tuxedo pants and white tuxedo shirts of the past two years had been replaced with a new ensemble, and everyone was eager to see what Camilla had up her sleeve.

At five-thirty the eight wait staff members gathered on Low Beach Road in front of Surf and Turf and began their first stroll together through Sconset to their destination on Elbow Lane. As they all knew, the trip could be hurried through in ten minutes, but tonight a leisurely pace would do just fine, and, of course, they had to stop in at The Sconset Market, the only spot to get provisions in the tiny village, and gossip.

Camilla and Billy stood arm in arm on the front porch. In keeping with the look of most buildings on Nantucket, Sconset House was all weathered grey shingles with the traditional dusty pink Nantucket Ramblin' Roses of Sconset virtually covering the front of the two story building and up onto the trellised roof. All the trim was sparkling white. Even though the roses wouldn't begin to bloom until late June, the foliage was green and the front windowboxes were filled with azalea colored geraniums surrounded by clouds of sweet white alyssum. The walkways leading from the parking lot and the street were paved with crushed white clamshells. In all, Sconset House looked like a pretty fairy tale and the waitstaff greeted the Smiths with compliments on how nice everything looked this year.

The inside of Sconset House was divided into three dining rooms. The main dining room, the one you entered first, was The Chester Smith Room, named after Billy's grandfather, from whom he inherited the property. It was usually referred to as The Main. Two smaller rooms on either side of a long hallway that led to the verandah were called The Lily and the Rose Rooms, named after the flowers which decorated their respective tables. Each of these opened onto the verandah and served as a wonderfully private setting for small weddings, anniversaries, birthdays and the like. Tonight, the staff was ushered into the Rose Room, where a winebar and buffet table stood before the windowed wall overlooking the verandah and the ocean.

Camilla had employed Mrs. Camden of Sconset to keep house at the restaurant ever since their first season. This year she had her granddaughter Diana working with her, and the restaurant was already at its impeccable standard of cleanliness. Again, Mrs. Camden was like family, and Camilla never made any decorative changes in any of the rooms without first consulting her and oftentimes taking her advice.

The Rose Room was painted creamy white with a border of hand-painted rambling roses at the top of the wall. Dusty rose tablecloths with white lace over cloths and crystal candleholders adorned each table. Light from the white candles flickered on cut crystal glasses and bounced off the crystal globes of the wrought iron hanging light fixtures. The staff took their places and Billy made the rounds pouring champagne into each glass. Following the toast for a prosperous season, Camilla made her usual speech about schedules and the everyday running of the restaurant. She couldn't help noticing that Jasmine never took her eyes off of her, and she made a mental note to see if everything was okay. Her next task was to distribute the new season's uniforms. This was the one item of the evening she was a little nervous about. She'd never get over the fuss the staff made about wearing Hawaiian shirts four years ago. They had been packed away by July first and the waitstaff happily re-donned the tux ensemble. Camilla was still using the Hawaiian shirts as painting garb during the winter.

This year she had ordered collar-less white piqué shirts from a trendy men's clothing store downtown. The shirts were paired with Nantucket red trousers for the men and trim knee-length skirts for the women made of the same tomato bisque hue fondly known as Nantucket Red. Matching red espadrilles with a short wedge had been custom made for the women and white boat sneakers were in store for the men. As she passed out the uniforms, Camilla explained that these outfits were for regular service and the black and white tux ensembles would be worn for weddings and other private events.

Camilla noticed she was holding her breath as the group unfolded the new clothes and stood up to hold them out and mock model the uniforms. All were silent. Just as Camilla let out a big sigh, Maeve O'Connor exclaimed, "Brilliant! These are brilliant, Camilla!"

Jeffrey Tomkins continued the praise. "This is a perfect Sconset look. I always thought we were a bit overdressed for the consciously rumpled Brooks Brothers crowd we serve. Congratulations, Madam."

The others began to talk among themselves, smiling and nodding at Camilla. Dottie ran up to her with a hug and planted a kiss on Camilla's cheek. Everyone knew how much Dottie hated ironing the pleats on her tux shirt. "Thanks, Camilla," smiled Brian. "A season free of starched pleat complaints from Dottie." Everyone applauded.

Now Camilla stepped back to a seat at a vacant table to the side. Billy took over along with chef Brandon Gates. The two sous-chefs, Raul Fernandes and John Brooks began to tote examples of each dish from the menu out to the buffet table for a rundown on the items from Billy and Brandon. The waitstaff gathered around and after a quick and succinct explanation of each item, everyone took a plate and sampled the meals. To say the least, it was a feast. As the meal progressed, a free forum of comments and ideas surged amongst the wait and kitchen staff. It was the democracy of Sconset House in action with everyone feeling comfortable with praise as well as criticism of the dishes.

Camilla sipped a glass of chianti and simply observed her people reconnecting and making an effort to include Jasmine. Her sense of contentment was overshadowed by the blanket of weariness that was settling down over her. Camilla's high level of energy had always been a matter of pride with her. While others were dragging at the end of an evening, she was usually still chipper and ready for a bit of fun. Tonight she had the thought that perhaps she wouldn't make it through the season without more help. This desperate feeling brought a sob to her throat, which she was glad no one noticed. With a wave and a kiss blown to everyone, Camilla said her good evening and made her way to the Explorer and the quick trip to their home, nearby on Baxter Rd. She left lights on for Billy and headed straight for bed.

CHAPTER THREE

Sunrise the next morning found Camilla waiting for her coffee to drip while she poured out her bowl of cornflakes. A gentle tap at the kitchen door startled her at first and then a smile began as she walked to the door to greet Jared Miles.

"Mornin', Lovey," Jared crooned as he entered the room and took Camilla, who matched his five foot nine frame, in his arms. After a long, hard embrace, Jared pushed Camilla back and said, "A bit boney there, girl. What's up?"

"Nothing. Nothing at all, I think...Well, Annie wants me to go see her favorite specialist in Boston today. But, I'm okay. Just a little run down is all, I guess."

"Camilla, you know I love you as much as a man of my persuasion can love a woman. You know I'd kick Billy's can out of the way in a flash if I could and marry you. You know that, don't you?"

"I know, Jared.... Okay, what do you think?" asked Camilla.

"Well, first of all, I want to tell you how much I've been waiting to have our little morning rendez-vous. You know, nothing beats a bowl of corn flakes with you to start the day off right! Camilla, cornflakes and sunrise: any man's dream."

They chuckled together as they sat down at the little kitchen table in the bay window and spent a moment inhaling their coffee and gazing at the sun. Without taking his eyes off the sunrise, Jared said, "Something is wrong with you, Lovey. You're way too thin, you have deep circles under your eyes, your skin is as white as snow and your hair has lost its lustre." Touching her hand and looking her in the eye as she turned her gaze to him, he continued, "I was shocked when I saw you at the airport. I had to get myself calmed down a bit so I waited until now to bring it up. How do you feel? And don't lie to me. You were gone by seven last night and I'd wager you went straight to bed. Right?"

"Right. I guess something is going on. It's more like a sense of dread. I feel like I've lost something and I can't find it and it's taking all my energy to try to find it....Does that make any sense?"

"Yes. I guess"

"I was working really hard to finish up my last painting before I had to open the restaurant. So I skipped some meals, and I've been blaming that on how I feel and look. It kind of scared me, though, when Annie was concerned, and now you're making me even more worried."

"That's not what I intended. But I'm going to make sure you find out what's wrong. Okay?"

"Okay."

"That's all I'm going to say about it for now. So, you had a productive winter?" asked Jared.

"Great. Best ever. Annie says the Guggenheim wants to show one of my paintings. Let's go down to the gallery later this morning." Camilla's eyes began to light up at the prospect of sharing her winter's work with Jared. "How's Prescott?"

"Just fine. And I have a surprise for you. He left last night for a month reviewing shows in London and in return for that bit of drudgery, he has July and August off this summer. Isn't that great?"

"You mean he'll be here two months?"

"He lands in New York June thirtieth and leaves for Sconset House July 1. He hoped you'd be pleased."

"I was wondering last night how I'd make it through the season, and now this. I'm thrilled. Tell him I'm thrilled, Jared. And please don't worry him until I find out what's wrong. I promise I'll do something next week. Just let me get the restaurant opened and then I'll go see Annie's Dr. Anderson. Deal?"

"Deal. I just want to know one thing, Lovey. Hasn't Billy said anything to you? Isn't he worried about you?"

"When Billy looks at me, he sees something else, I'm not sure what, but something else. No, he hasn't noticed. He's so wrapped up in his own world I don't think he'd notice if I shaved my head."

"Really?"

"Really."

Laughter bubbled through the kitchen as the sun began to cast a serious glow on the two at the table. "It's good to be home," sighed Jared.

"So, what do you think of the new girl?"

"Classy," was Jared's quick response. "If Dottie doesn't scare her off, I think she'll fit in okay. I did notice, though, that she can't seem to take her eyes off you. Did you catch that?"

"I did. And I thought it might be a bit of hero worship or something. She's in museum restoration and seemed to know a lot about my work when I interviewed her on the phone. Maybe you should spend some time with her. Tell you what, I'll pair her up with you for the opening preview tonight."

"Great idea. The usual crowd coming?"

"You know it. They're the backbone of our clientele during the shoulder season, so I shouldn't complain, but I'm really looking forward to old age so I can spend my time painting year round.

I'm dying to be a total recluse. You know what I mean?" Camilla asked.

"Exactly. No more kissing butts. But seriously, Camilla, you *should* be painting year round. I swear that you would except you love your staff so much you can't bear to spend the summer without us, right?"

"That's true. And I need to do this with Billy. It's what we do together."

"Yeah...Hey, check out Jeffrey and Jessica. I think something's been going on there this past winter. She full of smiles and did you notice the new do? And I'm almost positive he's colored his hair. Lovey, the grey is gone and that head had snow on it! They're being discreet about it, but I'll wager he's doing her or getting ready to."

"What a way to phrase it. Hmm, wouldn't that be interesting. We haven't had a romance here since Johnny Parker got Wendy Cassidy pregnant about seven years ago. Remember?"

"I remember round the clock morning sickness starting in August. You had to fill in for her one night, as I recall. They actually got married, didn't they?" chuckled Jared.

"Married with three children. They send me a photo at Christmas each year. I think Wendy still feels guilty. I must have really given her a hard time. Oh well, let's hope Jeffrey and Jessica use precautions if they start 'doing' each other... I can't believe I said that. Oh Jared, you bring out the worst in me and I love it!"

After Jared left, Camilla eased into her sweats and began her morning walk on the beach. Weather permitting, she took her exercise each morning and returned to a second cup of coffee with Billy. It was their planning time, and the unspoken rule was that no one expected to see them between eight and ten. The sun seemed a bit too hot this morning and instead of walking, Camilla found a comfortable spot to sit in the warm sun with her back against a big old worn rock. She just relaxed and let her mind roam, and it soon returned to her first summer on Nantucket, a time she did not allow herself to think of often. But today, she couldn't seem to keep the old memories away. Maybe it was because the new girl Jasmine was beginning her Nantucket experience and it took Camilla back to hers.

Camilla spent her first year after art school working in an avante garde gallery in Harvard Square. It was 1973 and the art scene was really wild. The strange groups of people represented by the gallery and the eclectic group of customers distracted Camilla from the heart break she had just endured the past year. All she would say to her co-worker Anne Hitchcock was that the love of her life was lost and she would never be as happy again. Anne liked Camilla and thought her talent was enormous, but the post-beat, all-too-hip atmosphere of Cambridge seemed to be spiraling Camilla into an even deeper depression. Artists were supposed to suffer and Camilla was getting an A+ in that course.

When the warmth of spring settled over the northeast, Anne suggested to Camilla that she accompany her to Nantucket for the summer. She was sure she could get Camilla a job waitressing with her at The Opera House, the trendiest spot on-island at that time. Camilla begged off but was finally persuaded to go when Anne pointed out that Nantucket was becoming a haven for artists. And waitressing at night left days free for painting.

Camilla had grown to trust her little red-headed friend. Just looking at Anne's mane of strawberry blonde curls and her smiling blue eyes gave Camilla a lift and she didn't think she could bear spending the hot summer in Cambridge without her. Since Camilla was avoiding her family this summer for reasons Anne was not privy to, she was free to just pack up her belongings, most of which were art supplies, and make the trip to the Nantucket boat in Hyannis.

The first distinctly Nantucket experience Camilla registered after the long boat ride was the high-pitched sound of the grinding winches locking the bow of the ferry into place on the wharf. It was a new sound to Camilla, one which now, thirty years later, had not changed and meant home. Camilla allowed Anne to take her over that summer. They occupied a tiny guest house on her family's summer property on Cliff Rd. The light there was beautiful in the morning and soon Camilla was back at work with her oils, painting her version of the vistas that spread out from her door.

Her job was okay. The knack of waitressing clicked with her and Camilla, although somewhat reserved, was making a splash with the social set. People, especially young men, were intrigued with her stunning tall stature. She possessed a natural grace and seemed at home gliding through the restaurant with her long mahogany braid swaying behind her to the rhythm of her stride. Her withdrawn emotional state was mistaken for mystery, and a long list of young and not-so-young men wanted to date her. But Camilla was not interested. And so after work, instead of going out for a drink with Anne and her social set, Camilla walked alone through town and up to her perch on the cliff.

Anne had made it her quest that summer to find out what was hindering Camilla from enjoying herself like any other pretty young lady on Nantucket. She was not able to pry anything out of Camilla and was about to give up trying when she finally persuaded Camilla to accompany her to a late August house party at Billy Smith's family estate in Sconset. Camilla went because she heard Sconset was fertile ground for landscape material and she was planning on staying through the fall to expand her Nantucket portfolio. Already, her oils had sold well in several galleries and Camilla was hopeful that she would make her name there.

Camilla followed Anne up the steps of a gorgeous old summer home set high on the Sconset cliff. The Smith Place, as the village referred to it, had been purchased by Billy's grandfather Chester Smith, as a summer retreat for his Wall St. brokerage firm during World War II. Many New York families made Sconset their summer destination following the elegant yet laid-back times they had spent with the Smith family. When Billy's father Jonathan took over the firm in the mid-sixties, he chose to entertain in the Hamptons instead of Sconset. This left the Smith Place pretty much abandoned for several years until Billy was in college. Billy was the only one of the three Smith boys who preferred Sconset over the Hamptons, and he began to summer in the old mansion with a group of his classmates from Yale. Billy was famous for throwing a great party. He hired the best caterers and always invited an interesting cross-section of young people to his festivities and tonight was not an exception.

The foyer was sparkling with more lit candles than Camilla could count, and the soft strains of live jazz floated in from the long verandah which spanned the entire back of the sprawling home. Billy came forward and enthusiastically hugged Anne. His six foot three frame dwarfed Anne, and he lifted her feet up off the ground as he hugged her. When he turned to Camilla, open admiration flowed from his ice-blue eyes to her deep green ones. He took her hand and found himself at a loss for words. Camilla looked like a goddess. Her dark waves hung beautifully from a simple gold headband and her calm, deep eyes engulfed him.

Camilla was a bit confused by this large blonde young man. Her first thought about him was Ivy League. Her second thought was handsome. Really handsome. Anne stepped in and relieved the awkward moment by introducing them. And that was it. Kind, somewhat shy Billy Smith and the artistically remote Camilla Stuart became a couple that night. Billy was enthralled with Camilla and Camilla, in her heart of hearts, knew instantly that this man was safe. She would never have the passionate love for him that had almost stole her soul earlier in her life. She would be safe from her own emotions with Billy.

Billy was naïve. In spite of his wealth and education, he was naïve, like a large boy full of wonder. As the youngest of three boys of privilege, Billy had been loved and protected all of his young life and his innocence appealed to Camilla in a way that turned off many other young women who expected him to be more worldly. Camilla had shifted all of her passion into her art and yet she needed security in her life. Billy would give it to her.

That first evening, Billy was practically tripping over his feet trying to make her comfortable. Anne whispered that she'd never seen him so flustered, and Camilla whispered back that it was because he had just met the woman he would marry. Anne thought Camilla was kidding, but when the engagement was announced at Thanksgiving, Anne made a quick trip back to Nantucket to get the full story from Camilla.

Camilla had rented a beautiful old captain's home on Centre Street where she had set up a studio. The living room was completely taken over by several easels set up with works in various states of completion. Tables strewn with paints, pencils and sketches dotted the room. When Anne entered without knocking, as Camilla had instructed her, she stood for a moment watching her close friend work on a sweeping panorama of the moors with a gentle mist undulating over it. A photograph was tacked up on the easel and seemed to be what Camilla was painting from, although Camilla, the paints, the brush, the canvas, and the scene seemed to be one. Anne had the sense that Camilla was not painting, she was the painting. That image had continued over the years in Anne's mind when she attempted to describe Camilla's work. Camilla was able to break all ties with the mundane and enter the sacred space of her muse.

Anne was only able to watch this for a few moments. It seemed wrong to eavesdrop on such an intimate minute. Clearing her throat, she walked over to Camilla and murmured, "Hi, dear one."

Camilla gave a start and looked over at Anne with a confused expression in her eyes. That passed in a second and Camilla placed her brush on a workspace, pulled off her painting tunic, and enveloped her small-framed friend in a deep hug. "I'm so glad you're here, Anne. Let's go make a cup of tea."

And so the two friends sat at the rickety little table in the old kitchen and caught up on each other's news. "I told you we were going to get married, Annie. He's perfect for me. He has his own interests, which will always take him away for long periods of time and so I'll always have time to paint. You know I've made more money on my paintings this fall than I did at the restaurant all summer. And I have a plan."

"A plan, Cammie? What a surprise," laughed Anne in reply.

"Now, don't make fun of me. I found out that there's a spot open on Old South Wharf next summer. A lot of people are opening galleries down there and I thought maybe you could open a gallery and sell my work. You're great in a gallery, you know, and I thought…"

"Oh my God, Camilla. That's perfect. Maybe I could get a couple of other artists from the Artists's Association and make a go of it. Hitchcock Gallery. How does it sound?"

"Beautiful. Just beautiful."

"And what is Billy going to do with himself?"

"He's off with his college chum Dave Collins taking pictures for some kind of outdoor magazine. He'll be away on and off all winter and next summer he's going to do some renovations on the Smith Place for his grand-father. We'll move out there after the June wedding and if we can get it heated, we'll live out there forever. Oh, Annie, I'm so happy about this. Wouldn't that be a great place to raise a family?"

"You want kids?" asked Anne in amazement. *"Why?"*

"We just do, that's all," answered Camilla, looking down at her hands gripping her mug. *"I want a baby, several babies if I can."*

"You're not pregnant, are you?" asked a puzzled Anne.

"No, silly. Why would you say that?" Camilla almost snapped.

"I didn't mean anything by it, Camilla. Relax. So, what about the wedding?"

"Oh, I'm leaving it all up to my mother. She's been hoping for this since my first breath and I told her to just do it. She's in heaven. The wedding will be on June 6 in the back yard of my parents' house in Hingham. It's a really pretty spot on the main street running through town. So with Mrs. Efficiency at the helm, I don't have a thing to worry about now. All I have to do is show up. I've finally found a way to please them."

Anne looked at her friend with surprise at the bitter edge she had when speaking about her mother. It wasn't like Camilla to be this way and Anne found it puzzling.

"I'd love it if you'd be my maid of honor, Annie. Will you?"

"*Of course I will,*" answered Anne shaking off any misgivings she felt.

Camilla shifted back to her usual demeanor, a smile taking over her lovely features in the wake of the tense moment when she spoke of her family. Anne had the sense that Camilla was happiest as a solitary woman, one with no ties and obligations to her family. It just didn't make sense that she would want to marry and have a family of her own. Anne was confused and feared that her friend was making a serious mistake. She changed the subject from the wedding to plans for the gallery, a subject on which they could connect and feel comfortable again.

CHAPTER FOUR

Jasmine Hunter grew up in Greenwich Village in New York. Her family background was interesting in that she had been adopted at birth by her father's sister and husband, Yolanda and Byron Hunter. Jasmine called her adopted father Pops and her real father Daddy. She had an older brother Hakim (actually her cousin) who doted on her and always called her Princess. Jasmine had been a serious little girl who was well cared for and excelled in school. She often seemed preoccupied as there were two things she was always looking forward to; her frequent visits to her father Lincoln Jones' spacious apartment overlooking Central Park West on the Upper West Side and Sunday dinner at her grandparents home in their close-knit neighborhood in Alphabet City on the Lower East Side.

Jasmine's grandparents had moved to Manhattan from Brooklyn in the early sixties when they realized that their two children were blessed with talent, and the cultural advantages of living in Manhattan off-set the financial burden the move caused. Yolanda was a singer. As a little girl she was the one who stood in front of the youth choir, belting out her Gospel solos. Even though it seemed that every child in choir could sing like a bird, Yolanda stood out and members of the congregation would nod at Milly and Desmond Jones in approval after each of their daughter's performances. Yolanda was accepted to Julliard for voice and the family could make it work if Yolanda lived at home. They decided the shorter the subway ride the better, hence the move. Lincoln was sixteen.

Lincoln was the artist of the family. From the time he was ten until his graduation from high school he drew and captioned his own comic strip *Captain He-Man*. Each Saturday morning, in honor of Saturday morning cartoons, the next installment of *Captain He-Man* was presented to his mother at the breakfast table. She would then take the previous week's strip off the bulletin board, date it, and place it in that year's shoebox of strips. The new episode would reign over the kitchen for the upcoming week. Eight boxes, each containing a year's worth of strips, were stored in the attic of the Jones' home.

By the time Lincoln had entered high school he was showing an uncanny ability to draw portraits. His school notebooks were full of the faces he drew during tedious moments in classes that failed to capture his interest. This did not mean he was a poor student. He was actually quite brilliant and was able to draw and absorb lessons at the same time. During his junior year at his new high school, Humanities, his art teacher, Mr. Robinson, introduced him to sculpture in clay and that was it for Lincoln. Every spare moment he could manage and long after school hours were spent sculpting. His knack for drawing faces now became three dimensional and a special art show his senior year featured his remarkable work. A professor from Pratt Institute attended the show and within a week Lincoln had been granted a full scholarship to study sculpture.

Lincoln was ecstatic. His guidance counselor was disappointed, as he had hoped Lincoln was aiming for an Ivy League education, but Lincoln held firm. His parents were full of pride for their tall son with the long, sensitive fingers. Secretly, his father had hoped he'd opt for a basketball career as his agility and speed on the court had helped his team achieve an undefeated season. Secretly, his mother had hoped he'd become a surgeon. Fortunately, they kept their secrets to themselves and showered their praise on their son.

Yolanda formed a Gospel group called Celebration! during her years at Julliard. By the time she had graduated, Celebration! was in demand from the Bible Belt to New England. Every weekend of the year a new destination was booked and Yolanda handled all of the group's business. One snowy night in the Roxbury section of Boston at a church concert, Yolanda met a quiet young man with a smile that lit up her heart. Byron courted Yolanda with a vengeance and within two months had asked her father for Yolanda's hand. They were married the day after Yolanda graduated from Julliard and their son Hakim was born a year later. Byron got himself a secure job on Wall Street and slowly began to earn a solid reputation as a wise broker. They bought a second story co-op on Greenwich Avenue and proceeded to raise their family.

An abrupt change occurred when a frantic Lincoln called from Boston, where he had been teaching sculpture at the Museum School of the Museum of Fine Arts. It was his second year away from home and his family had not heard much from him for the past year. It seemed that Lincoln had fallen in love with a student at the school and she had become pregnant. During the delivery of the child, the young woman had died and a seriously frantic Lincoln now had a little daughter. Yolanda drove to Boston that night and was shaken when she saw her brother's state. His place was cold and messy. All the shades were drawn and Lincoln looked as if he hadn't eaten or slept in a week. A tiny cry came from a make shift crib and Yolanda walked over to peer at the tiny girl.

"What's her name?" Yolanda asked as she took the tiny babe and held her to her ample bosom.

"I haven't done that yet, Yo," answered Lincoln. He began pacing in the living room in a random, distracted way.

Yolanda was scared to death for him. Even though he was twenty-four, he looked and sounded like a lost little boy. Her plan popped out of her mouth fully formed. Yolanda Hunter took charge. "We're going home, Lincoln. Call the school and tell them you have a family emergency. We're all going to be okay."

Lincoln collapsed on the couch and made the necessary call. When it was done he began to feel the security his family had always given him in his sister. She was already on the phone with Byron, making plans for him to arrive the next morning with a U-Haul truck. Her next call was to her parents to inform yet not worry them. They would have Hakim's old crib waiting for Lincoln and the baby when they would arrive the following night.

Like a bad dream, Lincoln's distress began to lift, and by the time Byron arrived the following morning, he was ready to organize his belongings for the move.

Yolanda never let the baby girl out of her sight. She was a little angel with huge greenish-brown eyes and soft curls. Looking at her features and hair, Yolanda was shocked to realize that the baby's mother must have been white. She didn't want to upset her brother any more than necessary, so the topic of the mother was never brought up. But, moment by moment, she was falling in love with her brother's little daughter, and by the time Byron had arrived she had made up her mind that they would adopt the little bundle.

Byron scooped the baby up in his strong arms and softly cooed to her. "Why you're as sweet as a flower, my little Jasmine." The baby had been named.

Milly Jones was furious with her son and vowed to let him know it. She was devastated that her brilliant son had made such a mess of things. Milly and Desmond had been excessively proud of the way they had raised their family, and now this. It was a difficult moment for her to endure, but Yolanda had learned to take charge from her and decided she would not spend another moment in anger.

Desmond was dispatched to Greenwich Avenue to retrieve the crib and Milly busied herself in the attic unearthing the boxes of baby things Yolanda had stored there in hopes of a second child. By midnight she had everything laundered and Desmond had assembled the crib. Milly sat back and waited for the next chapter of her life to unfold.

Milly was not surprised that Yolanda and Byron wanted to adopt Jasmine. Who wouldn't want to have a gorgeous child like that? Even Hakim seemed part of the plot, holding the baby in his chubby arms with his mother's help. They looked like a happy family and Milly was not about to deny anyone this unexpected happiness. But what about Lincoln?

Of course he had agreed to the plan, knowing that his child would thrive with his sister. They decided that Jasmine would always know that Lincoln was her father and that he would spend as much time as he wanted with his child. Within a week, the legalities were taken care of and Jasmine took up residence as the Princess of the Hunter family. Lincoln stayed with his parents for a time and at their insistence, rented studio space in So-Ho. He began to work practically non-stop. His work took on an abstract quality and he began experimenting with carved marble. Within six months Lincoln Jones had mounted a very successful show which earned him accolades in the *Times*.

His profits enabled him to purchase a fabulous apartment on the twelfth floor of a lovely building on Central Park West and Seventieth Street. He kept his studio space in So-Ho and life went on. No one was surprised when Jasmine showed artistic promise, and her father made certain that she had the best art lessons available.

⊷╬⊷

Jasmine never thought to question her family situation. She grew up well cared for and contented. She always thought she was especially lucky to have two fathers in her life when so many of her friends had no father at all. She didn't begin asking about her birth mother until her best friend Adele asked her why her eyes were greenish and why her long dark brown hair lacked the expected kinkiness. Jasmine was twelve at the time and asked her Grandmother if she knew why.

Mrs. Jones had allowed Lincoln to keep his secret to himself and her only advice to her granddaughter was to ask her father. That happened on the evening of Lincoln and Jasmine's annual visit to the Radio City Christmas Show. The question Lincoln had dreaded for so long was now hanging in the air like an icicle about to drop from a roof. Lincoln told Jasmine that her mother had been a beautiful white woman named Camilla. She had been a fabulous oil painter and he had loved her with all his heart.

Lincoln stood at his living room window for a long time after he had spoken. He quietly wiped tears from his eyes as he stood gazing at the festive lights of the city. Jasmine was doubly shocked to hear this news and to see her father's emotional state following his admission. The fact of having a white mother didn't really matter that much to Jasmine, but her father's sorrow tore at her heart. Long silent moments passed with Jasmine at a loss. She had an inspiration, though, and taking a tall bayberry pillar candle and a pack of matches, she moved to the window and stood next to her father.

"Let's light this candle in memory of my mother, Dad. We'll leave it here in the window so she can see it burning for her," Jasmine suggested.

Lincoln turned to his daughter and managed a smile through his tears. "I think that's a lovely idea." He lit the match and passed it to Jasmine to light the candle. "For you, mother."

The Christmas candle for her mother burned in the Central Park West window every night of the Christmas season for the next eighteen years. During those years Jasmine attended high school and then received a degree in museum restoration from Pratt. No one was surprised when she landed her teaching spot at the Metropolitan Museum of Art. Not only had Jasmine become a competent, self-assured young woman, but she also became a name in her field almost over night. She had been hired on a temporary basis at the Met right after college to do some last minute, unexpected cleaning and restoration on several pieces in an upcoming Rembrandt show. Her work earned her raves and a great new position. Everything was wonderful in Jasmine's world and she stopped to buy a bottle of Dom Perignon to share with her father as she hurried up to her father's apartment for their annual candle lighting. The city was festive and everyone really did seem a bit friendlier this time of the year, Jasmine mused. Maybe Dickens was right, she smiled as she passed the sparkling array of lights outside Tavern on the Green and headed across the street to her father's home.

It was Christmas, and Jasmine was planning to meet the new man in her life, Cameron Jackson, at Café des Artistes, following her visit with her father. Jasmine was brimming with the news of her new love and couldn't wait to tell Lincoln all about him. Jasmine entered her father's home and was instantly absorbed into his reclusive world of sculpture and painting. She always felt she was going into another world and indeed she was. Lincoln lived outside the normal pace of the city. His studio had been moved to the apartment next door, which he had purchased some years ago. A door leading into the studio had been added and with eager delivery people roaming the Upper West Side, Lincoln was able to remain in his creative seclusion for long periods of time if he wished. Soft strains of jazz or classical music always filled the air of Lincoln's home and added to the dreamlike quality of his home.

But tonight, Jasmine was not going to sink into the quiet world her father inhabited. She brought her energy into the apartment with her and after she hugged Lincoln he stood back and said "My goodness, Jasmine. You're about to burst! What's going on?"

Jasmine proceeded to tell her father about Cameron. She was pacing around the living room telling her father about his incredible future in fashion design when something that had always been on the periphery of her perception of her father's home suddenly came into sharp focus. She realized that his collection of artwork was dominated by the work of one painter, C. Stuart. Spinning around to face her father, she interrupted her litany of Cameron's qualities with "Who's C. Stuart to you, Dad?"

Lincoln was caught off guard and fumbled a bit. "Well, she's… she was…Well, she's very famous, you know and I admire her work."

"I know that. But why do you have so many of her paintings, Dad? When I think about it, it seems like you've added at least one of her paintings to your collection every year. They're worth a fortune, Dad. Are they an investment?"

"Of course not, Jazzy," Lincoln was quick to answer.

"Well then, why?"

"I knew her when she was a student in Boston. We were friends and I like to keep track of her progress. That's all."

"They say she's reclusive and mysterious. Kind of like you. I've always wanted to know what the C stands for. Since you knew her you must know. What is her name, Dad?"

Lincoln picked up his glass of champagne and fingered the stem, gazing into the bubbling liquid for a long pause. After taking a sip he cleared his throat and said "Jasmine, come sit down next to me."

Jasmine slowly walked over to her father and noticed how grey his hair was becoming. She wished he had a woman in his life to keep him company as he advanced in years, and felt a familiar stab of worry about her father as she sat down next to him. She reached over and took his hand and said, "I love you, Dad."

"I love you too, Jazzy. This is not easy for me to say and I've been dreading this moment your whole life. Now, don't interrupt me, girl, just listen to what I have to say. The C stands for Camilla. Camilla Stuart Smith. She is your mother."

Jasmine jumped to her feet and stood looming over her father. "You mean to tell me my mother's alive? You mean to tell me she's not dead? Who else knows this, Dad? Has it been a family conspiracy to keep me from knowing my mother's a world famous artist?"

"No one in the family knows, Jazzy. They all believed me when I showed up with you and said she was dead. And she has been dead for us or for me, anyway. Her father made sure I'd never see her again. You don't know what it was like. She came from a lily white old Boston family in the suburbs. When she brought me to meet them and say we were going to get married a fury was unleashed on me that equaled the fires of hell. Jasmine, that old man did everything he could do outside of lynching me to keep me from his daughter. And when he found out she was pregnant, I thought he might actually lynch me. Someday I'll tell you the whole story of the measures he was willing to take to get us out of his life forever, but the main point of it is that a judge friend of his falsified your birth certificate, saying your mother had died in childbirth. The judge brought you to my Roxbury door one evening, I called Yolanda, and here we are."

"But Daddy, it wasn't Mississippi. It was Boston. How could that have happened?"

"Boston was one of the most prejudiced places in the country, honey. The white people tore up the city when they desegregated the schools, which was happening at the time of your birth. Camilla's father was a lawyer with powerful friends. I made promises to them. I was forced to sign papers. They threatened to go after my parents. I couldn't let anything happen to Mom and Pop. I did what I had to do to save myself. And I've had you."

"Are you secretly in communication with Camilla? Do you still love her? Is that why you've never married?"

"I've never spoken to her, seen her or written to her since before you were born. I kept my word to those people. That's why I have so many of her paintings. It's like having a bit of the only woman I have ever loved with me. That's why. That's why…"

"But do you still love her?"

"Yes. I will always love Camilla."

"Where is she? I have to know, Daddy. Where is my mother?"

"No, honey, I can't tell you that. It could be dangerous for you."

"I don't care. Where is she, Father? Don't make me go behind your back to find out. Because you know I'll find her. You know I will."

Lincoln slowly rose to his feet and went to his familiar spot at the window. The peace and serenity he surrounded himself with was not enough to protect him from his past. He had known this day would come and it had. Turning to face her from the window he simply said, "She lives on Nantucket where she paints in the winter and runs a restaurant with her husband, William Smith, during the summer. It's called Sconset House."

Jasmine arrived late for Sunday dinner that week. The Jones and Hunter family was all seated at the table and Desmond had just finished the blessing when Jasmine burst into the dining room. "Sorry I'm late," she said as she shrugged out of her coat and took her place.

"That's okay, honey," answered her grandmother. "Where's your father?"

"I suspect he's not coming. In fact I'm certain he doesn't want to face all of you after I tell you what he's been hiding all these years."

"Lincoln's been hiding something from us?" asked Yolanda. "You tell your family what it is, girl."

Jasmine had arrived full of energy, ready to scream out her news to her family, ready to malign her father, ready to justify her fury. But, as she looked around the table at her grandparents and parents, she felt her anger begin to seep out like a slowly deflating balloon. And to her chagrin, tears filled up the space left by the anger. She began to experience a bit of her father's pain and her love for him suddenly overwhelmed her. Jasmine put her hands to her face and began to weep quietly.

The family exchanged bewildered glances and as one steeled itself for the difficulty they sensed was next. Milly broke the silence. "We love you, child. We all love you."

Jasmine looked up at her beloved ones and slowly began. "When I was born, my mother didn't die. She's still alive. She's a very famous painter."

The family stared at Jasmine in shocked silence. The only sound was the grandfather clock ticking away the moments.

"Well, if she didn't die, where has she been all of these years?" fumed Yolanda. "What kind of mother would do that?"

"Quiet, Yo," cautioned Byron.

"Daddy says she came from an uppity white family in the Boston suburbs. Her father was a lawyer who had influential friends. He threatened Daddy. I don't know exactly how it happened, but he made Daddy sign papers that he would never see my mother again. And he had a judge change my birth certificate to say that a woman whose name they made up was my mother and that she died in childbirth. I think Daddy was ready to stand up to them though, until he threatened to ruin Grandpa's name and career. Daddy gave up then and the judge brought me from the hospital to him. I think that's when he called you, Mom."

"I always knew something was really wrong with the whole situation," Desmond muttered. "Lincoln had always been so self-confident. We made sure nothing ever broke his soul when he was a boy. But he had been broken when he came home with his little baby. I told you, Milly. I told you to talk to him."

"I do believe you know how to speak. You should have opened your mouth, husband," Milly spat back.

"Please, don't fight," Jasmine pleaded. "He's been so lonely all these years. I can see now why he's so absorbed with his sculpting. It's his escape and salvation."

"You and his art are his salvation," Milly corrected.

"Anyway, everyone, I've made a decision. I'm going to find her. It's not that I haven't been happy all my life or that I've lacked anything at all from any of you. I just want to get to know her. I want to meet the only woman my father ever loved."

"I suppose my brother knows where she is," snapped Yolanda.

"She lives on that tourist island Nantucket. She married a man named William Smith and they run a summer restaurant. I'm going to try to get a job there. If they won't hire me, I'll find work out there somewhere and eat at her restaurant. That's my plan for my summer break."

"I'm afraid for you, Jazzy," Yolanda said. "What if she rejects you? I don't want you to be hurt."

"I'm not going to tell her who I am," assured Jasmine. "Daddy made me promise not to. He's still afraid of what her father might do to us. I'll be okay with it. I just have to know her. She's the woman who painted all of those beautiful landscapes Daddy has in his apartment."

"She paints those moody things? The person who paints those paintings is as lonely as Lincoln is, husband or no husband," pronounced Yolanda. "I fear for my brother, I truly do."

⇒‡⇒

As Jasmine left the cozy surroundings of her grandparents' home she felt alone for the first time in her life. The familiar aroma of her grandmother's spices mixed with the scent of the fresh roses that always adorned the Sunday dinner table stayed with her as she made the commute to her West Village loft. She knew that this summer the protective spell of her family would slip away from her and she would be facing challenges she never imagined would come her way. She was compelled in a way that mystified her and excited her at the same time. By the time she reached her home, her resolve was ironclad. She would summer on Nantucket.

And so during the winter she sent her resume to Camilla Smith, received a letter back, had a spine-tingling phone interview, and took a position at Sconset House for the summer. During the late spring, Jasmine read every book on Nantucket she could find and by the time she boarded the little plane bound from LaGuardia to Nantucket she felt she knew what to expect. Unfortunately, words cannot convey the magic of Nantucket, and an unsuspecting Jasmine arrived unprepared for the otherworldly atmosphere of the Faraway Isle.

CHAPTER FIVE

B illy entered the sunny kitchen looking for Camilla. Returning from his early morning ritual of tending Sconset House's books, he looked forward to his leisurely meeting with Camilla over a second cup of coffee. When it was obvious she had not yet returned from her morning walk, he decided to climb down the cliff and meet her on the beach. He felt a slight annoyance gnaw at the back of his mind that Camilla was not in the kitchen waiting for him as she always did. The feeling quickly shifted to dread as the image of Camilla slumped back over a large rock came into view.

Calling her name as he ran to her, Billy stumbled in his dock-sides and kicked them off into the sand. Camilla didn't hear his call and only responded when he gently shook her shoulders, still calling her name. Coming to, she seemed disoriented for a moment before she smiled into his concerned blue eyes.

"What's wrong, Cammy? Are you okay?" Billy questioned.

Straightening herself up, Camilla adjusted her hair and looked out to the sparkling blue water before speaking. "I must have dozed off, sweetheart. I was remembering my first summer here, meeting you….., just rehashing the past. I'm fine, Billy." Glancing at her watch, she seemed startled at the time. "I'm really late. Here, give me a hand up and I'll get the coffee going."

Billy helped Camilla to her feet and steadied her for what seemed to him to be a long time before she was ready to make her way home. "Camilla, do you feel okay? You've never done this before and now you've got me worried."

"Probably my age, sweetheart. I'm at that time in life, you know. It's absolutely nothing to worry about. Let's get going. I have some changes I'd like to make tonight and I'd like to have the seating set up so I can set out the placecards this afternoon."

Billy followed Camilla up the beach with a puzzled expression on his face. He needed Camilla's steady strength to anchor him through the rigors of the up-coming season. Little waves of fear licked over him as he hurried forward to catch up with his wife.

One of the many charms of Nantucket is the island's dedication to its own special festivals. Daffodil Weekend, which christens the spring season, Christmas Stroll, which ushers in the holiday season, and an old fashioned Fourth of July which ends on Jetties Beach with fireworks are a few of the highlights island folk look forward to. On a more intimate, almost secretive note, Sconset has its own series of traditions during its short moment in the summer sun. The yearly musical at the Sconset Casino, opening day of the Sconset Market, and Mrs. Clark's openhouse rose festival are high on the Sconset social calendar. But for those who arrive early, an invitation to the Sconset House preview of opening night is particularly coveted. This year was no exception.

The one hundred guests began to arrive in staggered seatings from six thirty until nine. Traditionally, the evening gave the wait staff a chance to get back into the swing of Sconset House and allowed Billy and Chef Gates to circulate through the dining room getting feed-back from their most trusted critics, the regular crowd. A chilly spring rain had settled over the island, which seemed to spawn an even greater feeling of camaraderie among the guests as they took their seats in the cozy dining rooms, each of which had a small fire kindled in its fireplace. Warm greetings and winter updates circulated through the air as Sconset House took up where it had left off the previous fall. Camilla hoped for what she called a "seamless event," and that was what she got.

The waitstaff worked in male/female teams with two teams in the Chester Smith room and one team each in the Rose and Lily Rooms. The teams usually remained constant throughout the season, with perhaps a minor change made during the first week. Tonight, as promised, Jasmine was paired with Jared Miles, Dottie Kelly with Dave Johnson, Brian Folger with Maeve O'Connor, and by special request, Jessica Raymond teamed up with Jeffrey Tomkins. Camilla chuckled to herself: it seemed Jared had been right about Jessica and Jared. Everything was moving along gracefully and Camilla had a chance to circulate from table to table greeting so many familiar faces. Camilla's smiles were genuine as she realized how much she loved Sconset House and the magical evenings she and Billy had been creating over the years.

After greeting and seating her diverse crowd of mostly year round people, Camilla had a chance to pull up a chair and sit with Anne Hitchcock for a moment. Anne was dining with Mary Carver, one of the few fulltime Nantucket doctors, and Camilla let out a contented sigh as she leaned on the table toward Anne and asked, "What do you think?"

"It's almost too perfect, Camilla. That new girl is stunning. What did you say her name was?" Anne replied.

"Jasmine. Jasmine Hunter. She's really fitting in. And take a look at Jeffrey and Jessica. They absolutely glow."

"Looks like love to me," Mary noted. Now with Camilla's full attention, Mary quietly questioned Camilla. "How are you feeling, dear? You look a bit drawn. Is it a bit of last year's Lyme Disease?"

"I think you're right, Mary," Camilla smiled, obviously relieved. "I have been feeling fatigued lately, as Anne has probably told you," She offered a pouty nod to Anne. "I bet it's Lyme again."

"Most likely. I'm going to call in ten days' worth of antibiotics for you tomorrow and when you're done, come for a check-up to see if we've licked it."

Camilla took Anne's hand. "See, Annie? I'll be just fine. And I like the idea of a new wardrobe."

Camilla noticed Billy discreetly motioning her over to Ambassador White's table, and she quickly made her way to his side, where they stood arm in arm, beaming down at the Ambassador's table.

"This is a close as Camilla and Billy get," Anne noted. "She's so alone most of the year. I wish she had more happiness in her marriage. She's so determined to make up for it with her restaurant and staff." Looking up, she noticed Mary's questioning look.

"Don't mind me, Mary. I'm just rambling."

"I understand what you're saying," Mary replied, "but don't you think that her painting would suffer if she wasn't driven to it the way she is? I've always thought the painting came from her loneliness."

"I used to think so too, but I've known her for over thirty years, and whatever drives her to paint comes from a much earlier event. Her ability is much more than simply talent. She has a muse that totally inspires her. She could set up her easel in the middle of this dining room right now and go to into the magic of her creativity. I've seen her do it since we were in our early twenties. Her arrangement with Billy simply gives her the time she needs without interruption. I don't think a little wintertime happiness would change her work except to limit her time a bit."

Both women watched Camilla a few minutes longer and prepared to depart. As they approached the front door and searched for their umbrellas in the oriental umbrella stand, Anne turned back and saw Camilla sway backward and steady herself against the fireplace mantle. A cold dread snaked its way up her spine, and Anne had a certain realization that her dearest friend in the world had a much more serious ailment than Lyme Disease. The cold raindrops as she hurried to her car seemed to tap at her, saying, "Yes, yes, yes. You're right, you're right, you're right."

—≺‖≻—

By eleven o'clock all the guests had left and Sconset House had been re-set for the following night which would be the actual opening night of the season. A group of very self-satisfied people stretched out on the comfortable couches in the foyer and toasted themselves with champagne Billy had poured for everyone.

"To a wonderful season," Billy declared. "You are all terrific."

With his champagne glass in hand, Jeffrey stood and after clearing his throat began "I have an announcement to make. Jessica has accepted my proposal of marriage and we hope to be married here on the Fourth of July. We're always closed that night for fireworks and I had hoped that we could all join together for this on the verandah if it's okay with Camilla and Billy."

Camilla jumped to her feet and embraced a rather embarrassed Jeffrey. "It's more than okay. It's terrific!" Looking over at Jared she winked. "Jared, we begin the plans tomorrow at six over cornflakes, okay?"

"You've got it Lovey."

"Please, Camilla, don't go to any trouble. Let's have it simple. We wanted to do it here because this is where we fell in love and we want to share it with all of you, and..." Overcome, Jessica stopped to brush tears from her eyes.

"Jessica, we're all so happy for the two of you. You just let us take care of it. You and Jeffery will just have to show up." Camilla sat back down and as if on cue, everyone else got up amidst squeals of delight and back-to-back toasts for good luck.

Sconset House was definitely alive and ready for business.

CHAPTER SIX

The golden early summer sun began to blaze its way through the feathery morning mists wafting over Sconset. Brian and Dottie leisurely enjoyed their coffee on the deck behind Surf when Jasmine emerged, steaming mug in hand. Jasmine felt the scene was like a moment out of time, a vignette so outside her usual life that it was difficult to take in the experience of actually being there. Her sense of viewing a tableau from afar was a feeling she was becoming familiar with.

Lazy conversation about the success of the previous preview evening flowed around the table in a comfortable, congenial way. Jasmine slowly eased into the conversation and began to feel a bit more connected to the moment, as if her feet were more solidly on the ground. Soon she was asking questions about the clientele of the previous evening, and laughed at Dottie's anecdotes about what seemed to be her limitless knowledge of everyone on Nantucket's idiosyncrasies. As she stood to go back into the kitchen to refill her empty cup, Jasmine noticed that the mist had disappeared and bright, sparkling morning had taken its place. The sun invigorated all three of them and Brian suggested they go for a bike ride. Dottie, sensing the energy passing between Brian and Jasmine, declined, leaving Brian and Jasmine alone picking out bikes in the basement from years gone by hand-me-downs.

Jasmine liked Brian. His calm, straightforward manner helped still the inner turmoil she felt might spill over at any moment; and the fact the she and Cameron had broken up just before she left New York over her mysterious need to summer away from home left her free to connect with Brian. As they checked out their bikes and prepared to take off, Brian began to talk about his family and gradually moved the conversation to Jasmine's background.

"So, what does your father do?" he asked after Jasmine explained about her mother's Gospel group.

"He's a sculptor," Jasmine replied without thinking. She immediately felt panic creep up her spine and realized how easy it would be to make a mistake and reveal who she really was.

"I don't know too much about sculpture, but Camilla has some beautiful pieces of sculpture in her yard that I like a lot. Shall we pedal up by her house so you can see her stuff on our way to Wauwinet?" Brian suggested.

Jasmine hesitated a moment, fearing where the sculptor conversation might lead, but then decided that going there would deflect the conversation away from her father to the artist who had done the sculptures.

The ride through Sconset village and out to Baxter Road heading toward pristine Sankaty Lighthouse took about ten minutes. Jasmine was enchanted by the rambling, weather-greyed home that Camilla and Billy owned on the cliff. Rambling roses already starting to bud had crept up to the roof and several manicured gardens were coming alive in the early summer sunshine. They parked their bikes against the split rail fence in front of the house and Brian led Jasmine to a large garden situated to the left of the home. In the center of it stood *Rapture,* a marble sculpture of a young woman raising her face to the skies. Jasmine knew the piece

47

intimately because as a young teen she had posed for her father as he had sculpted it. She had assumed it was in storage, for she had always hoped that someday it would become hers. And now here it was in Camilla's garden. She found herself speechless, and stood staring at the somewhat abstract likeness of herself, heart pounding in her throat, hoping against hope that Brian would not see her face in the sculpture.

"Amazing, isn't it," Brian spoke to break the silence.

"Sure is," Jasmine whispered.

Brian walked her around the house, where four smaller Lincoln Jones sculptures stood as focal points in the remainder of Camilla's flower gardens. As they slowly made their way from garden to garden, Jasmine realized that Camilla had collected her father's work just as he had collected Camilla's. She felt numb and answered Brians's words automatically. In the back of her mind she hoped he didn't think her behavior was strange. She felt such a pull toward him, and yet she couldn't quite focus on their conversation as the full impact of what she was seeing flooded her senses. At her suggestion, they took back to the road and Brian led the way from the Smith's house.

As they pedaled along, the cool breeze calmed Jasmine a bit, and as her mind cleared she had a deeper realization. She knew that her father loved her mother and his collection of her art had been solid proof of that for Jasmine. And now here was Camilla doing the same thing Lincoln had done. *She still loves Daddy. She still loves him* echoed in her mind. "Oh, my God!" Jasmine exclaimed out loud.

Brian looked back and asked what was the matter. Frantically, Jasmine looked around and spying a swan on Sesachacha Pond pointed to it.

Brian smiled back at her in agreement.

━≺┼≻━

As Brian and Jasmine spread their blanket on the white stretch of sand to the right of The Wauwinet, an exquisite resort perched at the beginning of the conservation area leading to Coatue and Great Point, a deep sense of elation filled Jasmine, causing her to positively glow in the high sun. Grabbing Brian's hand, she pulled him toward the water, and kicking off their shoes they stood knee deep in the clean blue sea. Brian reached over and took Jasmine's slim expressive hand in his own large calloused one and the two stood for a long moment, watching sailboats bob along in the light breeze.

Brian turned to Jasmine, his heart filled to bursting with longing. Slowly and gently he took her chin in his other hand and kissed her lips. Jasmine reveled in his gentle manner and warmed to the promise of his warm embrace. Pulling back, they looked deeply into each other's eyes and slowly made their way back to the safety of the blanket and their picnic things. But a seed had been planted, one which both hoped would grow.

Easy conversation flowed between the two as they spent the next few hours sharing their hopes and dreams for the future. By the time they packed up their belongings for the ride home to prepare for opening night at Sconset House both knew they stood at the brink of a deep relationship, one which both of them had long dreamed of.

Jasmine went straight for her cell phone after returning to her room after her day with Brian. Her father picked up her call on the second ring.

After establishing that Lincoln had been extremely worried about her and now fairly angry that she had not called and that he had been busily fielding accusatory calls from his mother and sister, who were upset to say the least, Jasmine and her father finally settled into their conversation.

"Daddy, she collects your work," Jasmine began.

"That can't be," Lincoln quickly replied. "How do you know that?"

"I saw it, Daddy. She has *Rapture* and four small bronzes."

"*Rapture?* My God." Lincoln began pacing in front of his windows overlooking Central Park. Usually the view soothed him, but today nothing was going to do the trick.

"I hope no one notices that my face is on that statue."

"It's just and impression of you, sweetheart," Lincoln replied. "Don't give it a thought."

"Don't give it a thought? Daddy, let's get real here. The woman is married to nice guy who Dottie says she treats like he's a little brother or a son..."

"Who's Dottie?"

"Oh, Daddy, you drive me crazy. Dottie's one of the waitresses who's been here forever. Camilla is married to a grown up spoiled rich kid who goes hiking all winter long with a guy who takes pictures for a magazine. She's alone painting all winter. They have no kids. And she collects your work. What does that tell you, Daddy?" Jasmine demanded.

Lincoln stopped pacing and stared out over the emerald leaves of the park. It would be a great color for the kitchen he thought.

"Daddy, are you there?"

"Yes, Sweetheart, of course I'm here."

"Okay, I'll spell it out for you. She is still in love with you just like you're still in love with her."

"No, Jasmine. She has a full life. Don't try to make us into a family after all these years. You have a big family right here that loves you and is really frightened for you. Leave Camilla alone. You've seen her. Now come home. We'll spend July in Italy. We'll rent a car and visit all the places you've wanted to see. Just leave, Jazzy."

"I can't. You know I've made up my mind to spend the summer here. It's really beautiful in an other-worldly kind of way and the people I work with are wonderful. And besides, I couldn't leave Camilla high and dry like that. What would she do?"

"She'd hire someone else, Jasmine."

"You don't understand, Daddy. How can you be so dense? The woman you love feels the same way about you. It's Kismet or destiny or star-crossed or something."

"Look, Jasmine, I think you should calm down a bit. This will look different in the morning. Why don't you call your mother and for God's sake, don't mention a word about this to her or to your grandmother. Don't confuse them."

"Okay, I'll call them," Jasmine sighed. "I miss everyone so much. I'll call them and I won't upset them."

"Good girl. Now call me tomorrow morning and we'll set everything straight."

"Wait a minute. You have to tell me honestly, Daddy. Do you still love her?"

Lincoln began pacing again and after clearing his throat twice answered, "Yes."

The phone call shook up Lincoln more that he ever thought possible. His pacing continued and gradually included all of his apartment with a snifter of cognac now in hand. He had given Camilla up. Everything had ended except his feelings for her. And now *Rapture*. Why did she have to buy *Rapture*? The thought of it took him back to a lush summer day over thirty years ago. They had gone hiking at World's End in Hingham, a double-hilled nature preserve that poked its way into the harbor.

Lincoln had sat down to sketch a particularly gnarled tree that he wanted to sculpt and Camilla had wandered around on her own. Lincoln made a quick sketch of an ecstatic Camilla, head thrown back to the glorious sun as a smart breeze coming in off Hingham Harbor blew her hair and dress back. They had called the sketch *Rapture* and Camilla framed it to hang over his bed. The sculpture came from the sketch with Jasmine posing so that Lincoln could get the modeling correct. The face was Jasmine, it was Camilla. It was both of them.

Lincoln wondered how she'd found it, although once she knew of its existence he knew in his heart that she would have had to possess it. She must have had her agent deal directly with his to even know of the statue's existence. He remembered setting an exorbitant price for it when Harry Field, his agent, approached him about the sale.

He felt such a fool not asking Harry who had bought the piece, the piece he had planned to give Jasmine for her wedding.

He wondered if Camilla thought of that wonderful day at World's End when she looked at the sculpture. Upon reflection, he was certain she did. The realization made him feel strangely happy. Jasmine's words that Camilla still loved him echoed in his mind. If Jasmine knew the whole story of the sculpture, she'd probably go to Camilla and identify herself in a flash. In his heart of hearts he wished she would, but knew that would unleash a whirl of backlash no one could stop.

He did not want Jasmine to ever have to face the wrath of Camilla's father, her own grandfather.

CHAPTER SEVEN

Camilla took a seat at the corner window table in the Rose Room and leaned back in her chair, a cup of steaming cappuccino in her hand. A comforting sense of completion settled over her as she looked forward into the main dining room. Everything sparkled with readiness and the scent of fresh flowers made the moment seem hopeful and new. Now that she felt ready to open the restaurant later in the day, she allowed herself a mid-day indulgence of rest and began to think about the plans for Jeremy and Jessica's wedding she and Jared had begun to formulate that morning.

Never before had two of her employees married each other at the restaurant, so this would be a landmark moment for Sconset House. They wanted to create an evening with the ambiance of an at-home wedding. In her mind, her staff was family, so this was not too far-fetched. As she mulled over possibilities in her mind, she decided to hire caterers and waiters to prepare and serve the meal so that no one on the staff would have to work. She decided to set that aspect up immediately, hopeful that she could snag some good people at the height of the season. Menu themes were be-ginning to drift through her mind as Anne Hitchcock made her way from the foyer to Camilla.

With a smile Camilla motioned her dear friend to take the seat opposite her.

A flushed Anne rushed in on her tiny quick-stepping feet carry-ing files of paperwork along with a bulky, overstuffed Coach Purse, which seemed to be digging a permanent furrow in her round shoulder. The files and purse hit the floor in a heap as Anne sur-rendered to the comfort of the padded dining chair awaiting her.

Camilla laughed lightly as Anne got herself organized and finally relaxed. "You look like a postcard that would be called 'Height of the Season Jitters,' Anne. What brings you out here this time of day?"

"Cammie, you're not going to believe the phone call I just had with Blake Channing."

"Who's Blake Channing?" Camilla replied.

"You're kidding me!" Anne fairly screamed. "I can't believe how isolated you are out here in your little Sconset world. Blake Channing owns The Channing Gallery which is only one of the most prestigious art galleries in Manhattan. It's on Park Avenue, for God's sake. Any artist in the world would sell his soul to be shown at The Channing. It's a gateway for international exposure and fame."

"Anyone but me," Camilla returned. "So, what are you about to tell me? And mind you, my soul's not up for sale."

"Blake wants to plan an exclusive showing of your work for September next year. He's fielded so much interest in your work my way that he feels the New York trade would support a full and complete show there. Of course, I would receive a nice percentage from him for my part. Who would have thought all those years ago when we opened the gallery to sell those first early Nantucket paintings of yours that it would lead to this!"

"But wait a minute, Annie. How could I possible produce enough work to fill your gallery next year and still have enough to do a major show in New York? It's completely impossible."

"You could do it if you let Billy run the restaurant alone next year and stayed home to paint all summer," Anne answered. "Now come on, Cammie, don't look at me like that. I'm your best friend, remember? I know that you pry yourself away from what you really love to do so that you can run this place with your husband out of some kind of obligation you feel to him. I've never understood it, Cammie. If it's a money thing, you know that one week at The Channing would bring in more than you could ever realize in a Sconset House Season. As I've said before, you can hire someone to take your place here, but no one will ever paint like you do. Think about it."

With a deep sigh, Camilla looked out over the glistening pale blue ocean. It's the same color as Billy's eyes, she thought and with a start realized how often she registered colors, shadows, nuances of gesture. . . as if she was continually planning to paint everything she saw. She knew at that moment that she could paint the color of Billy's eyes perfectly without looking at him, by just thinking about the ocean before her. A chill came over her.

Reaching across the table to take Camilla's hand, Anne softly murmured, "It's because you couldn't have a baby, isn't it? Cammie, lots of women never have babies, but they don't let their guilt over it dominate their lives like you do."

Camilla looked over at her friend and gazed into her eyes. "It is about the baby we couldn't have. I've told you that, but there's more, Annie. It's a secret I've kept from you and from Billy and from the whole world. And now that my parents are dead, I'm carrying it alone except for one other person. It's a total blot on my soul and now it's a payment I owe Billy."

"What are you talking about, Camilla?" Anne demanded straightening up and holding her friend's hand more firmly.

"Can I truly trust you, Annie?" Camilla asked, rising from her seat. She gripped the back of the chair so fiercely her knuckles turned white. "I had a baby about six months before we met at the shop in Cambridge. I was pregnant at the end of my senior year in art school and when we told my parents about it and that we planned to marry, they totally flipped and made horrid threats to him. They gave him the baby and forced him to sign papers to never see me again on threat of horrible things happening to his family."

Anne sat for a moment in shocked silence. "Why would your family do that to you, Cammie? Your parents were educated, sophisticated people. How could they do that?"

"They did it because he was black. They did it because they would never claim a black child as their own. It's such a strange thing. You would never call a child of a mixed marriage white. It's always called black when in reality it's only half black. It's as white as it is black and the whole concept just drives me wild." Sitting back in her chair, Camilla continued, "And so anyway, my father, being the big time lawyer he was pulled in all kinds of favors and had a fictitious birth certificate created that listed the mother as a deceased Jane Doe. I don't even know if the baby was a boy or a girl." Camilla sobbed, looking up at her friend with tears streaming down her face. "I never knew, and I had such a difficult delivery that I was never able to conceive again. I never told Billy why we couldn't have a baby. I saw specialists and had tests and they all said the same thing. Irreparable damage from childbirth. I just told him I was infertile. Eventually, he gave up hope, and at that moment I felt tied to him for all eternity. Like the lie was a weight I could never free myself of."

Long moments passed as neither friend knew what to say to the other. Camilla felt like she had fallen into a vacuum and all the air was being sucked out of her. Anne had never felt so entirely blank.

She finally said, "That's the saddest thing I've ever heard. Did you love the father of the baby?"

"With all my being. We were one. And ever since our relationship ended I've felt like half a person. Billy made me feel safe, Annie, but he couldn't make me feel whole again. Remember what I told you that night I met him? I knew he needed to be taken care of and I knew he'd never intentionally hurt me, so I pursued him until he married me. But I never felt connected to him like I felt to Linc. I think that only happens once in life and that one time only, if you're lucky. I feel very guilty about Billy. The need to feel safe from the kind of hurt I endured is not all a marriage should be based on. Sconset House is my penance, because it makes him so happy and I've made myself find satisfaction in it. So, you see, I can't paint next summer."

"Why didn't you try to find the father?" Anne asked.

"I always thought he'd get in touch with me secretly. Every day I expected a messenger to approach me with news from him. Every time the phone rang I thought it would be him telling me he had to hear my voice. I guess his fear for his family meant more to him than me and then we came to Nantucket... and you know the rest."

"You were so reserved and moody then. I'm almost glad I know why now. I thought you were a real spoiled brat, especially the way you treated your parents around your wedding. It's all falling into place now, Cammie. I'm sorry I had such harsh judgments about you."

"You mean you don't judge what I've done? How I've cheated Billy out of a family?"

"Billy made his own choice. If a child had meant that much to him, he would have moved on, Cammie. People do get divorced."

Camilla smiled weakly through her teary eyes. "I feel a little better."

"Good, my dear. You should have told me years ago. I'm staggered that you've made yourself suffer all these years," Anne softly answered. "Did you say the father's name was Linc?"

"Yes. Now Annie, don't go getting any ideas about reuniting us. It's all over with. I'm sure he's happily married with more children in addition to ours."

"So, what's his name, Cammie?"

"Lincoln Jones. He's a sculptor."

The news shocked Anne to her feet. She paced in front of the window a moment before wheeling back on Camilla. "He buys your work, Camilla. He buys at least one painting a year."

Camilla simply stared at Anne.

"I speak to him at length about which painting I think he would like to add to his collection. And I've noticed you have some of his work in your gardens, dearie. Oh, and by the way, he's never married."

"Are you sure of that?" Camilla demanded, a crimson flush moving up her neck to her face. "How would you know a personal thing like that?"

"Look, Cammie, it's not so strange. He's obviously a very good customer and last year I mentioned to him that I would be in Manhattan for a show in the fall and he offered to take me to dinner."

"Did you go?" Camilla shouted jumping to her feet, sloshing her cappuccino all over the tablecloth. Oblivious to a blunder which would normally have driven her mad, Camilla took her turn pacing.

"Of course I went. We ate at Tavern on the Green, across from his home."

"So, what happened? What did he look like?" Camilla exclaimed, clutching her heart as she paced.

"Slow down, Cammie," Anne said softly as she sat back in her seat.

"Slow down? How can I slow down? This is the most important thing that's happened to me in thirty years and you tell me to slow down?"

"Okay, okay."

"What did he look like, damn it!"

"He's one of the most handsome men I've ever seen. Come on, Cam, you know what he looks like. He's the kind of good-looking that only gets better with age." Anne took a moment gazing out the window and Camilla stopped pacing and stared down at her friend.

"He told me he had to leave early to help his daughter with a problem she was having at work. He has a daughter."

"We have a daughter." Camilla murmured, this time grasping the lower right side of her back. "Did he say anything else about her? Please remember, Annie. Did he say anything else about her?"

"No, honey, he didn't. He's pretty reserved, you know. But he did ask a lot of questions about you, which I answered. Stuff like you have Sconset House with Billy, you don't have any children, you're alone in the winter, and basic things like that."

"He asked about me?"

"Now that I think about it, I suppose that's why he had me to dinner. He wanted to know about you. I left feeling I knew practically nothing about him. He was so mysterious. Now I know why."

"I don't know what to do, Annie. What should I do?"

"There's nothing to do, sweetheart. This is about how you feel, Cammie. Pay attention to how you feel."

"I feel like I've gained everything and lost it at the same time. A grown daughter I've missed out on. The love I couldn't have. Oh, Annie, this feels like a soap opera and you know how I hate soap operas!"

"I'm glad you haven't lost your sense of irony, Cam," Anne spoke, reaching up to take Camilla's hands in hers. "You have a lot to sort out. I have to go. Talk tomorrow?"

"Of course," Camilla smiled back. "I'm the most orderly person I know and right now I feel like I'm in the middle of the biggest mess of my life. How can I put myself back together?"

"Don't. Fall apart for awhile and see where it takes you."

Camilla remained at her seat lost in a haze, feeling hollowed out inside. The questions and fears she had held in check for so many years began to spill over and she wondered if she'd be able to carry on or if she'd lose her mind over it all. The operation of the restaurant that had always consumed her, kept her at a distance from her tragedy now seemed only a superficial burden. Anne was right. Sconset House was really not her soul's delight, but rather a distraction to keep her mind busy and her heart tucked carefully out of sight.

Looking down at her hands she saw the soiled tablecloth and with a sigh stood and began to unset the table to repair the damage. The futility of it brought fresh tears to her eyes and through them all she could see was Lincoln's dark eyes brimming with love.

On unsteady feet she slowly made her way to the kitchen to toss the dirty linen.

CHAPTER EIGHT

Camilla sat in her office a long time after Anne left. The shining blue vista beyond the window soothed her a bit and allowed her to drift back to a bright fall day in 1969.

It was Moratorium Day, October 15, 1969. The anti-war movement had called for everyone to stop their daily activities and join in nationwide rallies against the war. Thousands of people, mostly students and professors, thronged Boston Common at mid-day to hear Abbie Hoffman whip the crowd up to near a near riotous frenzy of anti-war zeal. Camilla, who was studying at the Museum of Fine Arts School, joined her fellow students and made her way with them, walking from the museum up Boylston Street to the Common.

The bright colors and exotic clothing the hip crowd wore dazzled Camilla and inspired a carnival-colored impression of the scene she later painted, winning a school award. As the day wore on and the crowd listened to speaker after speaker with a folk singer thrown in here and there, the tension of the group mounted, and when Abbie Hoffman finally took the stage, most members of the vast audience had taken to their feet, fists pounding against the puffy white clouds in the Indian Summer sky. The menacing tone of the afternoon made Camilla nervous, and as everyone else screamed and applauded en masse, she began to weave her way off the Common. But the crowd was so frenzied, she had difficulty making her way around the tightly massed, arm waving crowd. She began to panic, and as she stood looking around her for an exit route, she felt a strong hand on her back and a soothing voice say, "Let's veer to the right. There's an opening over there."

Trusting the firm guidance on her back and liking the voice, Camilla let her guide lead her to a small opening where she was able to turn around and meet her escort. He was a tall, strongly built black man with a neatly trimmed afro and large kind eyes. He had a warmth around him that was immediately palpable to Camilla. She had never felt an energy like his, and for a moment she stood in front of him mute.

"I didn't mean to get too pushy," he smiled expectantly. "You okay?"

"I'm fine now," Camilla smiled back. "That speaker scares me. Look what he's doing to the crowd. He's making a supposedly pacifist event look absolutely violent."

"My sentiments exactly. Care to join me for coffee?"

Camilla nodded and followed the slightly older man out to Tremont Street. She held his hand as they wove in and out of the crowd, and she found herself wondering if she would ever want to let go of him. It was a strange thought for an independent young lady like Camilla, and it surprised her. And yet she felt his energy drawing her into him like a magnet. What she didn't know was that he was having the same experience with her, and when he suddenly turned around to face her and the crowd jostled them together, the embrace and kiss that followed didn't surprise either one of them.

Camilla said it was love at first sight and Lincoln always agreed.

CHAPTER NINE

Billy loved socializing with his circle, as he called it, and Sconset House provided him the perfect spot to do what he loved most: connecting with old friends (some of them childhood buddies), planning golf outings and arranging summer sails on various yachts. Everyone loved Billy and those who knew him would smile benignly in the direction of the cocktail lounge off the Main Dining Room when his boisterous laugh punctuated the quiet elegance of a Sconset House evening.

Most of Billy's work took place early in the morning when he settled the books, checked on supplies with the kitchen staff, and met with Camilla. This arrangement left him plenty of time to enjoy his summer. He had found early on in his career that people could be hired to take reservations and care for the property. His days of fussing over the restaurant's gardens and famous roses were over. 'Let someone else do it,' was Billy's solution the past few years.

Once the restaurant opened at six and Camilla stood at her podium ready to seat their guests in the dining rooms, which she had inspected for perfection, Billy would spend some time in the kitchen hanging out with Chef Brandon. Oftentimes, they had played a round of golf at Sankaty in the late morning and either re-played their shots or planned their next adventure. When he saw enough orders pile up to indicate a good seating, Billy would ad-just his trademark bow tie, square his broad shoulders in his navy blazer, and amble into the dining rooms. His always sun-streaked blonde hair and prep school good looks beamed as his wide smil-ing eyes surveyed the area seeking old acquaintances to greet and share a laugh with.

Billy made his appearance at six thirty on opening night. He noted that Camilla had scattered guests throughout the three din-ing rooms thoughtfully and experienced the safe feeling he always had when Camilla was taking care of things. Her organization and efficiency were two of the qualities he loved most about her and as he took his first stroll through his restaurant he felt awash with happiness. 'It doesn't get any better than this,' he thought as he made his way to touch base with John and Karen Bates at their usual window table in the Lily Room.

After the predictable questions about the previous winter's activities, Billy slowly made his way from table to table. By the time he had made his circuit all the way to Camilla's spot in the front, a number of comments about Camilla troubled him. Several women had asked about her health, noting her weight loss and wondering why she frequently sat at a stool, new-ly placed behind her podium. People were concerned about her, and suddenly Billy's sense of well being was replaced with a wash of dread as he looked carefully at his wife for the first time in a while. Her usually radiant smile seemed pasted on her mouth and two bright red spots glowed on her cheeks as if she had a fever. When she turned to greet the Hamiltons he no-ticed that last year's light blue cashmere suit jacket hung from her shoulders as if it were on a hanger. Billy didn't know what to do. Camilla always took care of everything, including him. He felt frozen to his spot as he watched his wife slowly take the Hamiltons to a table which was not their favored location. At a word from Biff Hamilton, Camilla changed course and brought them to their usual spot.

As she ran her hand through her hair and made her way back to the podium at an even slower pace, Billy realized that something was terribly wrong. Rushing over to intercept her at the podium he gently took her arm and led her out onto the front porch.

"What's wrong with you, Cammie?" Billy asked, dread literally pouring out of his expressive blue eyes.

"Looks like a flare-up of last year's Lyme Disease," Camilla softly answered. "Seems to be taking away my energy a bit. Don't worry, Billy. I'm fine." She started to return to the foyer and abruptly turned back around and kissed Billy lightly on the lips.

"I want you to go home early tonight and get some extra rest," Billy insisted.

"Yes, sweetheart, of course," Camilla agreed.

With the Lyme Disease explanation safely stored away in his mind, Billy decided to forget the situation and enjoy his evening. After all, it was opening night and he had already made plans with Kendall Douglas to enjoy a cigar and port on the verandah later that night. Camilla would be just fine.

As the evening progressed, the sheer momentum of energy surrounding the opening of the restaurant invigorated Camilla to the point where when everyone was seated around ten she was ready to take her traditional table with Billy near the podium for their dinner. They had ordered earlier, so as soon as they were seated, Dottie appeared with their salads and a bottle of champagne for them to celebrate with.

Dottie bubbled with excitement as she served the Smiths their dinner. It seemed that one of her dates from last year, a patent attorney from Manhattan, was waiting for her in the cocktail lounge.

"He's got a bottle of champagne and strawberries dipped in chocolate in a basket in the trunk of the car," Dottie enthused. "We're going down to the beach later to get re-acquainted. I'm so happy to be back. It was a long cold winter up there in Maine."

"We're glad you're back too," Camilla returned. "And give my best to, what was it, Don?"

"No, Don's the doctor from New Jersey. He doesn't come out until August. Harry's the lawyer."

"That's right, good old Harry. Tell him to stop over to say hi," Billy smiled.

Dottie nodded in reply as she sped off to finish up for the evening.

"Oh, to have half of her spunk," Camilla wistfully smiled.

"Speaking of spunk, did you see how well Jasmine did tonight with Jared? I think they make a great team."

"I got a lot of great comments on her," Camilla agreed. "Looks like we have a new member in our little family."

"Brian's pretty happy about it. They've been spending a bit of time together during the days and while Brian protests that he's just showing her around, I think he's really interested in her." Billy confided.

"Hum, I wonder about that. She's a very sophisticated young lady. Brian might be getting in over his head, I think..." Camilla stopped as Anne and her husband John Price arrived at their table.

"Hey, you two," Billy boomed. "Glad to see you!"

"Ready for a cognac at the bar?" John asked. "I'm sure the ladies have plenty to talk about."

"Sure," Billy said, rising from his seat and managing to give Anne a peck on the cheek as he linked his arm in John's and they moved into the cocktail lounge.

"So, how are you doing?" Anne queried with a worried look on her brow.

"I feel like I'm losing it. I keep thinking about, you- know- who, and wondering what he's doing and, you know. . . everything. I can't keep my mind on what I'm doing. I almost sat Biff and Janey Hamilton at the wrong table. Can you imagine? I never make mistakes like that. I'm so confused, Annie. Oh, God, what am I going to do?"

"I don't know what to tell you," Anne answered leaning in close to her friend. "But you're going to have to do something about this at some point. Are you feeling okay?"

"No. I'm so flustered and tired and wired at the same time. I want to go check into a hotel for a few days and just sleep and think. Unfortunately, that will have to wait until October."

"Come on, let's get out of here. I'll drive you home," Anne literally commanded getting to her feet. "Hey Dottie, tell the guys I'm driving Camilla home, will you?" Anne asked as Dottie swung by to give her a hug.

"Sure thing," Dottie smiled, and darted off on yet another errand.

Camilla and Anne sat in the moonlight on the garden bench looking at *Rapture*. The soft moonglow suited the statue, gently caressing its sensual shape, revealing the artist's passion.

"When I look at this statue I can almost feel Linc's hands on me, smoothing my skin, caressing me as he must have run his hands over the sculptured shape. I will never forget the heat of his touch. I remember . . . no, I have to stop this. It's madness." Camilla moaned, her hands to her face.

"How could you leave this part of your life behind like this? You're so cool and capable all the time. You just . . . wait a minute.

I see it now. All this passion and longing comes out in your painting. And look at that statue! He's as cool and together as you are, but look at the statue! His passion comes through in his sculpting. Oh, Camilla, we have to take a trip to New York. I'll set it up so the two of you can meet. We'll go in September when the season slows and..."

"No, Annie. I can't do that. I just can't!"

"You are a stubborn woman, Camilla. But I'm going to cross you on this. You haven't heard the last from me. I promise you," Anne threatened, standing up to leave.

"We'll see about that, my dear," Camilla softly replied.

For a long pause Camilla gazed at the statue after Anne had left. Rising to her feet, she finally approached the statue and fell to her knees, weeping. "Lincoln, Lincoln," she sobbed over and over.

Jared stood at the edge of the garden watching his friend. He did not want to startle her and yet he couldn't just let her suffer. When Camilla's crying began to slow down, he approached Camilla and from a short distance called to her quietly, so as not to startle her. "Lovey, let's go in. I'll make us some tea."

Turning around, Camilla looked over to her friend and rose to her feet, arranging her skirt and fluffing her hair. "Oh Jared, I'm so embarrassed. Why are you here?"

"I wanted to make sure you were okay. Dottie said you left early, and I saw how you were struggling. The Hamiltons, sweetheart. It scared me."

"Scared me, too," Camilla answered as the two moved towards the side door near the garden.

"Who's Lincoln?"

"Someone from the past. Please don't speak of this, Jared."

"You don't even need to say that. Must have been a great love."

"A great love."

"Earl Grey or Sleepytime?"

"Definitely Sleepytime."

"Well, I have a great idea for the wedding, to change the subject," Jared enthused. "How about Mexican food? I know it's a bit lowbrow for Sconset, but Jessica told me that she and Jeffrey went to Acapulco last Christmas and that's where they totally fell in love. Isn't it just too much? Can't you just see old Jeffrey tangoing with Jessica in a ballroom overlooking the ocean? He dances her to the wrought iron railing, takes her in his arms, kisses her, and proclaims his love."

"You've definitely missed your calling, Jared. You should be writing romance novels. Nora Roberts beware!" laughed Camilla.

"But won't Mexican be great?"

"It will. And I know just the person to do the cooking. Hillary Clement from Twenty-One Federal in town used to own a trendy Mexican restaurant in the West Village. I'm sure she'll do it. And I'll go to Pier One to get some Mexican stuff to decorate the verandah."

"Or a dining room if it rains."

"Right. I've been stumped about this. Thanks, Jared. I can always count on you. Don't the Mexicans have a traditional wedding cake or something? I'll have to look into that. What's Billy doing?"

"He's out on the verandah with his circle, a bottle of port and cigars. They're having a puffed up grand old time of it. In other words, nothing unusual."

"Billy."

"Yeah, Billy."

CHAPTER TEN

The first two weeks of the season fairly flew by. During that period of time Sconset reawakened fully for the new season with seemingly endless plans for parties, shows, golf, and boating. Flocks of tourists biked down the Sconset or Polpis Bike Paths to get a glimpse of the rose covered cottages and taste the delicious ice cream at Sconset Market. It was a Sconset summer and Sconset House had taken on a life of its own.

A lingering early summer northeaster had increased business at the restaurant as many outdoor dinners and picnics had to be canceled in favor of indoor activities. And where else to go to escape the biting damp wind but the cozy Sconset House, with its crackling fires in each dining room when the weather demanded it? Everyone at the restaurant was thrilled. Camilla was exhausted.

She discovered that an afternoon nap was the only way she could make it through the evening's business. That nap and several cappuccinos during the dinner rush got her through the bustle and kept her mind sharp. Her course of antibiotics had ended and Camilla felt worse if anything with a nagging ache radiating from the right side of her back. She had an appointment scheduled for Tuesday morning with Mary Carver to run some more blood work, but her first priority was a shopping trip with Jessica on Monday, the only day of the week Sconset House was closed, to buy a wedding dress. Maeve O'Connor declared she just had to go and at the last minute Jared announced that he would love to share his two bits, and so the happy group of four headed to the airport and bumped its way across Nantucket Sound in the usual ten seater and landed in Hyannis fifteen minutes later.

Camilla had never spent too much time on the Cape, but had shopped at an exquisite boutique in Chatham a number of times with Anne. The little shop sold only exclusive designs by several very talented local dress designers.

Jared had called ahead and in the spirit of the festive time had rented a Lincoln Town Car for the ride to Chatham. Camilla was elected to drive. After several wrong turns and a pit stop for coffee the Sconset foursome arrived at their destination by late morning. Jessica immediately selected four lovely dresses to try and the other three gathered on overstuffed velvet chairs outside the dressing room to judge her selections. Each of the dresses could have worked out, but a stunning antique white voile sheath with exquisite Irish lace and discreet beadwork was everyone's choice. The slim lines of the dress coupled with a dramatic neckline and discreet slit up the side, turned Jessica into a suave, somewhat provocative bride, just the look she wanted. A jaunty little hat with similar beadwork and stunning voile pumps completed the ensemble.

"Jeremy is going to go wild when he sees you," Maeve proclaimed.

"The old boy won't know what hit him," Jared agreed.

"You're gorgeous," was all Camilla could manage through tear filled eyes.

Since the shopping had taken so little time, Camilla took Jared's suggestion and began trying on clothes that complimented her new shape. Her three friends help create a new look that made

Camilla look stunning instead of sickly in clothing that was too big for her. She had gone from a twelve to an eight.

Maeve also found a couple of outfits, one of which she planned to wear at the wedding. Spirits were soaring as the group left the boutique and went next door to the men's shop to help Jared find a new linen blazer for the occasion. They emerged with a gorgeous light grey blazer and stunning tie for Jared.

The lunch hour had arrived and almost passed them by when they finished shopping. Jared suggested a wonderful sushi restaurant in Yarmouthport for lunch. With several more missed turns and stops for directions, the four friends finally pulled up at the sushi restaurant at 3 o'clock. They had a tiny dining room in the back to themselves and happily recounted their purchases after ordering plates of California rolls, sushi and miso soup. While the tea was being poured, Camilla got up to go the ladies room. Suddenly, with a scream of pain, she fell to the floor clutching the right side of her back.

Maeve, Jessica, and Jared surrounded her immediately and tried to determine what had happened. The pain was so intense that Camilla was unable to speak. When Jared asked if they should call an ambulance, Camilla was only able to nod.

Long minutes passed as the four waited for the ambulance. Maeve found some pillows from a couch in the foyer to place under Camilla's head and the owner brought a blanket to cover her with.

"You'll be okay, sweetheart," a frantic Jared tried to say calmly. "Can you tell what it is? Is it your appendix?"

"Kidney," was all Camilla could say.

Trying to say the right thing, Jared reassured her "Well you have two, if this one won't work."

Shaking her head no, Camilla held up one finger.

"You only have one?" Jared practically screamed.

Again Camilla nodded. Jared kneeled over her and held her in his arms, tears threatening to stream down his face. They remained this way until the EMTs arrived some minutes later. After a torrent of questions to which Camilla could only nod or shake her head or mutter monosyllabic answers, the paramedics gently placed her on a gurney and rolled her into the ambulance.

"It's an organ in distress," was all they could tell Jared, Maeve, and Jessica who piled into the Lincoln and sped off after the ambulance heading toward the now seemingly at the end of the earth, Cape Cod Hospital in Hyannis. Upon arrival, Camilla was whisked into a trauma room leaving her three friends to wait in panic in the waiting room.

"I'm calling Jeremy," Jessica said.

"Wait. I think I should call Billy first," Jared suggested.

"But Camilla said he was on a boat all day and then she was supposed to meet him at a cocktail party at the Clark's house," Maeve pointed out.

"Okay, then, I'll leave a message for him to find Jeremy... where? At the restaurant? And then you should call Jeremy and tell him to go to the restaurant to meet Billy. Okay?" Jared suggested, pacing all the while.

"Okay."

The trio moved a secluded spot on the side of the waiting room and the phone calls were made with all three looking back toward the trauma rooms, hoping for word from the doctors.

After the calls were made, the three friends sat in miserable silence until about an hour later, a middle-aged male doctor signaled for them to meet with him in a little conference room to the right.

"Hello, I'm Dr. James. It appears that your friend is suffering from progressive kidney failure, which claimed her left kidney about thirty years ago. She is on the dialysis machine as we speak and she will respond to that treatment almost immediately. We've placed her on the kidney donor list and hope that produces something. She has no family for us to test for a match, so that leaves us totally dependent on the list."

"Will she come home soon?"

"Will she get a kidney?"

"Is she going to make it?" All three bombarded the doctor with questions.

"We're going to keep her in the hospital here for at least a week. She has been very sick for quite awhile. Why hasn't she done something about it?" Dr. James asked.

"She thought it was a flare-up of her Lyme Disease from last year and just finished taking the antibiotics for it." Jared answered. "She has an appointment with Dr. Carver on Nantucket tomorrow."

"I see. If she doesn't improve in the next two days, we will airlift her to Mass General in Boston. Hopefully, that won't be necessary."

"Can we see her?" Maeve asked, fighting back the tears.

"Yes. She's been admitted. She's in room 210. Don't be put off by the dialysis machine. It's saving her life at the moment. And she's a bit groggy from the pain medication."

"Thank you," Jared spoke for all three, grimly shaking the doctor's hand.

Up in her room Camilla began to relax as the pain started to diminish. The whole situation took her back to shortly after she had given birth. She had developed severe pain in her left kidney and had been told that it was a further complication from childbirth… something about a latent infection she had harbored during the pregnancy. When she didn't respond to antibiotics and started to decline, her kidney had been removed. And now this doctor said what she'd really had back then was a degenerative disease and now she needed a kidney transplant. He didn't say in order to live, but he didn't have to. As an only child with both parents dead, she had one uncle in California and an aunt living in Italy as her only relatives to test for a donor. She had never met either of these people and was not even certain they were alive. Camilla's fear rose as the pain lessened. She wanted to see her friends. She wanted Anne.

A gentle tap on the door and Jared, Jessica and Maeve entered. Everyone seemed a bit awkward and standoffish, at first, until Camilla broke the ice. "I know that this is life threatening. Don't be afraid that you know something I don't know. Now listen to me carefully. I need for all of you to go back to Sconset now and sit down with Billy and figure out how to run the restaurant. Maeve, tell Billy I think you should go on a salary that will equal the amount you make in tips, and you should take my place."

"No, no one should take your place. You'll be back soon," Maeve protested, leaning forward to take Camilla's hand.

"I won't be able to work again for quite a while, my dears. You don't know how weak I've been for weeks. The doctor reprimanded me for pushing myself so hard. Now Jared, don't look at me like that. I'm only trying to be realistic. I want this to be as easy as possible for Billy."

"To hell with Billy," Jared angrily replied. "It's time he stood on his own two feet and actually did something instead of relying on you to carry all the responsibility on your shoulders."

"Now, Jared, it's not that bad."

"The way I see it, it certainly is that bad."

"Well, I'm glad to see I have so many people looking out for me. Jessica, go ahead with everything we've set in motion. I will be there to stand up for you at your wedding. I promise you."

"We'll wait for you, Camilla. We wouldn't think of doing it without you," Jessica stammered and turned away as her voice broke and tears began to run down her cheeks.

"Okay, Maeve, can you take down a list of the things I need you to do? Divide them up any way you like. I need Billy to pack me underwear, nightgowns, a robe, slippers and my toiletries. They can be sent to me by transport or someone who comes over here regularly. Don't interrupt, Jared. I can see you getting ready to spout off again and I don't have the energy to deal with it, okay lovey? I need to talk to Anne. Please have her call me and I need my appointment with Dr. Carver canceled. Oh, and tell Billy to send me the pile of books I have on my nightstand. Looks like I'm going to get to read them, finally."

"Is that all, Cammie?" Jared quietly asked.

"Yes, dearheart, that's all I need for now. You'll have to jumble the teams and wait stations to let Maeve run the show. I suggest letting Dave Johnson go solo for awhile with a small station with the other teams each picking up one table. It should work out and I think Dave would like to work alone. Just give everyone my love and go home."

"Okay, Camilla. I guess we better get started back and give you some rest," Jessica said, looking around at the others.

"You two go back, I'm checking into a hotel and staying here tonight so Camilla knows someone is close by," Jared announced, feet squared off as if readying himself for an argument. Instead, Camilla began to cry and held his hand tightly.

"Thank you, Jared. I do think I need you."

"Okay, so you two go home and I'll be either here or at the Hyannis Regency if you need to talk to me. Jess, I'll call you tonight at ten at Surf."

"I'll have my phone on," Jessica promised.

"And I'll track down Billy. Jeremy is actually already on the case, so I'll hook up with him and get your things together for you," Maeve stated.

"Good then, give me a hug and go."

After they left, Camilla sent Jared out to secure his room and told him to come back in two hours so she could get a nap. When she was finally alone, Camilla spent a long time looking at the photographs of Cape Cod beaches on the opposite wall. She was relieved to have Jared close by tonight, but upon deeper contemplation, the only other person she wanted with her was Lincoln. Lincoln. She fell asleep remembering the way he held her close as she fell asleep at night.

CHAPTER ELEVEN

Jasmine decided to take the day off to be by herself and think through her situation. Her first weeks in Sconset had flown by in a welter of new relationships with her quick connection with Brian proving to be more intense than any she could remember. Not since her college days had she bonded so intimately with a group of people. As she slowly made her way along the vast expanse of sand called Low Beach heading into Sconset she had the feeling she had been on Nantucket, absorbed in the magic of Sconset House, forever. She couldn't decide if the situation was mesmerizing because of the sheer isolation of living in a tiny outpost on an island thirty miles out to sea or if she was caught up in Camilla's spell.

Sitting down in the warm sand, stretching out her long legs to absorb the golden sunlight, Jasmine focused on Camilla. The woman who was her mother turned out to be the most brilliantly talented, generous woman she had ever met. Part of her was intensely proud of her, but a larger, more ominous sensation was loss. If only Camilla had been her mother all along. It would have been so wonderful to have been a part of the intricate web she wove for her entire life. And her dad would have been so happy to have been part of her world. He was right, Jasmine mused. His instinct to protect her from what she couldn't have had made her a happier person than she was now. She was beginning to understand her father's blues, as she always referred to his frequent periods of withdrawal.

She had been protected, not only by Lincoln, but by his whole family. Her life up to now had been full of love and the experience of truly belonging to a dynamic family. She had not suffered the absence of her real mother until now, and wondered how her father could have ever let Camilla go. None of the various women he had dated over the years had come even close to replacing Camilla in his heart. "Poor Daddy," Jasmine murmured.

"I never tried to contact her," Jasmine remembered him saying. That fact stuck in her mind and, with a start, she wondered whether it was actually true. Sure, she knew about the Stuart family's threats, but still. . . maybe they had had carried on a totally secret correspondence of passionate love letters. Given her father's secretive ways, that wouldn't surprise her a bit. Maybe they had even met secretly, like in the play *Same Time Next Year*. The more she thought about it the more she convinced herself that the two of them had carried on a clandestine affair all along.

"Okay," she promised herself. "Tonight he comes clean."

With a decisive nod Jasmine continued her hike up the beach. She decided to stop at Sconset Market for an ice cream cone, and there she bumped into Dottie. A two minute chat informed Jasmine of the wedding dress trip and the boating excursion Billy was on. With that information in mind, Jasmine decided to continue up the beach to Camilla's house where she could be alone for a moment with her father's sculpture in the garden.

Half an hour later found Jasmine on the bench facing *Rapture*. But she was realizing that the more she was alone with her thoughts, the more confused she felt. Grateful that the busy pace of the restaurant kept her mind occupied, she found herseld looking forward to tomorrow's hectic schedule to distract her. Footsteps on the garden flagstones startled her and turning around she saw Anne Hitchcock heading her way.

"Oh Jasmine, I'm surprised to see you here!" exclaimed Anne.

"I was hiking up the beach and decided to make my turn-around here," Jasmine explained nervously. "It's so inviting, I just thought…"

"It is positively delightful. Camilla and I often have lunch on this bench. I had a heck of a time getting this Jones sculpture for her a few years ago, but it was worth it, don't you think?"

"It's…so…beautiful," Jasmine stumbled over her words uncomfortably. "I'd best be getting back to Surf." Hastily, she rose to her feet and for a moment stood in profile next to the sculpture.

Anne started at the sculpture's mirror image and rose from her seat. She gently cupped Jasmine's chin in her hand and carefully studied her features, glancing at the familiar marble face for confirmation. Reaching down to grasp Jasmine's hand, she realized she had often watched the likeness of those very hands painting. Looking into Jasmine's panic-stricken eyes she gently drew her onto the bench beside her. "A few weeks ago, after knowing Camilla all these years, she told me she'd had a child. It's a heartbreaking story of a lost true love, full of racial misunderstandings and broken hearts of Shakespearian magnitude. But you have her hands."

"She told you about me?"

"My dear girl, she told me she had a child. She didn't even know you were a baby girl. Your father had mentioned to me last year that he had a daughter and I was able to tell Camilla."

"So they really never contacted each other."

"Never. The closest they came was when Lincoln took me to dinner on my buying trip last year. Of course, we've been speaking to each other over the years about his purchases."

"It was the paintings that led me to my mother, Anne. You know, they told me she died in childbirth."

"My God! Why would they do a thing like that?" Anne murmured in dismay.

"It was part of the deal Camilla's father made with Daddy. He has suffered over this, Anne. A large part of his heart has been closed down all this time."

"As has Camilla's, Jasmine. She has no idea who you are, you know."

"I realize that. I had to make a solemn promise to not reveal my identity. Do you really think Camilla's father would try to hurt me?"

"No, I can say with certainty that he will not. You see, Camilla's parents died in a plane crash five years ago. No one will hurt you," Anne assured patting Jasmine's hand.

"So I've lost five years I could have enjoyed with my mother. I *hate* that man, Anne, and I'm glad he's dead." Jasmine spat rising to her feet.

"He did a reprehensible thing to you and your parents, that's for sure. But let's look at the future. What are you going to do?"

"As soon as I get back to Surf I'm going to call my father and tell him the Stuarts are dead and that I'm going to tell Camilla who I am. By the way, *he* said no one would see my resemblance to the sculpture."

"The man doesn't know his own talent!" Anne laughed, also rising to her feet. "Here's my business card," she continued. "Call me if I can help you or if you just want to talk. You have no idea how much I want my dear friend to enjoy the rest of her years with her own daughter. And I'm eager to be an honorary aunt. Now I have to go into the house and grab some paintings for a show at the Artists' Association, so I must get going."

"So do I. Boy, am I glad I followed my instinct to come to Sconset."

"You followed your heart," Anne called over her shoulder as she headed towards the side door of the house.

"I sure did," Jasmine smiled to herself as she made her way to the street for a hurried hike to her room.

⊶⊰⊱⊷

Anne let herself into Camilla's studio, which was an attached addition to the house on the cliff side. Huge floor- to- ceiling windows opened on the ocean view and, more importantly, let in marvelous light in the winter for Camilla's painting. The studio was always in a state of disarray, unlike everything else in Camilla's life. During the summer her easels were stacked in piles along the inside wall, but during the winter, as many as six would be in place with paintings in differing states of completion sitting on them. Paints spilled out of cabinets and jars of brushes stood everywhere. Stacked against her antique roll-top desk stood seven small paintings waiting to be framed. Anne had arranged for a small show at the Artists' Association of Nantucket and had come by to pick them up for framing.

One by one Anne looked at the canvases and, as always, marveled at her friend's magnificent talent. Camilla had referred to them as "some little things" when she suggested Anne use them in the show. They were a series of exquisite studies of the moors in various seasons. Anne hoped they'd sell in groups of two or three, for it seemed a shame to break them up. Since her car was parked in front of the house, Anne decided to go through the house and out the front door to load them in her Range Rover. She was passing through the kitchen with the first two paintings in her hands when she heard Jared's voice calling on the answering machine. He sounded frantic and called to Billy to answer the phone. Placing a painting on the counter, Anne reached for the phone and caught Jared just before he hung up.

"Oh, Annie, I'm so glad you're there," Jared exclaimed. "You'd better sit yourself down, girl, I've got bad news."

"What's going on, Jared?" Anne fairly screamed, little flames of fear licking up her spine.

"Camilla collapsed in the sushi restaurant. The ambulance took her to the hospital where they diagnosed her with kidney failure. She was admitted and is on a dialysis machine."

"Oh, my God! No wonder she's been looking so bad. Have you noticed her clutching at her back? How serious is she?"

"Very. Did you know she has only one kidney? It seems she lost one in her early twenties. She needs a transplant and has no relatives to test for a match. She's already on the national donor list, but, to tell you the truth, I'm pretty scared, Annie."

"Okay, I'm flying over tonight. I'll pack a bag for her and be over as soon as I can organize my life here."

"Great. I'm at the Regency and I'll go down and get you a room. Thank God they keep several rooms open for people connected to hospital emergencies, even in high season. Camilla wants Maeve to have Billy pack the bags, so best leave a note for him that you've done it when and if she can track down the Sconset playboy. Oh, and she said to bring the books she has on her nightstand."

"I'm so glad you're with her, Jared. Stay strong. I'll try to find Billy, but I'm going to have to get to the airport before too long. I can see a bank of fog starting to drift in, and you know what that means."

"Right. Love you, Annie."

"Love you too, Jared. Bye."

Anne sprang into action, running to her car with the paintings. She would have her husband handle the Artists' Association. With the paintings safely stowed she bolted upstairs to the bedroom and filled a suitcase with everything she thought her friend might need. A hastily scribbled note on the kitchen counter informed Billy of what she had done. Glancing around the house one last time, Anne felt complete and grabbing the suitcase, made for her Range Rover.

Suddenly, Jared's words 'no relatives' thundered in her ears. Instead of heading home, Anne raced through Sconset, breaking the twenty miles an hour rule by quite a bit and headed to Surf and Turf. With any luck, Jasmine would still be there.

Anne met Dottie on the porch and was directed to Jasmine's room. Calling over her shoulder, Anne asked Dottie to wait a moment for some news. Dottie, sensing the urgency of the situation, began pacing and called to Brian next door to join her on the porch.

Anne knocked on the door and was greeted by an agitated Jasmine. "He's not home, Anne. I'm just dying to tell him everything." Stopping short at the expression on Anne's face she demanded, "What's the matter?"

"Camilla collapsed this afternoon. She's in kidney failure, Jasmine, and she has only one kidney. You're her only living relative and she needs a donor, or I'm afraid she'll die."

Jasmine stood speechless in front of Anne, her face a mask of astonished pain.

Anne took Jasmine's hand. "I'm flying to Hyannis now to bring her what she needs. Will you come? Will you be tested?"

Shaking off her shock, Jasmine whispered, "Of course" and went into high speed, throwing things she'd need in a duffel bag, swiping angrily at tears all the while. Just as she and Anne were about to depart the room, her cell phone began to ring in her purse. Jasmine seemed uncertain what to do.

"Answer it," Anne suggested.

"Hello?"

"Daddy, I can't talk now. Camilla is in kidney failure and she has only one kidney. She's going to find out about me now because I'm her only living relative and I'm going to be checked to be a donor."

"What about her parents?" Lincoln shouted.

"They're dead, Daddy. I'll be at...at..."

"The Regency in Hyannis," Anne filled in.

"The Regency in Hyannis. Call me in an hour. Pray for her."

Jasmine clicked off her phone, pocketed it in her purse and the two bounded down the stairs. In the meantime, Jessica and Maeve had arrived and filled everyone in. They were beginning to make their plans for running the restaurant, and everyone except Brian failed to notice that Jasmine was leaving with Anne. Brian broke with the group on the porch and bounded after Jasmine.

With a finger held up to ask Anne to wait, Jasmine went with Brian to the back of the vehicle and whispered, "You must keep this to yourself, Brian. I'm actually Camilla's daughter. She has no idea who I am. Anne is the only one who knows. I must go to her to see if I can donate a kidney to save her."

"And tell her who you are?" Brian asked, looking deeply into her eyes.

"And tell her."

Brian took her in his arms and kissed her gently on the lips. "She's like a mother to me. I love her so much, Jasmine. I'm glad you're her daughter. There's a part of her that's always been so lonely and melancholy. Maybe your news will give her a stronger will to fight. To live."

With a deep kiss and a tender smile to Brian, Jasmine jumped into the Range Rover and in moments she and Anne were on their way to the airport.

Lincoln held the phone against his chest for a long moment. Dropping it on the couch he took his place, gazing out over Central Park. He knew Jasmine needed him to be with her. He hoped Camilla would want him there too, but what about the husband? Lincoln felt totally unable to make a decision. He went into the kitchen and began chopping onions and garlic and every other vegetable he had in the refrigerator. Cooking always calmed him down, and as the aroma of the sautéing filled the air, he began to gather his thoughts. The ringing phone broke his reverie.

"Hello, Lincoln, this is Anne Hitchcock. I have Jasmine with me and we're about to fly to Hyannis. She's getting the tickets and doesn't know I'm calling you."

"I'm glad she's not alone."

"Right. She's got a lot on her plate, Lincoln, and I think she needs her father. And this could also be your last chance to ever see Camilla. Please come to Hyannis."

"But what about the husband? I don't want to cause a problem."

"He's a pompous lightweight, Lincoln. Don't let that stop you from coming. And Camilla..."

"What about Camilla?" Lincoln pounced on Anne.

"She will want to be with you."

"Are you sure?"

"I'm positive."

"Well, I guess I can...I think I might... I'd like..." Lincoln fumbled for words.

"Just come," Anne commanded. "Got to go. They're calling our plane."

Lincoln turned off the flame, dumped the food in a bowl, and placed it in the refrigerator. A very quick cleanup followed while he waited on hold for his travel agent. When she finally got back on the line, she told him there was a flight leaving LaGuardia for Hyannis in an hour with one seat open. He took the reservation and in a parody of his daughter, did the same throw together packing and was hailing a cab ten minutes later. Mercifully, the traffic was moving and he made it to the terminal as the boarding call was announced.

He was amazed to learn he would be in Hyannis in under an hour. Lincoln was simply not accustomed to acting on events this quickly and a dizzying sense of queasiness took him over as the under-sized plane jounced all the way to Cape Cod. It took all his energy to hold himself together during the flight. Thoughts and emotions ricocheted around in his head like ping pong balls and it was a very disoriented Lincoln Jones who took a cab to the hotel.

Lincoln had no idea what to expect next. All he knew was the events of the next few days would change his life.

Jared crossed the open expanse of the hotel lobby, heading for the front door, and was at first pleased to spot Anne emerging from a cab and then surprised to see Jasmine behind her. The two women gathered several pieces of luggage from the trunk and headed his way. An odd couple, mused Jared. Everything about the usually perky Anne sagged, from her droopy auburn curls to her loose fitting cream linen over jacket and pants. Her obvious state of stress was matched by the usually cool and collected Jasmine whose hair was slipping out of her trademark twist and cascading over her shoulder, from which both her silk blouse and travel bag hung awkwardly.

Spying Jared, Anne visibly brightened as he approached to relieve her of Camilla's luggage. "I was afraid I'd miss you, Jared," sighed Anne. "You're looking a bit ragged."

"I was just thinking the same about you," laughed Jared, running his hand through his already disheveled curly locks. Leaning close to Anne's ear he whispered "Why is Jasmine with you?"

"Long story," Anne whispered back. Looking over her shoulder at Jasmine, she motioned her with a snap of her head to move closer to them.

"Jared's wondering why you're here. Is it okay with you if we tell him?" asked Anne.

With a fatigued sigh, Jasmine nodded and smiled at Jared. In return he tucked a stray strand of hair that threatened to blow across her face behind her ear. For a long beat the three stood frozen, not willing to face the next moment.

"Well, let's get you two registered and then why don't we get a cool drink over there," Jared suggested, pointing at a dimly lit cocktail lounge to the right of the indoor pool.

Anne and Jasmine nodded in synch and headed for the front desk. Moments later, relieved of their bags, they made their way with Jared in the lead to a little table at the back of the bar.

"So?" Jared asked, his expressive eyebrows raised in expectation.

"Well… " Anne began struggling to get comfortable on the hard little chair. "Earlier this afternoon, before I knew anything was happening to Camilla, Jasmine and I found ourselves together on the bench in front of Camilla's sculpture *Rapture*. While we were there I noticed that Jasmine looks like the girl in the statue… and is in fact her."

Jared snapped his attention to Jasmine. Looking at her in profile, he realized that what Anne said was true. With a sinking feeling in the pit of his stomach, he remembered finding Camilla a few short weeks ago sobbing on her knees in front of the same statue.

Jasmine raised her hands to her face as if to hide from Jared's amazed stare. Sighing again and trying to come to terms with the fact that these two people were probing into the intimate details of her life, she slowly lowered her hands and turned to face Jared and began, "My father sculpted that statue. I posed for it when I was in my teens. My father is Lincoln Jones and he…"

"*Lincoln?*" Jared interrupted. "Camilla knew a Lincoln. I heard her sobbing his name a few weeks ago. Is it the same Lincoln?"

"Yes, most likely. It seems like. . . well what really happened," Jasmine stumbled, looking to Anne for support.

"Camilla and Jasmine's father were in love a long time ago. Camilla's family couldn't condone their relationship, and when Jasmine was born they forced Lincoln to take the baby and threatened harm to his family if he ever contacted Camilla again." Anne filled in. "Pretty horrid, isn't it."

"My poor Camilla. My poor dear Lovey." Jared murmured. "So this means that you are Camilla's daughter. Does she know?"

"No" both women exclaimed simultaneously.

"I'm going to see if I'm a match for donating a kidney for my. . . for Camilla."

"Well, that's the first good news I've heard. So you just decided this summer to get to know Camilla and you came to Sconset under false pretenses?"

"Jared, that's a little harsh, don't you think?" Anne cautioned.

"Well, what was it then?"

With a deep breath, Jasmine began, "I was told that my mother died giving birth to me. My birth certificate even says that. Camilla's father had a fake one drawn up when he gave me to my father along with threats to ruin my grandparents' reputation or something like that if he ever contacted Camilla again. Daddy had no idea until today that the Stuarts are dead. Anyway, I found out about Camilla last winter and against my family's wishes, came out here incognito because my father wanted to protect me from harm at the hands of my Grandfather Stuart. I simply had to know her, Jared. And now, I'm going to reveal my identity to her and see if I can donate a kidney and…"

"So, what do you think of our Camilla?" Jared asked, interrupting.

"I think she's magical. I don't know how my father has managed without her all these years, and I truly wish I had grown up as her daughter."

Reaching out to take Jasmine in his arms, Jared smiled, "Magical. That's the best description I've heard yet. And with any luck at all, you'll have plenty of time to be her daughter. Of course, Annie and I come along as part of the deal."

"That's fine with me," Jasmine sighed, allowing the warmth Jared radiated to fill her heart.

"Okay, let's get this show on the road. It's getting late and we should get right over to Cape Cod Hospital to see if the lab can test Jasmine now. And I want to see my dearest friend," Anne said, herding the others towards the double doors.

"Has anyone wondered how Billy is going to react to all this? Frankly, I think the old boy is going to have himself a hissy fit." Jared asked as they made their way to the Lincoln.

"He might just do that. But at this point, I could care less about him. Let's go save our Camilla!"

———

Camilla drifted in and out of sleep as the painkillers began to take effect. It was the most relaxed she'd felt in a long time and she wished she could stay in her foggy state forever. With a gentle rap on the door, Anne entered with Camilla's belongings.

"I'm so glad you're here," Camilla spoke weakly.

Anne swooped to Camilla's bedside and hugged her fiercely. Standing back she said, "I just know you're going to be okay. We'll fight this thing and you'll be back to your old self in no time."

"I have so much to think about with the restaurant and all that the danger to me hasn't really sunk in yet. Did you speak to Billy? I've been expecting his call."

"No, I guess he was still out sailing when I left. Jeremy's on the case, tracking him down so I suspect you'll be hearing from him soon. The good news is the staff was in a huddle planning how to run the restaurant when we . . . I mean when I left Surf. You've got some dedicated people there, old girl."

"Great," Camilla replied with a gravelly voice.

Anne was relieved she missed the "we" accident and realized the level of medication Camilla was on as she would have picked up on that and not have let it go by ordinarily. "I'm going to un-pack your things and you tell me what you'd like to wear first," Anne bubbled with false enthusiasm.

For the next half hour Anne arranged Camilla's things neatly in her drawers and closet and stowed her personal things in the bedside table. Camilla continued to drift in and out of sleep and when Anne was finished she found her friend in a deep slumber. Anne leaned over, kissed her on the forehead and quietly left the room heading for the lab where she knew Jared and Jasmine waited.

━━┿╍┿━━

Jared and Jasmine paced impatiently outside the lab waiting for Anne to join them. They'd been anxiously discussing just how Jasmine was going to break the news to Camilla when, with relief, Anne bustled into view.

"Okay, guys, they have her knocked out pretty well, so I think we should go back to the hotel and get a quick dinner."

Jared agreed. "Good idea. The lab was about to close when we arrived, so we won't know anything until morning. I want to call the restaurant, the house, Surf, anywhere I can to find Billy. Isn't it just like him to be out of the loop with Camilla when she needs him?"

"You got that right. And she asked about him. She wants to talk to him. She needs him to show a little affection and ease her mind about the restaurant."

"Little affection is right. That's about all the self-centered prick is capable of."

"Is there a problem with Camilla and Billy?" Jasmine asked, hoping against hope that there was.

"Let's just say that Camilla caters to his every need. And aside from supplying her with pictures taken on his long months away

91

from home, it's hard to determine whether or not he truly does anything for her. Camilla actually expects very little from him and seems happy enough handling his life for him. Her incapacity is going to throw him for a loop," Anne mused.

"It's going to be very interesting to see what old Billy is going to do now. I'm betting he's going to get mad and make her life miserable," Jared pronounced.

"Let's hope not," Anne answered, shaking her head. "Let's hope not."

CHAPTER TWELVE

Billy was exhilarated after his day of sailing with the Andersons and was looking forward to cocktails at the Clark's quaint old renovated shanty just up the road from Sconset House as he raced down Milestone Road, the top down on his vintage MG. As usual, he was late and was certain that Camilla had already returned and realizing that he was behind schedule, had laid out an outfit for him to change into.

As he bounded out of his car and sprinted towards the side door, Maeve seemed to materialize out of thin air in his path. Stopping short, hand to his heart, Billy stood facing her waiting for an explanation.

"Billy, I've got bad news. Camilla collapsed at the sushi restaurant this afternoon and was rushed to Cape Cod Hospital. She has kidney failure."

"What?" Billy shouted. "She has only one kidney. This can't be."

"I'm afraid it is. She has been admitted for a least a week and…"

"A week? I need her here! She can't be gone for a week. It's almost high season and she has a restaurant to run. No, she has to come home."

"I'm afraid she can't, Billy. She told me to tell you that I should take her place and re-adjust the stations so that all the tables can be served. The staff has already worked it out and Prescott is due to arrive July 1, so I think we'll be okay."

"Okay? No, Maeve, I won't be okay without her here *now*. I've got to talk to Camilla." Abruptly, Billy unlocked the side door and went into the kitchen, motioning Maeve to follow him. After fumbling with the phone book and finally allowing the operator to make the call, Billy was asking to be connected to Camilla's room.

"Camilla, what's going on?"

"I have kidney failure, sweetheart," Camilla whispered over the phone.

"You'll have to speak up. I can't hear you."

"I can't. Talk to Maeve. Jared and Annie are here. They'll call you. Call Dr. James. I…" Camilla wavered.

"Don't go, Camilla. Should I come over there? Should I stay home? What should I do?" Billy shouted hysterically.

"Don't come here. Keep the restaurant alive. Love you," Camilla whispered, hanging up the phone.

Turning to Maeve, Billy wailed, "She couldn't talk to me. I could barely hear her voice and then she just hung up the phone."

The ringing phone caught his attention and with a hopeful look in his eyes he said, "I'm sure it's her calling back. I'm sure she got a second wind and can talk to me now." Maeve had to turn away from the heart-rending expression on his face. She was quite sure Camilla had not experienced a second wind.

"Hello? Oh hi, Kenny… I left my cap on the boat? Why don't you drop it by the restaurant tomorrow… No, we won't be at the Clarks's tonight. Camilla has taken sick off-island and so we won't be able to make it tonight. Goodbye."

After hanging up the phone, Billy sat down facing Maeve. He was so used to Camilla organizing and facilitating the events of his life that without her input, he was pretty much at a loss. For a long minute, he sat and stared out at the ocean, his blue eyes glazed over, lost in his own bewilderment.

Maeve allowed him his peace for a few moments and then decided to light a fire under him. Feeling sorry for himself was not going to help anyone, least of all Camilla. "So, Billy, what did she say?"

"Not much," he replied moving his haunted eyes to her. "Anne and Jared are with her and she gave me the name of the doctor. She said to rely on you to keep the restaurant going. That's all."

"You know I'll do anything it takes to keep Sconset House operating at Camilla's standards. Don't worry about the restaurant. Please. It's getting late, so why don't we see if we can get the doctor on the line."

"She sounded so weak, Maeve. She sounded like…"

"Don't even say it, Billy. She's on heavy medication. Her pain when she collapsed was extraordinary. Let's call information and speak to Dr. James."

With Maeve's help, Billy was soon speaking to the doctor who told the same story. Camilla's only hope was a kidney donor. Dialysis would keep her going for an indefinite period of time and he hoped that she wouldn't have to be airlifted to Boston. Fear gnawing at his stomach, Billy ended the conversation and hung up the phone. "Now what?" he asked no one in particular.

"If you want my advice, let's get the staff together at the restaurant tonight and plan the season without Camilla. I'll call Brandon and have him come in and cook us a meal and then I'll shoot over to Surf and bring everyone back to the restaurant. All you have to do is send your regrets to your hosts tonight and show up at the restaurant in half an hour. Okay?"

"Okay."

A visibly shaken Billy presided over the Sconset House staff emergency meeting. Even though everyone was showing incredible support, Billy felt alone, adrift without his wife to center his life. A snifter of cognac seemed attached to his hand as he and his people planned the season without Camilla. Everyone wondered where Jasmine was and decided she was enjoying her day off and would be caught up on the details later that evening. Brian felt a bit off-guard, but kept his secret.

By eight o'clock the meeting had ended and Brian accompanied the somewhat inebriated Billy home. Brian was used to escorting Billy around when he had consumed too much. Billy was a passive, sometimes weepy drunk and Brian or Camilla usually had an easy time persuading him to get into bed. But tonight Billy was particularly morose and wandered around Camilla's studio touching her brushes and paints, stopping to gaze at the few paintings that adorned the walls.

When he knocked over her prize African violet collection, Brian hurriedly righted the plants and forcefully steered Billy upstairs to the bedroom. Billy asked Brian to stay at the house in the guest room, and Brian was torn between wanting to be there for his friend and hoping to get a call from Jasmine at Turf. He chose to go to his own room in case Jasmine wanted to touch base with him.

For the first time in his relationship with Billy and Camilla, Brian felt ill at ease. It was obvious Billy that had no idea about Jasmine's identity. He was willing to bet that Billy was totally unaware that Camilla had ever even had a baby, and he wondered how they could have been married so long with such a significant secret lurking behind the door. And if Jasmine proved to be a match with Camilla and the operation was performed, wouldn't her father want to be at her side? And wouldn't he want to see his daughter's mother as well? Billy was already falling apart and

Brian had no confidence that he would rally and act like a responsible husband in the matter. The longer Brian pondered the situation as he slowly walked home to Turf, the more concerned he became for his dear friends.

CHAPTER THIRTEEN

J asmine, Anne, and Jared were standing at the crowded front desk of the hotel checking for messages when Anne spied Lincoln coming through the front entrance. Nudging Jasmine and gesturing in his direction, Jasmine darted to her father and locked her arm through his. Jasmine projected an air of sophistication and culture which Anne had noticed and felt served her well at Sconset House, but seeing the urbane Lincoln with his daughter, Anne realized that Jasmine had been brought up in culturally sophisticated family and that she was genuinely the polished young woman she appeared to be. She was not the average young woman waitressing for the summer, and Anne realized the sacrifice she had made in order to know her mother. She deserved to be known for who she was.

Lincoln slowly made his way with his daughter to the desk and after what seemed like an eternity, secured a room and re-joined Jasmine who sat waiting for him. The others had gone to their rooms.

"You don't look well," Jasmine observed.

"I'm not well. You know I don't like sudden changes, and the flight in that little plane knocked me off my feet. I need to lie down and get my bearings. So, tell me, where do you stand in this?"

"I've had a test to see if I match, but it was so late in the day when we got here, I won't know until tomorrow if I can, you know…"

"Save your mother's life," Lincoln finished for her. "And what if you don't match? Then what?"

"I'm going to tell her anyway. If I don't match, she probably doesn't have long to live and we deserve to have some time together. She's my first priority, Dad. Nothing will keep me from her now."

"I can see that. I certainly can. I'm going to my room, so let's meet here for breakfast at seven. Does that suit you, my love?" Lincoln asked, putting his arm around her shoulders.

"Yes, Dad." Jasmine whispered in her father's ear, her arms hugging him tightly. "Sleep well. I'm so glad you're here. Are you going to see Camilla?"

Looking deeply into his daughter's eyes so full of hope and concern, Lincoln's heart softened and he said, "That's certainly a possibility."

"Oh, good! I just think that will be wonderful."

"Perhaps, Jazzie. But don't forget, she has a husband. And I don't care what you or your workmates think about him, Camilla chose him and has been married to him for a long time. Even if she still cares for me a bit, I have to respect her marriage. So it may not be a wonderful thing for me to see her."

"You'll see that I'm right about this," Jasmine returned, a determined expression taking over her elegant features.

"We'll take it one careful step at a time, sweetheart. Now let me get some rest. My head is spinning and my insides are about to follow suit if I don't lie down."

Lincoln took some time arranging his toiletries and clothing. Seeing his own possessions made the sterile little room seem a bit more comfortable. Lincoln hated sleeping anywhere but his own home, and he particularly disliked the mediocre room he had and its trite paintings of Cape Cod beach scenes.

"How can people stand these paintings?" he muttered as he moved around the room. When he was finally satisfied that he had done all he could, Lincoln took a quick shower and settled into bed. The late day sun was just going down and his last thought before slipping into sleep was it must be after eight- thirty.

At midnight, Lincoln woke with a start. For a moment he didn't know where he was and thought the voices arguing outside his door were intruders in his home. Slowly, he pieced together the events that had brought him to this little room and felt his racing heart slow down. A few deep breaths relaxed him further and he hoped sleep would descend on him again. It didn't.

Lincoln couldn't stop thinking about Camilla. She had been the focal point of his internal emotional life all those years, and the fear of her death washed over him with chilling intensity. And then he began to remember.

Lincoln constructed a small studio space for Camilla in his own studio at the Museum School where he taught sculpture. The room was isolated from the teaching areas and looked out from the second floor over the Fens. From the moment they'd met at the demonstration, it seemed they spent every available moment together. Lincoln loved to sculpt with Camilla painting in the studio with him.

He sometimes stopped working to watch Camilla at her easel. Her long, expressive hands delicately working her paintbrush as she gracefully moved her entire body to the rhythm of her brush strokes enthralled him, even inspired him. His love for her consumed him and made him feel whole. He was positive that his work was better since she had come into his life.

One day, several months into their relationship, they decided to switch places. Lincoln took up Camilla's paints and she took his chisel in hand

and began sculpting a piece of marble. Lincoln's subject choice was easy. The beautiful gardens that stretched forward from his windowpane had always enthralled him and he began work on a lovely oil painting of his favorite vista.

Camilla wandered around the studio a bit hoping for a spark of inspiration. Watching Lincoln open paints and sink into his creation was what she needed, and, began a marble bust of Lincoln himself. They worked on their respective pieces for days and when they felt complete, presented them to each other as gifts. Lincoln had always believed that that was the day Jasmine was conceived, and Camilla agreed.

The simple sculpture of Lincoln still sat on his night table looking over him as he slept. It was like having a bit of her at his side all night and he loved the piece.

Tossing around in his hotel bed, Lincoln missed the sculpture and began wondering if Camilla still had the painting of the gardens. At the time, she'd said it was the most beautiful thing she had ever seen. He wondered if she still treasured it. He wondered if it hung in her home. Sleep came over him, and still he wondered in his dreams.

━‹†›━

CHAPTER FOURTEEN

J asmine tossed and turned her way through the night and finally
gave herself up to a morning shower at five- thirty. As she dried
her long curly tresses and gathered them up into the usual twist
she looked at herself carefully in the mirror. Her complexion, of
course, labeled her as Lincoln's child, and her grandparents always told her that she had many of her mother's facial expressions.
They meant Yolanda, of course, and Jasmine never doubted that
what they said was true. But this morning she saw Camilla's stamp
on her features.

The tilt of her nose, the way her forehead sloped back to her
hairline, the cut of her jaw – the more she looked at herself, the
more she saw Camilla. For a moment she focused on her hands,
busy gathering her hair, and saw those same hands arranging
menus on the podium at Sconset House. She truly looked like
Camilla and wondered how Lincoln had felt about it all these
years. And didn't Camilla find it strange to see bits of herself in
Jasmine? They were even the same height.

With a final pat of her twist, Jasmine left the bathroom and
donned the slightly wrinkled linen shorts and vest outfit she had

hastily thrown in her bag. She disliked wearing clothes that were not perfectly pressed and with a sigh, threw herself down on the bed and watched early morning news shows, waiting for her breakfast date with her father.

><++>

At seven, the four converged on the lobby at the same time. Jared was up on all the restaurant news and planned to stay in Hyannis only until Jasmine's test results came back. Then he would return to Sconset and work with Maeve to keep the continuity of Sconset House intact.

Anne had no specific plans, but knew that one way or another her dear friend would need her today and that she would be there for her. The details of Anne's life were being carried on by her husband John, and once again, she gave thanks for the wonderful man she had married.

Jasmine was simply nervous and seemed to have withdrawn emotionally. She and her father hardly spoke, but shared long looks and seemed to be communicating on a level that transcended the need for words.

Together, they grabbed a quick helping of the continental breakfast the hotel offered, and with cups of coffee in hand, loaded into the Lincoln Jared had kept on loan and negotiated the short trip to Cape Cod Hospital.

Jasmine had an arrangement to meet Dr. James in the out-patient waiting room at eight and he was waiting for her as the foursome appeared. Motioning her into a doctors' conference room, Dr. James looked at her quizzically.

"You are a perfect match for Mrs. Smith," Dr. James began. "A match this complete usually only happens with offspring, siblings, or first cousins, at best. I don't understand this, Miss Jones."

"The truth is, I am Mrs. Smith's daughter."

"But she said she had no living relatives except for some distant ones who she wasn't even certain were still alive. How can this be?"

"Well, she knows she had a daughter, but she doesn't know that the daughter is actually me. It's... well, it's a long story that I'd rather not go into right now, but the proof is in the test. I am her daughter and now I have to go upstairs and tell her who I am."

"Does she know you?"

"Yes. I work for her. I promised not to... well, as I said, it's a long story and I really don't want to speak of it until I see my mother. So, what do I have to do next?"

"We'll have to do a complete physical workup on you. You do know this is major surgery, don't you? Mrs. Smith won't be strong enough for the surgery for about a week, and since she's responding well to the dialysis treatment, I don't want to rush this. So we'll get you ready and wait until everything is right for a successful transplant. You will be required to take it easy for three to four weeks afterwards, so you need to take that into consideration."

"Okay. Just tell me what to do and I'll do it. But first, I'd like to see Camilla. Is it okay to speak to her now?"

"Yes. Come see me at my office in the doctor's building across the street at ten. My staff will set up everything for you and I'll go ahead and call in a colleague from Boston who will perform this with me at Mass General."

Jasmine returned to the waiting room and approached the three sets of questioning eyes with a huge smile on her face.

"You're a match!" Anne exclaimed, jumping to her feet.

"A perfect match!" Jasmine beamed.

"Okay, lovey, I'm on my way back. And don't worry, I'm only going to say that there is a match. I won't say it's you until the time is right. Billy will have to know and I'm a bit worried about that," Jared said, glancing sideways at Lincoln.

"I'll be back to work tonight," Jasmine assured Jared. "It's going to take Camilla about a week to get strong enough for this, but after the surgery, I'll be out of commission for a large part of the summer. I'm afraid you'll have to replace me or something."

"Prescott will be here by then and he'll run the show so Maeve can go back to her waitress spot. We'll hire a hostess and pull it off. Old Billy will have to get off his arse and pull his own weight for a change, and I'll see that he does."

Lincoln's questioning glance at Jared caused Anne to take him aside and explain the dynamics of Camilla's marriage. It was an explanation that rather pleased Lincoln in a way he wouldn't allow himself to completely acknowledge.

Jasmine was suddenly tingling with dread as the moment she had hoped for suddenly became a reality. Looking to her father for support, he put his arm around her and said, "I'll be waiting right here for you, Jazzie. Anne will be here too. You go to your mother and then we'll see what needs to be done next."

"Good luck, Jasmine. You know what to say." Jared kissed her on the cheek. "I'll see you tonight."

Squaring her shoulders, Jasmine strode off and looked back saying, "Here goes."

CHAPTER FIFTEEN

J asmine took great pride in her direct manner of speaking. Her talent served her well with the interns she supervised at the museum. Restoration work demanded clear instruction and Jasmine's meticulous lessons had earned her respect in the New York art restoration circuit. But as she approached Camilla's door, Jasmine's facile grip of the English language failed her. She paused outside the door going over the number of ways she had rehearsed with Jared to tell Camilla her simple message.

Lost in her own reverie, she was almost knocked over by an aide hurrying out of Camilla's door. The commotion that ensued attracted Camilla's attention, and she saw an uncertain Jasmine at her now open door.

"Why Jasmine. What a pleasant surprise. Please come in."

"Good morning, Camilla. How are you feeling?" Jasmine asked, totally ill at ease with this woman with whom she had so carefully established a relationship.

"Much better, thank you. Come over and sit down and tell me why you're here. We really need you back in Sconset, you know.

I'm touched you came in to see me, but..." Camilla let the unfinished question hang in the air.

"I came up to tell you that I had a test yesterday afternoon to see if I was a match for donating a kidney to you, and the lab just informed me that I'm a perfect match."

"You're a perfect match? How can that be?" Camilla exclaimed, sitting up straighter in bed, a flush moving up her throat to her cheeks. A moment of shocked silence hovered in the air as the truth of Jasmine's statement began to settle over Camilla. "I always thought you reminded me of someone, Jasmine. It was the way you turned a phrase. The way you stand back and assess your next words before speaking. You've learned that from your father, haven't you?"

"If you mean Lincoln Jones, the answer is yes."

"My good lord, Jasmine," Camilla whispered, reaching to take Jasmine's hand. "My dear child. My daughter. Why didn't you say who you were? Why did you wait so long? I thought surely..."

"They told me you died giving birth to me. I only found out about you this past winter."

"Oh, my God!" Camilla cried in her raspy voice. "They told you I died?"

"Yes. As soon as I knew who you were, I had to see you, know you. That's when I decided to apply for the job."

"But you didn't have to work for me to meet me. All you had to do was identify yourself."

"My father made me promise to keep my true identity a secret because he was afraid of what your father might do to me and my family."

"Yes, I can see why he would do that. And of course, he didn't know my parents are both dead now. But let's forget that. You're my daughter. My beautiful daughter. I have a daughter. I can see Lincoln in you. Oh yes, I can see him shining through you."

"And I can see you in me. We have the same nose. And look at our hands," Jasmine bubbled, placing her hand next to Camilla's.

"We're a match," Camilla smiled, tears filling her eyes. Pulling Jasmine forward, Camilla hugged her with all the strength she could muster. Jasmine's heart broke to feel how weak and frail Camilla had become, literally before everyone's eyes.

"But what about your name, dear? Why do you call yourself Hunter? Are you married?"

"No. Daddy's sister Yolanda and her husband Byron Hunter adopted me when I was a couple of weeks old. I grew up with them and spent as much time with my father as I could. You must know, I never lacked for anything in my life and as I believed you were dead, I never felt it was my mission to locate you."

"But as soon as you knew about me you had to find me. You don't know how much that means to me, Jasmine. My heart is bursting."

"And I'm determined to have you for a good long time, Camilla. Dr. James says he can do the surgery in about a week. Isn't that great?"

"Are you certain you want to do this, Jasmine? What if you are prone to kidney disease like I am and at some point find yourself needing a transplant? I don't want to put you in that kind of jeopardy. After all, I've done nothing for you all these years and now you have to save my life. . . well, I think it's too much to expect."

"I'm going right over to Dr. James's office this morning to have a complete physical. I'm certain he'll be looking to see if I have any signs of kidney disease and I'll make certain he is as careful as possible checking me out. If he gives me the green light, please let me do this."

Smiling up at her daughter through her tears Camilla whispered, "Of course. We have so much lost time to recover. I'm so proud you're my daughter. You are any mother's dream come true."

"And you are any daughter's dream come true."

"This is going to be hard on Billy. I told him. . . Oh never mind what I told him. He'll either get over it or he won't. So, you're going to go see Dr. James now?"

"Yes," Jasmine said looking at her watch. "They're expecting me in ten minutes, so I guess I'd better get going. I'll come back as soon as I can."

"I wish you didn't have to go through this alone. Ask Annie to go with you."

"I know she'd go with me, but my father's downstairs waiting for me, so..."

"Linc's downstairs?" Camilla screamed, knocking over her water pitcher from her bed table as she lunged forward, grasping Jasmine's shoulders for support. "He's in the building? Oh my God, Jasmine, why didn't you tell me?"

"Well, I didn't think it would make that much of a difference to you."

"It wouldn't make a difference knowing my true love, my soul's only mate was nearby? Jasmine, I love him more than life itself. I always will. Do you think he'll come see me? Does he have someone else?"

With a huge smile, Jasmine lowered Camilla to her pillows and threw a towel down on the puddle of water threatening to soak her sandals. "Yes, I think he'll come up, and no, he doesn't have anyone. I believe. . . well I'll let him tell you how he feels himself."

"Will you bring him up later after your appointment?"

"Of course I will. I have to run now, but we'll be back as soon as possible."

Camilla tried to calm herself by gazing out the window at the white glow of high summer. As she knew she faced death quite clearly on the horizon, her most secret desires where coming to her. Overwhelmed with the emotion of it all, she wondered if the gods were playing a cruel joke or if she would actually live to enjoy her daughter. And Lincoln. What about Lincoln? He would be at her side in a few short hours. And she knew she looked like death warmed over. No, not even warmed over.

Slowly, as her rapid breathing began to slow, Camilla noticed a familiar scent in the air. She thought it smelled like the Somalian Rose Lincoln used to wear, a sensation she hadn't experienced in oh so many years. Just the slight whiff took her back to her life with him and she remembered melting in his arms, his beautiful fragrance surrounding them. As she was deciding that she had lost her mind, as he wasn't due to arrive for hours, she felt a hand on her shoulder and turned to face Lincoln.

Neither was able to utter a word. Slowly, as if floating on a cloud, Lincoln bent down and gathered Camilla in his arms and she truly believed she might have just gone to heaven. As if the thirty-two years were a second in time, all the love and passion Camilla felt for Lincoln re-surfaced. "Don't ever leave me," the last words she had spoken to Lincoln were the first words she uttered.

"Never, my love," Lincoln murmured in her ear. "Never."

After what seemed like an eternity, but may have only been a few seconds, Lincoln let go of Camilla and sat on the edge of her bed. "Why did you marry him?"

"I had nothing, Linc. When you and the baby disappeared my life went blank. All I had was my painting. My life with Billy allowed me the solitude to paint and keep my longing for you alive in my heart. He let me alone. He let me live in the part of my heart you occupied. He never demanded more of me, and I owe him for that."

"What do you think it's been like for me? I never trusted that your father would keep his word. I was always waiting for some inevitable evil to strike my family down. I knew I would kill him if he harmed Pops or anyone else in my family. I knew I would kill… "

"But you had our baby. Do you know that I only found out she was a girl a couple of weeks ago when Annie confirmed you had a daughter? Not knowing all those years ate away at me. And then no babies in my marriage. I had truly wanted a child. I thought it would force me back into the land of the living. Instead, I remained in my exiled world of art. Other than with Annie, the only happiness I've had has been with my staff at the restaurant. Those people were my link to reality."

"I am your reality, Camilla. Jasmine is your reality. Let her make you well. Let her be the miracle for you she's been for me. Please. I can't lose you again."

This time Camilla took Lincoln in her arms and pulled him into her bed with her. They held tight and fell back in love with each other as quickly and completely as they had the first time. Camilla felt his unmistakable heat seeping into her being, giving her strength to fight on. "I've never stopped loving you, Linc."

"Nor I you." Sitting back up and looking into Camilla's deep green eyes, Lincoln smoothed her long, tangled hair away from her face, fanning it out like a halo. "You have a husband."

"Yes, I do, Lincoln. And I'm going to have to divulge this to him now. You know, I never told anyone about our child, not even Annie, until a short time ago."

"How do you think he'll take it?"

"Not well. I'm sure it will be an utter fiasco."

"Well, you deal with that now. I'm not going to force you into any decisions while you have so many things on your mind, but you must know what I want, Camilla."

"I do, Linc. It's what I want as well. Look after our daughter, my love."

"Your eyes are closing, Camilla, so I'll go to Jazzie now and let you sleep."

"Yes," Camilla sighed, slipping into a deep sleep with a contented glow brightening her lovely features.

CHAPTER SIXTEEN

Allowing Camilla an hour of rest, Anne peeked in Camilla's room just as she was awakening. Stopping for a moment to assess the state of her friend, Anne rushed to her bedside enthusing "I've never seen you smile like this, Cammie. You're positively radiant!"

"It's been a long time, but trust me, Annie, this is how I always looked when Linc and I were together. It's like . . . it's like you and John. *You* know."

"Yes, I do know, sweetheart. It's what I always hoped you'd have with Billy. But with him you look overwhelmed with duty."

"My marriage is my job, full of tasks and monetary reward. I always knew Billy would never take Linc's place in my heart, but I thought that if we had a family, it would be a substitute for all I had lost. Why couldn't it have worked out that way? Why couldn't I be so happy in my marriage that the sight of Linc would only be a pleasant memory, a blip from the past?"

"He's a lot more than a blip for you, honey. You are head over heals in love with him and I would guess that you're on the brink of loving that stunning young woman you gave birth to."

"She's pretty amazing, isn't she? Can you imagine what she's been going through in Sconset, knowing I'm her mother and not being able to say so? I think it has probably been the first adversity in her life."

"I would say so. Lincoln's family brought her up beautifully, and I'm afraid you're going to have your hands full dealing with them, not to mention Billy."

"Billy. My God, how am I going to explain this to him? Speaking of adversity, this will be a first for Billy. All the coddling he's received from his family and then from me. He looks like he's together, but you and I know he's the most dependent grown man in the world. I know I'm to blame. I'm afraid I let him be my child when he couldn't cut it as my husband. I'm at a loss, Anne!"

"Look, honey, all you can do is get him over here and tell him face to face what has happened. Don't protect him from difficulty like you always do. Let him know the facts and send him back to Sconset. You're not going to be back for quite some time, so let him figure out where he stands. He has a lot of friends' shoulders to cry on. Believe me, he'll do a lot of that and then when he sees that the restaurant can go on without you, maybe he'll become a stronger man for it. Maybe you'll find that you have a marriage after all."

"I don't know about that. Do you think Lincoln and I could carve out a future together? It feels so right. I don't want to lose this feeling again, Annie. And I don't want to hurt Billy."

"You're going to have to decide which is more important to you and then do what you have to do without looking back. Sounds easy, doesn't it?"

"Yeah, sure. Easy as pie. Maybe I should just fade away. I could, you know. Without a transplant, that's what would happen."

"Don't even *think* that, Camilla," Anne shouted, rising to her feet. "Think of all you have to look forward to. Cut that albatross from your neck, Cammie, and live!"

"Live. That's what this is about. Living beyond my staff and my paints. I've had it so organized, so controlled, for so long. This is very scary, Annie. Everything is changing, pulling me along."

"One thing you can count on is that I'll be by your side every step of the way. Now, I'm going over to the mall to buy you some bright bedclothes to match the color in your cheeks and the light in your eyes. No more subdued pastels for you, Cammie. Bright colors. *Alive!*" Anne headed for the door, her arms gesturing outstretched and turning back called "Be back soon. Don't lose that glow."

<hr/>

Camilla settled back into her pillows, a smile on her face. She was the one everyone in her life looked to for advice and guidance, but it certainly was wonderful to be on the receiving end of it for a change. "Annie," she said out loud shaking her head. With a sigh she reached over and picked up her phone. It was strange to hear her own voice on the machine, and as she began to leave Billy a message he breathlessly picked up.

"I thought you were out, and I was going to call you at the restaurant," Camilla said.

"You sound so much better today. I was just going out the door to meet with Maeve when I heard the phone ring and I ran back in. What's going on?"

"I want you to fly over now and see me."

"Now? I can't come over now."

"Yes you can, Billy. Just let the staff know that you'll be back in a few hours and get on the first plane to Hyannis. I need to speak to you. Now. Please fly over."

Okay, okay, Camilla, I'm on my way. Do you think it's too early to start serving the Sconset Lobster special? The market price is low and I think we could sell some even though we don't usually offer it til later in the season. What do you think?"

"I think it's time to make changes. Buy the lobsters. People love the dish. Give them what they want. See you soon, Billy."

"Right," Billy answered hanging up the phone.

With a sigh, Camilla replaced her receiver and realized that he was unable to even make a decision about serving lobsters. Guilt settled over her like dense fog, chiseling the strain lines back into her forehead. Jasmine was on her way back to Sconset and Linc had to be back in New York this afternoon, preparing for an opening at the gallery that represented him on Park Avenue, so she had the late morning free for Billy. Thank God Annie was close by, bringing her colors. Colors, she thought, shaking her head. Black would probably suit her better.

⇒╫⇐

The phone never stopped ringing. First it was Jared, then Prescott from London, followed by Dottie, and lastly Maeve. Camilla had just hung up from her conversation with Maeve when a clearly distressed Billy entered the room, a vase filled with pink roses in his arms. Placing it on her bedstand, he leaned over and gave her a peck on the cheek, then sat in the chair next to the bed.

"Jared says they found a donor for you and the transplant will take place in a week. Is that true?"

"Yes."

"So that means you could be back to the restaurant in August then." Billy smiled.

"Wait a minute, Billy. First of all, don't count on me at all this summer. Dr. James ruled that out from the start. And I..."

"Damn, Camilla! What am I going to do? This is horrid."

"Look, Billy," an exasperated Camilla continued. "You can either work with the extremely competent, loyal staff we have or you can close the place. Frankly, I don't care at this point. We don't need the money."

"You don't care? This isn't like you," a perplexed Billy whined.

"Billy, I'm dying. Give me a break. I have something more important to tell you anyway." With a huge sigh Camilla began: "I have been keeping a terrible secret from you all these years. This is very difficult for me to say and it will probably be worse for you to hear it, and I won't blame you if you hate me forever, but a year before I met you I had a baby. The father was a black man who I loved very much." Camilla gauged the shocked expression on Billy's face and continued.

"My father could not accept the situation and after all kinds of threats to the father of the baby he forced the baby on him and made him agree to never seek me out. The reason I could never conceive again was because of irreparable damage I suffered during the delivery of the baby."

"You lied to me from the start. I can't *believe* it!" Billy shouted rising to his feet.

"Well, that's true. I never even knew if the baby was a boy or a girl until this very summer, Billy. I was never in contact with either of them."

"Oh, really, Camilla. I find that hard to believe."

"It's the truth. Anyway, when I got so sick yesterday, it happened that my daughter had become a part of my life, unbeknownst to me. It's Jasmine. She had a blood test last night and it seems we are a perfect match. She is my donor."

"You mean to tell me you have a black daughter? What will our crowd think? This is a total embarrassment."

"I don't give a damn what your crowd thinks. My God, Billy, now I know why my father liked you so much. You sound just like him. I'm appalled at your ignorance."

"I'm appalled at your betrayal."

"I should think you'd be happy that I have a chance to live. Without a transplant I'd die, you know. Maybe that would suit your stupid prejudicial self just fine."

"No, it wouldn't, Camilla. I'm just shocked."

"Well, take your shocked self back to Nantucket and run the business. The staff knows I have a donor and since you're going to need Jasmine for the next few days, don't reveal that it's her. Please don't tell anyone that she's my daughter. *Please* give her that consideration. She'll explain it all before she leaves to be admitted at Mass General later in the week. Jared just called to say that Prescott will be in Sconset Friday afternoon, so Maeve can take Jasmine's place on the waitstaff. I suggest you hire Diana, Mrs. Carter's grand daughter, to help Prescott at the podium."

"The cleaning woman's girl?"

"Mrs. Carter's girl, Billy. She's lovely and best of all, she knows where everything is and she knows most of our guests. Trust me, Billy, she'll be fine."

"Okay. I'm going home, Camilla. I'm too confused to say anything, so I won't. I'll probably call you tomorrow morning to let you know how things are going, if it interests you at all."

"Of course I want to know, Billy. Goodbye."

Billy left without looking back. Moments later Anne bustled in, laden with shopping bags. "I guess you told Billy. He was in such a snit going down the hallway he didn't even recognize me."

"Lucky you," Camilla replied. "Do you know that he was more concerned about our reputation with his elitist friends than he was with my health or what I thought he would be most upset about, our childlessness? Can you believe this?"

"Camilla, I don't think you know how stuck up your husband is. He is the epitome of East Coast snobbery. Of course this would shake him. Don't you realize you married a man quite a bit like your father?"

"My father was a very successful lawyer and a brilliant man. Billy is neither."

"But Billy does have your father's values, doesn't he?"

"I guess so, Annie. God, this is complicated. I have a raging headache."

"I'll go get a nurse. But first, let's get you into this gorgeous caftan," Anne said holding up a Hawaiian looking silk caftan flowered in red, turquoise, and yellow. This will brighten the whole room."

"I hope so. I wish I could snap my fingers and make all these dissentions disappear."

"And what would you do after it all disappeared?"

"I'd get on the first plane to New York and hold Lincoln in my arms forever."

CHAPTER SEVENTEEN

The medication given to Camilla for her headache finally began to work about an hour after Anne left her alone. Dr. James had her telephone disconnected for the remainder of the day and visitors were told they could not see her until further notice. The respite from the pain allowed Camilla the chance to relax and reflect on the chaotic circumstances she found herself in.

The essence of her dilemma boiled down to whether or not she was willing to leave the edifice of the marriage that she had carefully constructed for over thirty years to pursue personal happiness. The concept of acting in such a self absorbed manner was completely alien to her, and bits and pieces of her responsibilities to Billy and Sconset House kept popping into her mind as she attempted to focus on what her life might be like with Lincoln.

Who will see that the flowers are properly arranged on the tables? Who will pack Billy's clothes for his treks? Who will reassure his mother that everything is fine? Who will manage their hectic summer social schedule? She found herself asking questions that made her feel wild and out of control.

She had no doubt, however, that whether or not she left Billy to be with Lincoln, she would establish a relationship with Jasmine. That delightful nugget kept her spirits up as she mulled over her options. Camilla realized that guilt was the primary force that would continue to bind her to Billy, and that it had been dominating her marriage for a long time. She knew herself well enough to understand that her guilt could come forward and clutch at her heart at any moment. A helplessness washed over her in the wake of this knowledge and she had serious doubts about whether she could make a clean break with Billy. How could she be strong enough to fight for her relationship with Lincoln? she wondered as a deep drug-induced sleep closed her eyes for the day.

⟞⟝

Lincoln's trip home was smoother, and with a jaunty lift to his gait, he sauntered to the sidewalk and hailed a cab to Newsculpt Gallery on Park Avenue to keep his appointment with the press. As usual, his agent had drummed up a lot of coverage for this opening, and while he wished he could postpone it now, he knew he had to face the music, so to speak, and talk about his work.

The session progressed easily enough, even though snippets of his moments with Camilla kept intruding on his thoughts. She loved him, he kept telling himself. The magic between them was still there and he simply couldn't wait to see her again. For Lincoln, the situation was very simple. Camilla would divorce her husband and they would live in happiness for the rest of their lives. After all, he reasoned, they had suffered without each other long enough and deserved to have a new chance for happiness.

The only unpleasant aspect of the situation was that he had to tell his family about Jasmine's decision to donate her kidney, and he certainly dreaded that conversation. After debating back and forth in his mind how and when to do it, he decided to cab it down to the Village before going home, and tell Yolanda. He had put her through worse, he figured, stepping out of the cab and entering the old brownstone his sister called home.

Celebration's latest recording met Lincoln's ears as Yolanda let him in the front door. The aroma of chicken stewing and cornbread in the oven made him feel at home as he hugged his sister. After several minutes of conversation about the new CD and the gallery opening, the two found themselves at the kitchen table, iced tea glasses in hand, looking at each other with silence hanging between them.

"So, what's up, brother?" Yolanda began. "I can't even recall the last time you dropped in on me unannounced, so what's up with you?"

"I don't quite know where to begin," Lincoln sighed, running a hand over his close-clipped, softly graying hair. "It's about Jasmine."

Abruptly, Yolanda stood and moved to the counter, seeming to brace herself against it for support. "What's happening with my baby?"

In a labored, stop-and-go manner, Lincoln told his sister the story of Camilla's illness and Jasmine's determination to donate a kidney. His sister's silence, punctuated with various *humphs* and "*Oh my lords*" allowed him the space to tell the whole story. He ended with his hope that he'd re-connect with Camilla and they'd get married or something. When he finished, the silence in the room hung like a hot summer afternoon's stillness before a thunderstorm.

"You're going to let my baby give a kidney to some stranger and you think that stranger, who never made any effort in thirty-two years to contact you when she was very close by, is going to leave her wealthy, snooty white husband and go paint with you for the rest of her life? Are you crazy, Lincoln? What is Mama going to say? Is this woman a witch or something, to have my brother and daughter under her spell like this? She's using the two of you to save her life and then she's going to cut you back out again as soon as she's well," Yolanda stormed. "And what do you think her husband is going to say when he finds out his wife has a fully grown black daughter? Do you actually think this woman loves you so much that she's going to risk everything she's got to be with you?"

"Yes, I do think she will," Lincoln replied, believing in his words. "You have no idea what it was like for us back then. We were one, Yolanda, and I felt it again when I saw her today. I'm not going to lose her again."

"Look, Lincoln, we were all in love like that when we were young. But we're over that nonsense now. Look at you, gray hair peeking out everywhere and middle age spread around your waist. You don't even have your cute rear end any more and you're talking like you're about to make magic again at your age? Come on, Lincoln. Smell the coffee. She's *playing* you."

"It's not just a physical thing, Yo. My bond with Camilla is spiritual. I can't explain it any further. But I do know that we both want it back."

"No, you want your spiritual thing back. She wants to live, and that's a totally different motivation." Looking at her bother's set jaw and narrowed eyes, she continued: "The woman's got you bewitched. She's been keeping you in her clutches all these years, keeping you from marrying. And what was wrong with Aida or Maggie or Daphne? Any one of those women would have made you a fine wife. A black wife. But no, you're pining away for your long-lost white woman all these years. I bet she's a blonde."

"No she's not," Lincoln quickly interjected, having at least one point to solidly refute. "Her hair is just like Jasmine's. And her eyes, too."

"Her hair and her eyes, just like Jasmine's," Yolanda mimicked sarcastically. "You make me sick. I can see that you're a lost cause, so just tell me where my daughter is so I can call her and set her straight."

"I think she's gone back to Nantucket to work," Lincoln paused. "Please don't give her a hard time, Yo. She's so happy to have finally connected with Camilla. Don't spoil it for her."

"Spoil it for her? She has a perfectly good mother and family. She has two fathers, for God's sake. She doesn't need that woman to make her life complete. Let the bitch find another kidney and leave my daughter alone."

The argument spun around quite a bit longer, with Yolanda using her professionally trained voice to underscore her salient points. A thoroughly deflated Lincoln left a half-hour later and returned to his uptown home. All he wanted was to hear Camilla's voice, so he was further disappointed when the hospital would not allow him to speak to her. He panicked, demanded to know her condition, and was told "critical but stable."

The argument with Yolanda threw Lincoln severely off base and after stepping out as significantly as he had, he began to withdraw into his world again. Changing into his work sweats, he tackled a block of marble with vigor, beginning an abstract sculpture that had been lingering in the back of his mind. The rhythmic motion of hammer and chisel began to comfort and he was able to leave his troubles outside his studio, which had always been his accustomed way.

CHAPTER EIGHTEEN

Yolanda paced back and forth from stove to refrigerator muttering under her breath. She hated to bring dissent into her home and truly believed that the energy from arguments such as she just had with Lincoln left behind a residue that would affect her family. When in trouble, Yolanda always lifted her voice in singing praise and began singing along with her recording to no avail. It was up to her, she believed, to set the woman straight, face to face. No amount of singing in the world would do just that.

In a replica of her bother's activity the previous day, Yolanda got on the phone with her travel agent, turned off the stove, packed a quick overnight bag, left Byron a detailed note and hopped in a cab to LaGuardia. During the ride to the airport and flight to Hyannis she rehearsed her speech over and over in her mind with a menacing anger resulting from her focus on Camilla. *How dare she*, Yolanda kept repeating over and over, mantra-like.

After an hour of struggle with the information bureau and countless phone calls to hotels, inns, and motels, she finally procured a room in a little cluster of cottages on a lake in Yarmouth.

The slightly musty room with circa 1960 furnishings offended Yolanda and with a sigh she opened windows wide and sprayed her Ombre Rose on the faded green curtains with the hope of masking the odor by the time she returned from the hospital.

Another cab ride brought her to the hospital, where she attempted to find Camilla's room and was told that she might be able to see her tomorrow, but that the present early evening was out of the question. With at the end of her last nerve exasperation, she asked the receptionist to call her another cab, and while standing near the desk waiting to be picked up she heard a floral delivery person ask for Camilla's room number; and to Yolanda's amazement, the number was given.

In a minor crisis of conscience, Yolanda had to weight whether or not to simply go to the room, or wait as instructed. With a sweeping rationalization, she decided that if a delivery person was allowed to bring her flowers, then she should be able to go in and see her as well.

Yolanda proceeded into the hospital, took an elevator to the second floor, and followed signs pointing her in the vicinity of room 210. Waiting around the corner of the room for the delivery person to emerge from the room, Yolanda darted in as he exited, unnoticed by the busy nurses laughing together at their station, and found herself face to face with a very sickly looking woman propped up on a pillow reading *White Oleander*. For a moment Yolanda doubted her rash actions, but what had been set in motion continued as Camilla looked up startled from her book with a question in her eyes.

"Are you Camilla Smith?" Yolanda spoke quietly, not expecting her enemy to be so frail looking.

"Yes," Camilla replied, taking off her reading glasses and putting her book down. "What is it?"

"I'm Yolanda Hunter, Jasmine's mother. My brother Lincoln just informed me of your plan to take my daughter's kidney and I came here to stop this abomination." She began, her voice beginning to boom. "How can you do this after ignoring your child all these years? I cared for my girl since she was a tiny baby, soothing her hurts and celebrating her triumphs. And where were you? Nowhere, Mrs. Smith. You were nowhere, making my brother suffer the loss of you. Keeping your sick clutches in him so he wouldn't marry. But I see you married and had a successful life. Thank God Jazzie never knew about you,." Yolanda belted out, stopping only for breath.

Camilla, obviously taken aback, marshaled her meager resources to reply, "I felt it was best to let Linc and his family alone. There were threats made by my deceased father and I was afraid to do anything but go on in a different direction. I thought…" Camilla spoke in her raspy voice, struggling to sit up straighter.

"How many other children do you have? Why don't you take one of their kidneys?"

"I was unable to have another child after Jasmine was born."

"*Aha*! God slapped you down for the way you abandoned your own. I hope you suffered in your barrenness. And I'll tell you one thing, don't you think for one minute that I'll let Jazzie give you her kidney and don't you think for one minute that you can waltz back into my brother's life and break his heart again. I know your uppity type, lady, and frankly, I'm not impressed. I want you out of my family's life. Now," Yolanda demanded, arms crossed over her ample bosom.

"I had hoped that we might be friends," the ever-conciliatory Camilla began. "Jasmine came looking for me. She wanted to know me, Mrs. Hunter. And I have to admit, I'm delighted to have a second chance with her and with your brother, and there's no way for you to actually stop me."

"I'll get to them both. Don't underestimate the power of my family. My parents and I will convince them of your evil ways," Yolanda proudly responded.

"They're not children who can be controlled," Camilla began.

Leaning down and jabbing her finger in Camilla's face, Yolanda raged "You are not going to put my daughter under the knife to save your own skin. I don't care if you did give birth to her, you're not her mother and you never will be and I'll. . ."

Yolanda was interrupted by a nurse who grabbed her by the shoulder and pulled her away from Camilla. "Leave my patient alone. Get out of here now, before I call security," she commanded standing back, waiting for Yolanda to leave.

Yolanda straightened herself up to her full height and with a toss of her head stormed toward the door. Before leaving she turned back to say, "You are a despicable excuse for a woman."

The nurse assured Camilla that Yolanda would not be allowed to re-enter her room as she helped her settle back into her pillow. When the nurse finally left, Camilla burst into tears. Camilla hadn't been attacked that way since her father's performance following her disclosure that she was pregnant with Lincoln's child. She felt the threads of her life unraveling and drifting beyond her reach. Torn between her hopes and shame for needing the kidney, Camilla felt an uncontrollable need to escape. Escape from Billy, Lincoln, Jasmine, Yolanda, and her sterile hospital room.

With single-minded purpose, Camilla began to plan her departure.

Yolanda, still fuming with her own frustrations, hopped a cab back to her room in Yarmouth and upon her arrival phoned Byron. He allowed her to spout her accusations and recount her actions before breaking in with his habitually calm voice, asking her if she thought she had been a bit hasty. He suggested that perhaps she should have allowed Lincoln to deal with the problem, at which point she shouted, "He can't see straight with that woman, Byron!

You didn't see how ecstatic he was when he came over here. The man was floating up in the clouds and he was happy as hell to have our daughter give up a vital organ so he could get back with a healthy version of her sickly self. I just hate it when brothers choose white women. It's like the sun glinting off their shiny hair and white skin blinds them to their faults."

"But, Yo, love, you can't control Lincoln's or anyone else's heart. He's a very grown man and Camilla Smith has held her spot in his heart for a long time. You're going to have to face the fact that he is going to probably risk everything to have her back in his life. Everything, Yo."

"Well everything does not mean my daughter's kidney, Byron."

"Yolanda, Jasmine is going to make that decision on her own. Look at the risks she was willing to take just to meet the woman. She even gave up that new boyfriend she had to leave for the summer. Don't you realize how much this woman means to her? Our Jazzie is certainly not going to sit back and watch her die when she could save her. You know she'd do that for a stranger, so why are you surprised that she would even think twice about saving her mother. We brought up a magnificent woman, Yo. Think about it."

"All I can think about is my daughter risking her life to save that smug woman."

"You're bigger than this, darling. Look, while you're alone there tonight, pray on this and ask God for the strength you're going to need to see you through. And for goodness sakes, don't call your mother. Don't get her going with your upset until you've really thought it through. Okay?"

With a deep sigh, Yolanda said, "Okay. I'll be home by ten tomorrow morning. Can you arrange to be there when I get home?"

"Of course I will. I love you and I've been lucky enough to have the woman I love in my life since I met her. Cut your brother some slack."

CHAPTER NINETEEN

B illy stood at the entrance to the cocktail lounge watching the staff set the three dining rooms for dinner. It had been a long time, possibly years he thought, since he had observed the nightly ritual of preparing the front of the restaurant. He had anticipated his role as supervisory, and it was with a knot of nerves rolling around in his stomach that he approached the task. He was frankly at a loss as to what to say to the staff and had no idea how Camilla proceeded with the job.

But with the first feeling of relief he had allowed himself all day, Billy realized that Camilla had trained her staff completely and they simply prepared the restaurant like a well-oiled machine. He caught himself reverting to the customary sense of security Camilla provided him and had to remind himself that he had been betrayed by her, that he was hurt and angry and abandoned.

Maeve, looking lovely in a mauve print garden dress with her strawberry blonde curls caught up in a jaunty high ponytail, worked absorbedly at the podium organizing the seating arrangement. Billy's confidence in her warmed his heart along with the snifter of Hennessey he kept clutched in his hand. He was actually looking forward to watching her move through the dining room, her tiny waist accentuated by the wide sash of her dress, the full flowing skirt creating a ballet-like feel to her ensemble. As he approached the podium she looked up at him with concern beaming from her deep green eyes.

"Are you okay?" she asked in her lilting Irish accent.

"Well, I guess so. At least I feel a little better watching you hard at work," he answered, leaning over the podium to catch a whiff of the light flowery fragrance she always wore. With a smile Billy, turned around and slowly wandered through the restaurant. Dave Johnson set his small station alone since he would probably be working solo for the rest of the season. Billy marveled at how such a powerfully built man could place the silverware and glasses so delicately on the tables. Giving him a manly slap on the back, Billy moved over to watch Jeffrey and Jessica work together adjusting flowers and positioning the chairs just so. They were obviously absorbed in their work and in each other, and Billy saw they were the least of his worries.

Dottie and Brian held down the Lily Room. Brian was polishing the silverware with customary attention to the smallest detail and looked up at Billy cheerfully. The son I always wished for Billy mused, smiling into Brian's openly affectionate face. "Hey Dottie," Billy laughed, "don't scrub the glass away."

"There's a stubborn little spot here from last night, Billy," Dottie replied, looking at him over her shoulder as she busily buffed a small section of window. "Ah, success!" she exclaimed, turning her attention back to her task.

Billy now turned his attention to Jasmine and Jared in the Rose Room. Everything seemed set to perfection, and the two stood in the corner intently whispering to each other. Putting two and two together, Billy guessed that Jared knew Jasmine's secret, and a wave of anger threatened to spoil his growing good feelings. Just like Camilla and Jared he thought. Always something private and personal. The familiar sense of exclusion he always experienced when Jared was with Camilla washed over him, and Billy realized that Jared would always side with Camilla. He knew in his heart that he supported her relationship with Jasmine as was evidenced by the way he kindly touched Jasmine's arm and appeared to be giving the obviously agitated young woman his support.

Billy, whose scrutiny was shielded by the large floral arrangement separating the Lily and Rose Rooms, attempted to find bits of Camilla in her appearance. Well, the hair is identical, he nodded to himself. But a certain tilt of her head and the way she moved her hands also reminded him of his wife. Other than a similarity in their height, the rest of her belonged to the black side of her heritage, he thought with disgust. Again, his sense of revulsion that his delicate, refined wife had been intimate with a black man settled over him and he made strides to the cocktail lounge to refresh his snifter.

The evening proceeded rather smoothly, all the regulars asking about Camilla and many showing sincere concern. With a mixture of pride and growing disdain, Billy interacted with his customers in a hands-on fashion unfamiliar to him. Thankfully, the continual flow of Hennessey kept him loose, he thought as the last customers of the evening slowly meandered out into the warm Sconset night.

Jared took Brian to the side in the kitchen and whispered, "Billy's getting pretty tanked, old man. I know he counts on you to watch out for him. I was hoping…"

"I'll get him home," Brian smiled. "Hey, Jared, do you think I stand a chance with Jasmine? She's so dazzling. I'm just in awe of her and now that I know who she really is…"

"Ah ha. This is something to keep under your hat for now. Anyway, I do know she broke up with her boyfriend this spring over her summer plans. Seems he was jealous of all the male attention she would generate, although she seems pretty oblivious to it. He wanted to take her to the Hamptons. Just take it slow, Bri. I think we're in for some rough sailing."

"Sure will," Brian grinned gazing at Jasmine as she entered the kitchen.

Billy was lighting his customary late-night cigar as he walked toward the verandah to meet a group of his intimates for a nightcap when Maeve raced up to him and, grasping his arm, whispered, "The hospital's on the telephone for you, Billy. They have to speak to you immediately."

With an off-balance lurch Billy spun around and unevenly made his way to the podium. Maeve searched for Jared and, spying him emerging from the kitchen, rushed over and told him what was going on. Grabbing Brian by the arm, the two men literally ran to the podium to catch up with a red-faced, screaming Billy.

"*What do you mean*, she's disappeared!" he shouted in the receiver.

"It seems that Mrs. Smith gathered her belongings at some point in the last hour and left the hospital. Dr. James is very concerned and feels that she is in a life threatening situation."

"How could she leave unnoticed?"

"She was sleeping peacefully the last time we checked in on her at nine thirty and we assumed she was asleep for the night. There's something else, Mr. Smith. Earlier this evening we discovered a woman in her room screaming at her."

"I thought she was not allowed any visitors tonight."

"This woman must have sneaked in with the floral delivery person. We're very sorry, sir. Do you know anyone who would have been angry with Mrs. Smith?"

"No," Billy yelled, exasperated. "Everyone loves Camilla."

"Well, this woman didn't. We thought she was about to physically assault Mrs. Smith and it was on Mrs. Smith's insistence that we allowed her to leave the premises without police questioning."

"Who could it possibly have been?" Billy asked in total astonishment.

"All we can say is that she was a tall, sturdily built black woman with very short hair."

"My God," Billy exclaimed. "I'm going home and I expect you to keep me updated."

"It's out of our hands now. We suggest you call the Barnstable Police Department to begin an investigation. Dr. James will also call them to stress the urgency of locating your wife."

Billy slammed down the phone and looked up at Jared and Brian. "A black woman threatened Camilla tonight and she's left the hospital. Dr. James is afraid she'll die if she's not found. This is so insane! Camilla would never do anything like that."

"She must have been at the end of her rope," Jared mused, anxiety gripping his heart as he attempted to remain calm.

Billy wheeled around and, spying Jasmine, ran over to her with Jared at his heels.

He grabbed Jasmine's arm and began, "Some tall black woman with short hair verbally assaulted my wife tonight in her hospital room and drove her out into the night. I want to know who the woman is so the police can contact her to find out where my wife is."

A stunned Jasmine simply stared at Billy, unable to speak.

"I said, *who is the woman?*" Billy screamed, attracting the attention of the entire staff.

"Jasmine, we have to find Camilla. She's in real danger now."

"Your description sounds like my mother."

"What's her name?"

"Yolanda Hunter. But she lives in Manhattan. It couldn't have been her."

"Well, then, you come right over here and call her," Billy sneered, roughly pushing Jasmine toward the phone on the end of the bar.

With shaking hands Jasmine called her home and to her distress heard the phone answered by Byron.

"Hi Pops," she began. "Can I speak to Mom?"

After a few moments of simple chatter, Jasmine hung up the phone and told Billy that Yolanda had flown to Hyannis earlier that day after speaking to her father. With a horrid sense of dread, she told Billy where her mother was and helplessly listened to Billy report the situation to the Barnstable Police.

Forty-five long minutes passed as Jasmine sat alone at a window in the Rose Room staring out at the moonlight bouncing along the tops of the chop offshore. Jared stood nearby, protecting her from Billy and whispering the situation to Maeve and Dottie, who then told the rest of the staff. Brian sat with Billy at the bar listening to him rant his side of the story. The worry in the air became palpable as everyone waited as one, hoping to hear that Camilla had been found. Jasmine prayed that Yolanda would not be arrested.

Finally, the phone rang and the police asked for Jasmine. Holding her dignity together, Jasmine slowly came to the phone and in an even voice said, "Yes, this is Jasmine Hunter."

After a long pause, Jasmine replaced the receiver on the phone and turned to Billy, saying, "The State Police are sending a helicopter to pick me up so that I can go to Hyannis to identify my mother, Yolanda Hunter. They will release her into my custody. I'll be staying with her tonight. I hope someone can drive me to Surf so I can change and pack a bag."

"I'll take you," Jared assured her.

"And what about Camilla?" Billy screamed.

"They've alerted all the authorities in the state and are looking for her. They want you to call them back in thirty minutes to give the task force more information. I'm very sorry, Billy." Jasmine finished, looking Billy in the eye.

Billy turned his back to her and poured another drink.

Jared began to escort her to the door, the rest of the staff standing back in shock. Brian broke from the group and racing around to face Jasmine, embraced her and whispered assurances in her ear.

Jared continued to propel her to the door and when they entered the Sconset House Explorer, held the weeping Jasmine in his arms.

"Everything will be okay," he soothed her. "Don't worry, I'll go with you tonight."

"You don't have to," Jasmine managed through her tears.

"I must. Camilla would want me to."

CHAPTER TWENTY

"This is more than I can deal with," Jasmine sobbed as they made the short trek to Surf.

"I can only imagine," Jared returned, and after a moment continued, "When I'm in the middle of something that seems too big for me, I stop and make a list of things I need to do. Probably a bit of the old Virgo in me, but it works."

"Okay. That's a good idea. Let me see. I think I need to talk to my father first. I want to know what my mother said to him earlier today. Then I need to pack. Then I need to go to the airport. That's as far as I can get."

"Sounds good. While you're talking and packing, I'm going over to Turf and make you some sandwiches to take along. I know you didn't eat tonight and I doubt your mother had much either. A midnight snack will be nice to settle the nerves. A bottle of Bordeaux won't hurt either."

"Thanks Jared. I feel like you've been part of my life forever. Isn't it strange? We've known each other for such a short time, and yet…"

"You were always waiting in the wings, my dear. You know that Camilla is, well she can't be my wife, but I guess you could call us soul mates. I hate that New Age drivel, but it sort of describes our relationship."

"I can see that. Even though Daddy is my father and all, I think he's a soul mate for me. Having him close by never made me feel desperate for boys and then later men. It keeps things in perspective when you have someone like that. I don't think I've ever made any big mistakes in relationships."

"Brian will be happy to hear that. He was just telling me tonight that he hopes he has a chance with you."

"When all this is over, he probably will. He means a lot to me, but he'll have to wait before I can even start to think of anything at all romantic."

"I'll tell him."

"Again, I feel so to Brian in such a short time. Close to everyone, really, except Billy. What is it?"

"Camilla's magic. Don't you know? She's magic. Billy's not. Look at the paintings she does. You should see her in action if you don't believe she's magical. It must be like watching Leonardo or someone."

"Or like watching my father. He's magic with his chisel. He's so fragile inside, though. I'm afraid for him."

"Camilla's the same way. She protects herself so that she can continue to create her paintings and her magical summer experiences. Do you know she hardly ever travels? I've been trying to get her to come to Manhattan for years in the winter when she's alone, but she literally never goes anywhere."

"Dad's the same way. The trip to Hyannis made him physically sick. They're a pair, aren't they?"

"Yeah. And then you throw in Billy, who lives for his long trips away from home, and you can see he's really the odd man out in the picture."

⤃⤃

Jasmine was relieved to hear her father's voice on the second ring. Without preamble she launched in with, "What did you say to Mommy?"

After a round about account of his unpleasant encounter with his sister, Jasmine filled him in on the latest developments. Lincoln was first shocked that Yolanda would do such a thing and then frantic that Camilla had disappeared.

Jasmine told him that she rarely left Nantucket and her close friend Jared had no idea where she might go. Lincoln said he would call Anne to see what she thought and then he'd wait by the phone to hear that she and his sister were safe. With a Godspeed to guide her Lincoln hung up the phone and took to his spot over-looking Central Park West to keep his vigil.

True to his word, Jared had a sack packed with all sorts of sand-wiches and snacks, and as she boarded the ominous-looking state police helicopter, Jasmine felt taken care of and loved. In a whirl-wind of activity she was whisked from the Barnstable airport to the Hyannis Police Station, where she identified her mother and they were allowed to leave together in a cab.

When they were finally safe in the tiny cabin and eating a snack picnic style on the bed, Jasmine asked, "Why did you do it, Mommy? She's a really wonderful woman and Daddy loves her."

"She's self-centered and wrong, Jazzie. She abandoned you and now she expects you to undergo major surgery to save her sorry life. She's just plain wrong and I told her so."

"But couldn't you see how sick she was? They have her on heavy medication and, my God, I hope she's not driving a car." Getting up to pace, Jasmine repeated, "I hope she's not driving a car!"

Watching her daughter in dismay, Yolanda began to experi-ence the first inklings of regret. She had no idea her daughter was so involved and loyal to this woman. Her brother too. Yolanda's quiet was unusual and indicated to Jasmine that perhaps she was beginning to see the light.

With a sigh that originated in her toes, Jasmine sat back down on the bed and dialed her father again. This time his worried voice answered on the first ring. "What took you so long?"

"Everything, Daddy. Look, we're exhausted. Did you speak to Anne?"

"Yes. She's actually still in Hyannis at the Ramada and wants you to call her in the morning. She's stumped. She'll call Billy when she thinks he'll be sober in the morning and see if there are any special places he used to take Camilla. Does he have a drinking problem, Jazzie?"

"He has a drinking something. I'm no one to judge him at this point. He positively despises me, Daddy. The hate just oozes out of him. I think he's prejudiced."

"Probably. You're not to go back to the restaurant. Understand?"

"Yes."

"Let me yell at my sister for awhile and you get to sleep."

Handing over the phone to her mother, Jasmine went into the bathroom for a shower and when she emerged, found her mother sobbing in her bed under the covers. "He says if anything happens to Camilla he'll never speak to me again. Oh, what have I done? What have I done?"

"You tried to protect your family. Like a lioness. Like the time in fourth grade when you thought my Nancy Drew book report deserved an A instead of a B and you went in to see Mrs. Mullen. I know you weren't satisfied with the A- compromise, but Pops said you were the protector of the family and that was that. I'm not totally surprised at what you did, Mom, I just wish you hadn't done it. Good night."

⋙⊹⊹⋘

The two exhausted women fell into a shared deep dreamless sleep unlike Lincoln, who tossed and turned all night long and when he finally drifted off just before dawn had a vivid dream he hoped was prophetic.

In the dream, he was sitting on a hill overlooking the ocean drawing in his sketch book, and he kept seeing Camilla appear and reappear on the shore in front of him. She was so young and beautiful, and each time he called her name she disappeared. So he'd sit quietly and wait for her to reappear and then disappear again when he couldn't contain himself and called out her name. It became a nightmare and on fully awakening, although the setting was indistinct, Lincoln knew in his heart that the dream took place at World's End in Hingham, where Camilla grew up and where he drew *Rapture.*

With certainty, Lincoln knew that Camilla was either at or about to go to World's End. And he knew that he was the one to find her. It was five-thirty in the morning, and not wanting to wake Jasmine and Yolanda, Lincoln threw a few things into a knapsack and hailed a cab to LaGuardia. By six-thirty he was boarding the first shuttle to Boston and within an hour he had rented a car and begun his trip to World's End.

Although it had been years and the access to the Southeast Expressway had changed, Lincoln was easily negotiating his way south, heading towards Camilla.

CHAPTER TWENTY-ONE

Camilla thanked God that her room was at the end of the corridor, across from the elevator and quite removed from the nurses' station. All of her IV tubes had been removed earlier in the day, and her next dialysis session wasn't until morning, so she was free to get up and prepare for her departure. At first she was very wobbly on her feet, but after a few minutes she got her bearings and slowly packed only the absolute necessities in her small overnight bag. When this was accomplished, she had to sit back down and was dressed, but under the covers when the nurse made her half hourly visit at nine-thirty.

She pretended she was sleeping, and by the time the nurse left she truly was tottering on the edge. She knew from their routine that her room was the last one to be visited on the appointed rounds before the nurses met back at the nurses' station to organize the charts and chat. Forcing herself to her feet, her main concern escape from the overwhelmingly upsetting situation she found herself in, Camilla peeked out the door to see if the nurses were doing their usual thing, which they were. As she turned to the right to go back into the room, her eye spotted a stairwell not five feet from her door.

With pounding heart and throbbing temples, Camilla held her bag in her hand and, waiting for the nurses to completely turn their backs to her, bolted out her door, through the doorway to the stairs, and stopped, gasping for breath at the top of the stairs. As her heart began to resume its normal beat she felt strong enough to negotiate the stairs and, thankful that she was only on the second floor, slowly made her way down the stairs, one hand gripping the cold metal banister, the other lugging her bag behind her.

As she emerged from the stairwell, Camilla was thrilled to see an exit to the building straight ahead, and as soon as she knew it she had escaped. The thrilling sensation of daring, a totally new sensation, gave her a false burst of energy and Camilla headed for the road at a rather brisk pace. Stopping there to get her bearings and catch her breath she was pleased to see a cab stop in front of her asking if she needed a lift. With a thank you to the gods for looking after her, Camilla hopped in and asked to go to the airport, where she knew she would be able to rent a car. Since the season was in full swing and businesses remained open longer hours, she did just that and within a half hour was driving up Route 6 heading off Cape Cod.

At the Sagamore Rotary she had to use the bathroom rather badly and pulled into a McDonald's, emerging with a coffee in her hand and the realization that she had no idea where to go. Escape had been her sole reason for existence all evening. Destination had not even crossed her mind, and now that she was over the bridge and free to go anywhere she pleased, she realized she had no desire to go anywhere. Slowly sipping her coffee, Camilla began to think of all the people who would be worried about her and felt her level of guilt take her over.

Well, just one day, she promised herself. Just one day of freedom and then I'll call Anne. Knowing that her friend would help her sort through the barrage of indecision that crowded her mind, threatening to plunge her into deep depression, Camilla pulled back onto the highway and was able to drive as far as Plymouth, where she pulled into the Governor Carver Motel and booked a room for the night.

The refreshing shower helped wash away the hospital smells, which seemed to have permeated every pore of her body, and sliding between the cool sheets, Camilla plunged into a deep sleep. At four in the morning, the harsh throbbing pain in her kidney woke her, and for a moment she had no idea where she was. Slowly, the events of the evening before came into focus and Yolanda's damning phrase: "You are a despicable excuse for a woman" echoed over and over in her head. How could her life have gone so wrong so fast? Camilla asked herself as she rolled from side to side on her bed trying to find a comfortable position.

In desperation, she rose to rummage through her purse and gratefully downed four ibuprofen she found lurking in a pocket. Slowly the painkillers took effect and she fell into a restless sleep. She woke up and realized she'd been dreaming about World's End in Hingham. It had always been Camilla's favorite spot growing up, and while downing a second dose of the medication, decided to drive up there before phoning Anne.

Camilla hadn't made this particular drive since her parents' funeral following their deaths in a plane crash five years earlier, even though she still owned her parents' home, which she allowed her father's firm to use for various functions. During the years after she married Billy, Camilla and her parents had achieved a wary peace. As her father had aged he seemed to mellow a bit, and he particularly looked forward to visiting Sconset and playing golf at Sankaty. Camilla's mother had several Hinghamite friends with summer places in Sconset so she was in her element with the cocktail party circuit and had a certain pride that Camilla ran such an esteemed restaurant… although she could never understand why a woman of Camilla's standing would want to work in a restaurant or slave over paintings. Camilla had grown to accept her parents' values and limitations and had truly grieved their deaths.

Bittersweet memories of them darted in and out of her mind as she wove her way up beautiful Main Street. where her childhood home was, and proceeded to the harbor and up the hill that meandered its way out to the spectacular nature preserve called World's End. Nothing seemed to have changed there at all, Camilla noticed with relief. As her arrival coincided with the opening time of the park, she was able to snag one of the few coveted parking spots available and slowly made her way out of the parking lot and up the first hill.

The going was slow for Camilla, and several times she had to stop and rest before she reached the crest of the hill with its broad, rounded meadow leading to the harbor, where a fleet of youngsters in Turnabouts filed out to enjoy sailing lessons in the glistening morning sunshine. Camilla sat under her favorite tree, the one Lincoln had been sketching the day he was inspired to draw *Rapture.* She decided to close her eyes for a moment as the climb had winded her and the sun felt like warm blanket.

Camilla dozed for quite a while and awakened with the sun straight up overhead. Deciding to get back to civilization, she attempted to get to her feet and failed at the attempt when the pain in her back caused her legs to crumble under her like matchsticks. Twisting her ankle as she tumbled back into the trunk of the tree, she lay in a twisted fashion, the pain making it impossible to straighten her legs. Searching around for her purse, her cell phone, and the pills, Camilla remembered locking her purse in the trunk and pocketing the key for better ease in climbing. With no hope of diminishing the pain, Camilla settled back and tried to relax her breathing in the hope that it would help.

After another block of time passed with no hikers passing by to assist her to her feet, Camilla surrendered to the pain, which gradually robbed her of her consciousness. Her final thought before completely going under was *I wonder if I'll ever wake up.*

⛬

Lincoln pounded his fist on the steering wheel as he circled around the rotary at Hingham Harbor for the second time. He had found his way that far by dumb luck, he thought, but he just couldn't remember the last leg of the trip. Pulling into the nearest gas station, he asked directions and realized that he was almost there. Speeding up the hill, veering sharply to the left and taking the curving road to World's End on screeching tires, Lincoln followed his heart to the spot where he hoped he'd find Camilla.

Only a couple of cars sat in the lot as Lincoln lunged to a stop and ran out of the car, heading for the crest of the first hill. Stopping to search the encroaching forest on either side of the path here and there as he ascended the hill, he saw no sign of her, and as the summit came in view he ran full out, now calling Camilla by name.

As the tree he had once sketched came into view, he saw her lying in a crumpled posture, like a marionette cut loose from its strings. With a bellow of anguish, he stooped to cradle her head and gently called her name, stroking her tangled hair away from her head. *At least she's breathing* he kept reassuring himself as he continued to attempt to revive her.

As if in a dream, Camilla heard her name being called and with supreme effort brought herself to consciousness to see Lincoln's beloved face hovering over her. Unable to speak, she simply gazed up into his deep, dark eyes, eyes filled with tears that were now spilling down his cheeks and dropping on her; she wondered if she were alive or dead. The pain that caused her to shriek as he rose to his feet cradling her in his arms assured her that she was still very much alive.

"Sweetheart, just put your arm around my neck and I'll get you to the car. Just hold on."

"Lincoln," Camilla managed to whisper. "How did you find me?"

"Your heart called to me, my love. Your heart."

━┼ ┼━

With Camilla propped up as comfortably as he could possibly make her next to him, Lincoln navigated his way to the South Shore Hospital, following Camilla's whispered directions. Over and over Lincoln thanked God for helping him find Camilla for he knew that if she had not been rescued soon, she probably would have passed away at World's End. Lincoln reached over and held Camilla's hand firmly in his, attempting to pass some of his strength into her.

Lincoln stood back and let the emergency room staff take over when he carried her through the automatic doors. Filling in information Camilla was unable to articulate the doctor pieced together what had happened from Lincoln, and in a few moments had Dr. James on the phone. A quick review of her weak vital signs led the two doctors to send Camilla to Mass General Hospital in a helicopter to meet Dr. James' associate Dr. Halloran there.

With brisk efficiency, the emergency room doctor directed the nurses to start an IV for Camilla and began feeding her fluids and painkillers. Lincoln was asked to notify the donor and have her travel to the Boston hospital immediately. In what seemed like seconds, Camilla was being rushed through the trauma unit toward the waiting helicopter. As she was wheeled through the doors, in a burst of strength she screamed Lincoln's name. As he rushed to her side she asked the doctor if Lincoln could come with her, and after a brief discussion in which the doctor made Lincoln promise to call the donor as soon as he reached Boston, Lincoln and Camilla entered the helicopter for the short flight to Boston.

CHAPTER TWENTY-TWO

Lincoln believed he'd left his stomach behind as the helicopter lurched upward in a rapid, uneven ascent. The heat of queasiness rolled over him and he closed his eyes to steady himself, knowing he had to be strong for Camilla. The scene they left behind of cars abandoned, families arguing and general panic almost brought a smile to his face. After living over thirty years of carefully planned order, his coming together with Camilla was leaving a trail of destruction and chaos like the path of a tornado. What would those thirty-something years have been like if they had married? he mused.

Camilla squeezed his hand to get his attention. "When we get to the hospital please call Anne at the Ramada and then call Jared at Turf. Jasmine will give you his number. You can trust him to handle this with my husband...you know. So you won't have to call him."

"I'm not afraid to call him, Camilla. I'll only be filling him in on the facts."

"Call Jared. And remind him to tell Billy to get the keys to the Hingham house out of my desk. If he comes up, he'll want to stay there."

Pausing a moment, Lincoln said, "Jazzie's right. Here you are on an emergency flight to the hospital and you're thinking about what Billy needs. How come he hasn't come to you bedside? Why are you taking care of him when you're the one whose life is in danger? What kind of man is he, Camilla?"

"He's been pampered all his life and now…"

"Now he's going to have to deal with me."

"Oh Lincoln. This is complicated," Camilla sighed looking deeply into Lincoln's eyes. "I wished to be with you countless times. Truly countless times and now…"

"You had to practically die to get me here. Romantic scene, isn't it?"

"Not what I had hoped for," Camilla smiled as the pain killers brought her back to life. "What is going to happen with your sister? I cringe each time I think of her. She's quite right, you know. I did abandon Jasmine to you and your family, but…."

"You did what you had to do to protect me. I always knew it was the greatest act of love a woman could show a man. Never, in all these years, have I doubted that you loved me as much as is humanly possible. The mistake is mine in not telling my family the truth. They believed you were dead and now that you're resurrected from the past, they are in shock and out of control. I'm truly sorry that this happened to you, Camilla. I will speak to Yolanda as soon as I call Jasmine and Jason."

"Jared, Linc. Jared Miles. He and Anne are my closest friends. I trust them completely."

"The question is, do you trust me, my love?"

"Of course. I trusted you to do the best for our child and you certainly did. And now you've probably saved my life. How did you know where to find me?"

"I dreamt of losing you at World's End last night. I just knew you were there."

"Funny. I dreamt of World's End last night too. I woke up thinking about it and planned to go there for a few minutes before

I called Anne. I was just enjoying a few moments of freedom from all this."

"We used to dream together back in the good times."

"You're right. We did, didn't we, Linc. I love you so much."

"I love you so much too," Lincoln whispered in her ear holding her in his arms, breathing in the scent of her hair.

⇒⊰╫⊱⇐

Billy paced around Camilla's studio in complete confusion. A large portion of his peace of mind came from knowing that no matter where he was or what he was doing Camilla was either at home or at the restaurant making certain that their lives were being taken care of. Now she was not only sick, but missing. Billy truly had no idea what to do next and was relieved to see Maeve's bouncy strawberry curls moving above the hedge toward the kitchen door. Moving back into the main house he met her at the door and with a smile accepted the cappuccino she had brought him from the restaurant.

"How are you doing?" she asked with sincere concern and worry beaming from her cornflower blue eyes.

"Not well, Maeve. I'm lost without her. She runs my life for me and I don't know what…"

Taking Billy's arm by the elbow, she sat him down at the kitchen table and interrupted him. "I had a meeting with the staff at the restaurant and we all feel that we can run the restaurant without you, if need be. Prescott will be in place for the weekend and even though Jared is straining at the bit to go and find Camilla, he says he knows she would count on him to stay put and keep things going here. I'm going to man the reservations for now and limit the seating a bit so that we can do it with fewer people," Maeve said leaning forward toward Billy in earnest. "What I'm trying to say is if you have to go off island in this situation, we'll be fine. I just need the bank bags and such so I can make the deposits in the morning."

Reaching over to take Maeve's hand Billy replied, "Thank you, Maeve. You're so much like Camilla. You take away some of my worry and I'm so grateful to you. I can't even say how much you mean to me."

With a flush of embarrassment, Maeve pulled her hand away and, running it through her clipped curls, stood quickly, her chair scraping noisily as she rose. "Hungry?" she asked, shifting the focus away from herself.

"Actually, yes."

"Okay, then. I'll whip up some eggs and toast and you call the police or whatever you have to do to locate your wife."

Maeve had spent so much time in the kitchen with Camilla during the off season when they took their breaks during her painting apprenticeship that she was completely familiar with the kitchen and had breakfast cooking in what seemed to Billy to be moments. He enjoyed watching her strong, competent movements and the way she kept looking over her shoulder, smiling at him as he slowly sipped his brew, waiting to eat.

They were both startled to hear a tap on the door and looked up to see Jared coming unbidden through the door. "I've got news!" he boomed. "She's been found and has been med flighted to Mass General."

"Who found her?" Billy asked, rising to his feet.

"Lincoln. Jasmine's father."

Falling back into his chair, Billy said with disgust, "Did she run to him in New York?"

"No. He found her at World's End in Hingham. He said he followed a hunch and there she was. She had collapsed and he literally ran with her in his arms to his car and took her to the hospital."

"Shit!" Billy spat. "Her knight in shining armour. Her long-lost love. It makes makes me sick just to think of it."

"Well, look at it this way," Jared shouted, moving to Billy and grabbing him by the collar. "She'd be dead right now if he hadn't found her. At least he did something, Billy instead of feeling sorry for himself and drinking himself into a stupor. You're the sickening one, Billy," he finished, letting go of the shirt.

"How dare you?" Billy stormed clenching his fists. "I'll teach you a lesson, faggot."

"Later for that. Aren't you at all interested in how your wife is? Or have you already replaced her?" Jared asked looking over at Maeve.

"How is she?" Maeve interrupted, placing Billy's food in front of him.

"She is in very bad shape. Jasmine is flying to Boston to be ready when they stabilize her enough to do the surgery. She's on dialysis and they're keeping her heavily medicated. She did suggest that Billy get the keys to the Hingham house from her desk so he can stay there. Of course she's assuming you'd want to be with her, Billy, and I think that's quite an assumption."

"Of course I want to be with her. I'll go as soon as I speak to the Barnstable Police and pack a few things. You're going to stay here, aren't you?"

"Yes. I'll stay here. But only for her."

"Whatever," Billy replied dismissively. "I'm going to go to my room to prepare. Please lock the door on your way out, Maeve. Oh, the deposit materials are in Camilla's desk at the restaurant in one of her drawers. I don't know which one."

With that, Billy left the two alone in the kitchen. "Be careful with him, Maeve. He'll use you and you could get hurt."

"I can feel him reaching out to me in a way I didn't expect. Has he no loyalty to Camilla?"

"Billy is self-serving. He's only interested in what Camilla does for him so he can live happily. He calls it love. But it's only self-love, Maeve. Watch out."

"I will. But it would be a lot easier if he wasn't so damned good looking. Camilla means the world to me. Let's go get the restaurant going for the day, for her."

"Okay," Jared smiled warily, helping Maeve finish putting the kitchen back in order.

CHAPTER TWENTY-THREE

J asmine looked into Yolanda's eyes as she snapped her cell phone
closed following her conversation with Lincoln. "Daddy found
her. If you didn't think they're connected, you will when you hear
this. Daddy dreamed last night that he was at that place where he
did the sketch of Camilla for *Rapture*. He got on a plane to Boston,
rented a car, and drove to the spot and there she was. She had
dreamed of it too and went there."

"Your father told you all that?"

"Yes, Mom. That's what happened. She got there and collapsed. He carried her out to his car and took her to the hospital
and they were flown in a helicopter to Mass General in Boston."

"It's hard to believe that Lincoln, Mr. Stay-at-Home at all costs,
actually went to that kind of effort. She really has him bewitched."

"Cut it out, Mother. He saved her life and now it's my turn.
They're trying to stabilize her with dialysis and who knows what
else, and they want to do the transplant the moment they think
she can survive it. I have to go up to the hospital right away. And
I want you to go with me."

Standing up and pacing the tiny room, Yolanda countered, "I don't like this one little bit. I'm afraid for you. You're my baby girl and I don't think you know how serious this surgery is going to be."

"That's why I want my Mommy with me. I'm not looking for Camilla to take your place. She couldn't. What I want with her has nothing to do with being her baby girl, like I am to you. I want an adult relationship with her. I want to see what we can have together. It means the world to me right now. Please come with me."

"Does your father want me to come?"

"He said not to come without you. Please, Mom."

"Well, okay. But I have to call your grandparents first."

"Daddy already did. He also spoke to Pops and he's going over to spend the day with them. So you're free to come with me. Daddy says the two of you can stay in special housing they have at the hospital for families in this sort of situation away from home."

"Okay. Let's get some breakfast and see about renting a car."

"I can't eat. I'm preparing for surgery now and Daddy said they told me not to eat or drink anything."

"Well, if my baby can't eat, then I can't either. Let's get out of this dump and get on the road."

"Thanks Mom," Jasmine smiled as she gave her mother a long hug.

⥺╫╪⥹

Anne bustled into Camilla's room, arms laden with shopping bags filled with Camilla's possessions left behind at Cape Cod Hospital. Dropping everything beside the bed, she turned to her friend and demanded, "What did you think you were doing? You had me scared half to death!"

A long pause ensued during which a frail, pasty-white Camilla attempted unsuccessfully to sit up higher in the bed. Taking the bed control in her hand, Anne adjusted the bed up as she

155

smoothed Camilla's sweaty locks away from her forehead with her other hand.

"Yolanda came to see me."

"Who's Yolanda?"

"She's Lincoln's sister and Jasmine's aunt and adopted mother. She was furious about the surgery and about my relationship with Jasmine and Lincoln. She threatened me and called me despicable. I was so confused and upset and I just had to get away from it all. I had to escape. I couldn't go on keeping it all together."

"How did she get in? You were off-limits. I couldn't get in last night. She must have sneaked."

"She came in right after a flower delivery from our neighborhood in Sconset. I know it was a weak thing to do, but I felt so trapped, so vulnerable, Annie. I just hate being like this. I want it all to go away. I want to go back to my nice predictable life at the restaurant with my nice predictable husband and staff."

"Where you can control everything. Right?"

"Right."

"Well, my dearie, those days are over. Your deeper wishes are coming true and you're breaking out of the predictable, mundane life you've created and said you love. You're alive!"

"How come it feels like death?"

"Because you're sick. But when you're all better, just think of the possibilities. You'll have a daughter. You'll realize that the restaurant can survive without you and you'll be free to paint all year round. You'll have the man you love in your life…"

"And I'll have an angry, betrayed husband to deal with. No, I want my predictable life back, thank you." Camilla said with a grimace.

"You broke out of it last night, Cammie. Be realistic. What kind of woman would make a daring escape from a hospital when she knows she's critically ill?"

"An insane woman."

"No. A woman who's up to any adventure. A woman breaking out of her cocoon. A risk taking woman. A woman who's my best friend," Anne exclaimed, waving her short plump arms expressively, her elaborate silk scarf flowing from her arm like a gossamer wing.

"You should be on stage, Annie," Camilla weakly laughed. "Okay, you're right. I broke out last night and it almost killed me. So now I have to go on with what's been set in motion and I'm scared. I don't know where it's going to lead me."

"No one does. But I can guess where Lincoln hopes it leads. His finding you is about the most romantic thing I've ever heard of. It makes my tired old heart thump just to imagine what you have ahead of you with him."

"God, it was amazing. When I looked up and saw his face I thought I was in heaven. I truly did. That's how much I love him. It's just like before. He has a heat, an energy around him that draws me in and makes me feel reborn, complete."

"A little different from your ivy league cool husband."

"Billy's inanimate compared to Linc. All that blue blood, you know."

"Is he going to make an appearance, or will I have to phone your status to him?"

"He's due to appear later after he settles himself in the Hingham house."

"And visits the liquor cabinet. His drinking is getting out of hand. Brian's become his caretaker and I think he's getting a little tired of that role. I think he'd prefer to be playing the role of Jasmine's boyfriend."

"I thought so. I have no idea where that would lead at this point."

"Apparently Jared asked her about it and she said she was open to it after the surgery and all. Speaking of Jared, it's killing him to be stuck at Sconset House at a time like this. He says he's doing what you would want him to do, but it's eating him up inside. Thank God Prescott will be on island Friday," Anne continued.

"Prescott. I'm so lucky to have so many good friends. They won't let me have a telephone, so tell Jared I love him and that he is doing just what I would want him to do."

"I will, Cammie. I'm going over to the family housing to meet Lincoln and help him get Jasmine settled in her room down the hall. I don't know if they'll let me back in to see you, but you know I'm right down the street at the Sonesta. I'll know what's going on with you and when I can I'll be at your side."

"Thanks, Annie. Tell everyone at the restaurant that I miss them and I'm proud of them."

"Okay," Anne spoke over her shoulder as she left the room.

<hr/>

Lincoln continued to lead Camilla away from the mayhem ensuing on the Common and with quite a bit of luck found a table at Bailey's and ordered their drinks. Settling into their quiet corner on little wire-backed soda fountain chairs, they looked into each other's eyes over the cool marble tabletop, unable to think of anything to say.

Lincoln finally cleared his throat and introduced himself. Camilla followed suit and to their delight discovered their connection in art. The usual getting-to- know-you information was shared back and forth, but both of them really wanted to get out of the ice cream shop and see each other's work. That's where the true knowing would take place.

As soon as their drinks were emptied, Camilla asked Lincoln if he would show her his sculpture and with a grin that lit up his whole being, he moved her out the door and up Boylston Street heading for the Museum of Fine Arts.

The studio Lincoln occupied enchanted Camilla. Several of his sculptures stood on stands. Camilla was particularly attracted to the sculpture of an African woman in tribal dress. Running her hands over the satiny smooth ebony she closed her eyes and imagined Lincoln's hands running over the softly rounded contours of the figure and wondered what his hands would feel like on her own flesh.

As Camilla stood, caught in her private reverie, Lincoln came up behind her and gently touched her shoulders, moving his warm hands down her arms and back up to begin their descent down her back. Camilla thrilled to his touch and felt herself come alive in a way she had never experienced before. Surrendering herself to the magic of his hands, she allowed herself to be slowly turned around by Lincoln and when his lips met hers again she melted into the sensation and opened herself to him completely.

Lincoln felt this as a merging. In his life he had heard of two people having the experience of becoming one, but he'd never believed it could happen until this moment with this stunning young chestnut haired woman. He grasped handfuls of her luxurious hair and continued to kiss her for what seemed like an eternity. Gradually, they began to move apart, needing to gaze into the other's eyes as if to confirm that this was real.

Camilla whispered, "Now you have to see my work. You must know me like I know you."

"I'm dying to, Camilla. Take me."

The two slowly made their way out of Lincoln's studio and strolled hand in hand to Camilla's apartment on St. Botolph Street close by. The tiny apartment was in an old brownstone complete with intricately carved wrought-iron hand railings leading into an interior of rich old mahogany woodworking and elaborate hanging light fixtures. The living room was set up as the studio, and Lincoln took in the paintings with hungry eyes. One was a reclining man from her life painting class, and he stood in front of it, taking in the sensual touch Camilla had brought to the rendering.

The other paintings were landscape scenes from the mountains of New Hampshire, the rocky coast of Maine, and World's End. Lincoln stood in front of the World's End piece, entranced by the beauty of the place, the work. "I want to go there," Lincoln murmured to Camilla, never taking his eyes from the painting.

"Of course," Camilla whispered in his ear, her hand resting lightly on his broad shoulder.

When Lincoln turned to Camilla and took her in his arms, words were not needed to communicate the depth of their connection. They drank each other in like parched desert dwellers finding fresh water.

They remained together, only leaving the other's side when classes demanded, until they were driven apart by Camilla's father's scorn. By that point, they felt no barriers between them, their racial difference obliterated by the intensity of their love. The enforced rupture was like death for them. A living death.

CHAPTER TWENTY-FOUR

Jared and Maeve sat together at a table in the Rose Room planning how to run Sconset House, as the afternoon deepened into arrival time for the staff. Jared had trouble focusing on the tasks at hand, his gaze repeatedly attracted to the sun glinting off the rippling blue sea so close at hand. A large part of him sat beside his dear friend as she fought to hang onto life. He swore he could feel the rhythm of her breathing, the beating of her heart so far away in Boston.

"Jared. *Jared*," Maeve raised her voice, reaching for his hand and giving it a shake.

"What?" he answered, returning his eyes to Maeve, a far away look in his eyes.

"I know this is horrid for you. But could you please focus on this for a moment? Billy's counting on us and I don't want to let him down."

"Let me be perfectly clear with you, Maeve. I don't give a damn about Billy. I'm here because of Camilla. I hope our differing allegiances won't get us into a stew."

"I'm here for Camilla, too," Maeve quickly added, her cheeks reddening, however. "You and I are in charge of Sconset House now and I want us to be a team. So, when is Prescott coming?"

"He'll be here day after tomorrow, and of course he'll be working with you. Prescott has a knowledge of the clientele that almost equals Camilla's. He loves it here and you really won't have to supervise him at all."

"Oh, I don't plan to. Don't forget that we've been friends for years. I'm going to let him run the seating of the restaurant during operating hours and I'll simply go back to waiting tables. During the day I'll handle the banking and the reservation phone in Camilla's office. Prescott can spell me there as he wishes."

"I'm sure he'll be fine with that. After all, we'll be living upstairs, so don't hesitate to holler up the stairs at any point."

"Brilliant. So, what I'm worried about now is the ordering of the food. Billy normally takes care of that."

"I've already worked out a system with Brandon. He actually makes out the orders and picks out the fresh fish from local vendors himself in the morning. Billy simply calls in the orders on Monday and Thursday mornings and the provisions come like clockwork. With that in mind, I might be able to pop up to see Camilla now and then." Jared continued.

"What a great idea. If you fly up early in the morning, you can certainly be back by afternoon."

"Exactly. And if I don't see for myself how she's doing, I think I might lose my mind. She is as dear to me as . . ." Jared hesitated.

"A wife," Maeve completed.

"Yes. A wife."

"She's lucky to have you and Billy and that mystery man, Jasmine's father."

"She's not lucky to have Billy. Billy has been lucky to have her. Period. And as for Lincoln Jones, they must have had some kind of magic together for him to know where she'd be after all these years. It must have pissed off old hung over Billy totally."

"Well, he was in a terrific snit when he heard this morning," Maeve said with a small giggle. "I think Camilla's in for a time with him."

"Probably. I'm sure he won't even take her condition into consideration. Thank God I'll never have kids. I'd be afraid of ruining them the way Billy's mother did."

"I can't wait to have some of my own."

"Is there someone back home waiting for you?"

"Oh, just the local fellow I've been datin' since we were teens. A bit of a problem with the bottle he has and I wouldn't want to subject a child to that. No, there's no one I'm in love with or serious about. I've really been putting most of my winter hours into painting. I'm having a show in New York just before Christmas."

"Be sure to let me know about it. Prescott and I will be there."

"Brilliant, Jared. Now, about tonight..."

━┿┿━

Billy picked up Camilla's rental car, which had been retrieved from Hingham, at the airport. The car had another five days' rental paid on it and he hoped that all this would be over by that point so he could return it and fly back to Nantucket. The short distance from the airport to the highway in Hyannis took forever, as the full onslaught of summer time traffic bogged down his progress completely. By the time he pulled onto Route 6, Billy was exasperated and wanted a drink.

Taking a deep breath, he visualized the liquor cabinet in Camilla's father's study and prayed the firm had kept it stocked. Billy had so much on his mind with no one to ease his burden that he felt desperate and out of control. Going over things he let go of any nagging worry about the restaurant, knowing it was left in good hands. Of course he was concerned with Camilla's health, but what really consumed him was Lincoln Jones.

How was he going to deal with this ghost from the past and his gorgeous daughter? On the one hand, he was happy that Camilla would be saved by this unknown daughter. But a profound sense of embarrassment overtook him when the ramifications of explaining Jasmine to their crowd began to pop into his mind. This was unheard of in his narrow circle of experience. He would be the laughing stock of Sconset, he thought, and he focused all of his anger and frustration on Lincoln Jones.

Billy decided that Lincoln had put Camilla under some sort of voodoo spell when she was young and vulnerable. There was absolutely no way for Billy to ever accept that his wife would have had an intimate relationship with a black man unless she had not been in her right mind. And what concerned him now was that she would fall back under the spell of this black man and leave him. That would be a total humiliation for Billy, one that he was not willing to face.

And so as Billy pulled into the driveway of the Main Street Hingham home of his wife's parents, he was blind to the exquisite beauty of the colonial mansion he was about to enter and instead narrowed his vision on how to keep his wife in his life without her daughter and her former lover.

After he stowed his belongings in his room and greeted Maria, the housekeeper the firm employed to maintain the house for guests and meetings, Billy found the liquor cabinet and toasted his resolve with a snifter of Remy. The warming liquid soothed his jangled nerves so beautifully that he made a second toast to his late father-in-law's firm for keeping the cabinet so well stocked, and then he left for the trip to the hospital in Boston.

━╾┼╼━

It seemed that every doctor in the hospital managed to check in on Camilla that afternoon. Their unending questions and remonstrations about her behavior exhausted her, and all she wished for was sleep. And she was worried. Worried that Billy and Lincoln would show up in her room at the same time. She was fervently hoping that Lincoln would come back soon so she could talk to him about it when he finally came in the door.

"I'm so glad you're here," Camilla murmured with a sigh.

"You look like you need some sleep, my love, so I'll just be a minute. Jasmine is admitted to the hospital and is ready for the surgery as soon as your team of doctors gives the green light."

"That's so wonderful, Linc. Give her all my love," Camilla said through the tears in her throat.

"I will. That will make it all worthwhile to her."

"Billy is about to arrive, I think."

"I know. I'm going back to Jasmine's room and I'll only come in to see you when the charge nurse says he's gone. I'm not going to put you through any changes like that when you're so. . ."

"So close to death. It's okay. I know how bad it is. Every Tom, Dick, and Harry doctor has told me as much. You really did save my life, you know."

"I saved my own." Lincoln bent over Camilla whispering in her ear. "I wouldn't have wanted to go on living if there was no hope of ever seeing you again."

"What are we going to do?"

"You're going to get well. We'll discuss it then. But know that my love for you has not changed or diminished over the years. You are the love of my life."

"As you are mine," Camilla whispered, closing her eyes and drifting off into sleep.

Billy bustled into Camilla's room just before five. He was completely annoyed to find her sleeping and promptly woke her up. Camilla had difficulty coming out of her medication-induced sleep and had even further difficulty following Billy's stream of conversation. What she did notice with clarity was the liquor on his breath, a familiar smell with Billy over the last few years.

After a brief update on the restaurant, to which Camilla was unable to even respond, with complete oblivion to Camilla's condition, he launched into a diatribe against Lincoln in which he attempted to show Camilla how unsuited the man was for her and how he, Billy, was the perfect husband for her. He went on and on, it seemed to Camilla about how they would conspire to keep Jasmine's identity a secret to save face or something like that, Camilla surmised.

When he had finally wound himself down and Camilla was on the brink of unconsciousness again, Billy asked, "Well?"

Camilla answered with a whispered, "No."

This set Billy off on another list of arguments designed to sway Camilla to his way of thinking. He began pacing around the room, waving his arms, his voice rising to a near shout. An incoming doctor startled the bombast issuing from Billy for a moment, and when he actually looked over at Camilla he discovered to his dismay that she was deeply asleep. The doctor asked who he was and then firmly said, "How dare you come into this room and accost my patient? Get out!."

"But I'm her husband."

"And I'm her doctor. Do you even care that your wife is on the danger list? Don't you have a shred of compassion for her? I don't care what bee is in you bonnet, get out. And you will not be allowed back until Mrs. Smith and I agree that she is up to your, pardon my language, bullshit."

With a grunt of dismay, Billy turned on his heel and left the room, almost colliding with Anne in the hallway. "Asshole doctor kicked me out," Billy raged as he stalked down the hall muttering under his breath.

Quietly, Ann inched the door open and peeked in. Dr. Franklin, who she had met earlier in the afternoon, motioned her in. "What is that man's problem?" he asked Anne.

"There are a lot of issues involved here and I think Billy's having a hard time right now," Anne answered.

"You mean like the daughter down the hall and Mr. Jones?"

"Exactly."

"Well, I don't care what Mr. Smith thinks, frankly. He's forbidden to enter this room until further notice. I hope my patient slept through his abuse. You could hear him down the hall, for God's sake. No wonder Mrs. Smith fled. I would have, too."

"Is it okay if I stay here for a while? I don't want her to wake up with no one to talk to about her husband's behavior."

"Yes, please stay. I think it will be good for her."

"Is there any thought about the surgery?"

"Dr. James is flying up tomorrow at eight and we will consult with each other then. We might proceed at that point. Her vital signs are quite bad, but have not deteriorated since her arrival. That's a good sign that I hope will improve."

"Wonderful," Anne sighed, taking a chair next to Camilla as Dr. Franklin left the room.

CHAPTER TWENTY-FIVE

Billy sat in a maroon leather armchair in the Hingham house study staring into space. He felt cut off, set adrift from the stability of his life, at a loss. Glancing at his watch, he realized the restaurant was open and decided to call Maeve to see what was happening there.

He smiled for the first time in quite a while at Maeve's sweet-sounding Irish accent, saying, "A pleasant good evening. Sconset House."

"A pleasant good evening to you too, Maeve," Billy returned.

"Billy, where are you? Is everything okay? How is Camilla?"

"She's not good. Did you know she's on the danger list?"

"Jesus, Mary, and Joseph," Maeve whispered. "Oh, Billy, I pray the saints be with her. How are you holding up?"

"I'm. . . I guess I'm making it. I'm back at the Hingham house. Maria's preparing me a meal and then, I don't know. I almost wish I could be back there. Being alone like this is unnerving. I don't know what to do."

"Have you spoken to her doctor yet?"

"Yes," he answered, avoiding the circumstances of his conversation with Dr. Franklin and portraying himself as a model husband. "A decision about the surgery will be made tomorrow morning. I'll be there, of course, when they decide."

"I must go, Billy. The Swanson's just arrived for a birthday dinner and I must escort them to their table."

"Then by all means, go," Billy replied, a patina of annoyance coloring his voice.

"Okay then, goodbye."

Billy slammed down the phone and rose to refill his snifter at the liquor cabinet. Left to his own devices, unable to speak to anyone and totally unable to accept any responsibility for his actions, Billy began to brood again about Lincoln Jones. His hate for the man burned in his throat like acid. After finishing the light meal Maria prepared for him, followed by two more large snifters of Remy, he decided to call the hospital to see if Jasmine had been admitted.

When he had ascertained her room number, Billy made the somewhat inebriated decision to pay her a visit and find out where her father was staying so he could confront him and force the man out of his wife's life. The plan was to offer Lincoln money if he agreed to disappear from Camilla's life, and as he made the trip back to the hospital, Billy went over various figures in his mind and settled on one hundred thousand dollars. In his limited scope of consciousness Billy thought the man would jump at the chance for cash like that. Billy chuckled to himself with superiority, noting that the amount meant relatively nothing to a man of his means.

With the feigned charm of a truly concerned stepparent, Billy greeted Jasmine, thanking her repeatedly for what she was about to do to save Camilla. With contrived concern for her well- being, he asked if she had any family there for her, and Jasmine quickly reassured him that she had her father and mother close by in the housing provided by the hospital for families of patients.

Billy made a quick departure, saying he had to tuck Camilla in for the night. Jasmine was at first pleased that Billy had stopped in to see her, but as the moments passed she became suspicious of his intentions. After all, her last encounter with him had been so bad her father had forbidden her to go back to the restaurant. With a sinking feeling in her stomach, Jasmine realized she had told the man where her father was. With fingers lightly trembling from rising panic, Jasmine dialed her father's room and shouted at him, "Daddy, I think I just made a terrible mistake."

"What could you have possibly done, Jazzie?" Lincoln smiled.

"Billy Smith was just here in my room, making like he was all close to me, thanking me for saving his wife and all. I let him trick me into telling him where you're staying. I'm afraid he's going to try to find you and do something."

"What could the man do to me, Sweetie? I have nothing to fear from him. He was not in the picture when Camilla and I were together. He came along later."

"But Daddy, he's sort of drunk."

"I'll bear that in mind if he shows up," Lincoln reassured his daughter. "Now get some sleep. I'll be up to see you the moment they'll let me in the morning. Love you."

Jasmine settled back on her pillow, unable to focus on the novel in her hands. She just knew something bad was about to happen and she assumed she had set the whole thing in motion.

⋇

Within minutes, a phone call from the hotel-like hospital accommodation front desk announced that Mr. Smith would like to pay Lincoln a visit. Taking a deep breath, Lincoln said to send him up, and with more of a sense of adventure than apprehension, awaited Billy's arrival.

Lincoln opened the door after a quick knock, and the two men stood for a few moments, sizing each other up. Lincoln's first impression of Billy was that he was soft. Soft around the middle, soft facial features, soft fluffy hair. The thought drifted through his mind that Camilla's father must have been thrilled with Billy Smith.

"Good evening, Mr. Smith." Lincoln began and, stepping back, continued "Please come in."

Without a word, Billy entered the spacious accommodations overlooking the twinkling lights of Cambridge across the Charles River. "What can I do for you?" Lincoln asked the silent Billy who took a seat on the couch Lincoln motioned him to. Sitting in the leather recliner opposite Billy, he leaned forward, waiting for the large blonde man to speak.

"I want you out of Camilla's life."

"Can't be done, Mr. Smith. I lost her once and I won't repeat the mistake."

"Do you actually think she'll divorce me for you? Are you *insane*?" an incredulous Billy asked.

"I don't know what Camilla wants at this point and I certainly would not push her into anything in her present condition. However, when she's better, I intend to speak to her seriously about our future."

"You don't have a future with my wife. Look at what I have given her. What on earth can you give her to compare with the life she has on Nantucket?"

"Well, for one thing, I can share my daughter with her. Secondly, we have a deep connection in the realm of the creative art arts, and thirdly, well, that's pretty personal and I wouldn't want to…"

Jumping to his feet, Billy screamed, "Don't you even *suggest* intimacy with my wife. It makes me positively nauseous even thinking about it. I won't allow it, do you hear?"

Lincoln stood to stop the advance Billy was making toward him. While Billy stood a good three inches taller, it was obvious that Lincoln's wide shoulders and firm stance proclaimed him to be the stronger of the two. "How much will it take to get you and your daughter out of my way forever?" Billy asked.

With a shake of his head Lincoln answered, "Are you serious? Are you talking about buying me off?"

"That's it exactly. I'm prepared to wire one hundred thousand dollars into your account in the morning if you promise to stay away from Camilla forever."

"Well if this isn't déjà vu, I don't know what is," Lincoln laughed. "You're as bad as her father was. No, Mr. Smith, you can't buy me off. I'm not budging on this."

"But just think what a hundred thousand dollars could buy for you and your daughter. You could own your own condo and…"

"I own the entire floor of a building on Central Park West and Seventieth Street and would you believe that just yesterday I sold a piece of sculpture from my new collection for two hundred fifty thousand dollars. I'm not interested in your piddling, insulting offer, Mr. Smith, and I'd appreciate it if you would leave now."

Billy stood staring at Lincoln; his mouth dropped open in awe. The man's actually rich, he realized with a start. This realization shook him, and for a moment he let Lincoln's firm grip on his arm propel him toward the door. But suddenly he stopped and wheeled around face to face with his adversary. Leaning away from Lincoln he swung his free arm around and punched Lincoln in the stomach.

With a lurch forward, Lincoln took Billy by both shoulders and rammed him up against the wall. Grabbing Billy by the collar, he banged his head against the wall twice, shouting all the while, "Get your bigoted ass our of my space. You want a fight? Well, you've got one and I don't think you have any idea who you're messing with."

"Let me go! Let me go!" Billy squealed in what was the first fight of his protected life.

"What's going on in here?" Yolanda screamed, bursting in through the door. "I heard the banging on the wall and I was. . ."

"It's under control. Mr. Smith is just about leave, aren't you?"

Straightening his clothes and clutching his bruised head, Billy inched his way toward the door, which was blocked by Yolanda.

"You married to that Camilla woman?" Yolanda asked.

"Yes, I am Camilla's husband," Billy replied attempting to regain some semblance of dignity.

"Mr. Smith offered me a bit of money to keep out of Camilla's life. Oh, the deal included keeping Jazzie out of her life too."

"You think you can buy off my daughter? What kind of trash are you? Get out of here before I bang you around myself."

"You'll hear from my lawyer," Billy threatened weakly as he passed through the doorway.

"You were the one who came into my room and you were the one who threw the first punch. I'll press charges and see you behind bars. And in addition to assaulting me, I'll get you for slandering my daughter and giving her a hard time. You're in for a fight, Mr. Smith. I'm afraid it's a fight you can't win."

"All I want is my life with my wife back."

"Your wife wouldn't have a life if it wasn't for my daughter. Face it, your happy little Sconset existence with your happy little Sconset friends and your happy little Sconset wife is over. You never had any idea who she is, did you? I bet you aren't even aware that the Guggenheim is showing one of her new paintings this month. All you want her to be is a caretaker and hostess at your little restaurant. She's too extraordinary for that and I plan to appreciate her for what she is for the rest of her life."

Unable to think of a retort, Billy slammed the door and ran out of the building, his heart pounding up into his throat, his head throbbing.

Yolanda and Lincoln burst out laughing as they heard Billy's footsteps recede down the hallway. "That's one pathetic human being," Lincoln managed between gales of laughter.

"Wonder if he'll make it to the bathroom?" Yolanda asked to renewed laughter from her brother.

"What I don't understand is what she saw in him in the first place."

"Well, from a woman's point of view, if what she felt for you was as intense as you seem to think it was... "

"Is," Lincoln corrected.

"Then he was safe. I'm certain she could control him in a way that probably made her feel very secure after the horror you and her father put her through. He makes perfect sense to me, Lincoln and you're going to have to realize that he serves a big purpose for Camilla. A purpose she might not want to give up."

"What do you mean?"

"She's in her early fifties, I would suppose and she's going through a major health problem. Do you think she'll be able to handle the intensity you plan to bring into her life when she gets better? No matter how much she loves you, Lincoln, she may not be equipped to deal with you again. Billy might be the safe harbor she needs."

"I don't believe that will happen, Yo. I won't let it happen."

"I hope you're right," Yolanda said taking her brother in her arms.

CHAPTER TWENTY-SIX

B illy had never been so humiliated in his entire life. Emerging on the sidewalk in front of the hospital's family lodging he stopped, unable to decide what to do next. The thought of returning to the emptiness of the Hingham house was more than he could deal with. All he wanted to do was sit on the verandah of Sconset House and sip cognac with his friends. Glancing at his watch he realized that he had enough time to do just that and with resolution in his step made his way to the rental car.

After turning in the vehicle at the airport, Billy found that he had missed the last flight to Nantucket. In his frustration he lashed out at the young clerk, who nervously got on the phone and arranged a private flight for Billy. Feeling his self-confidence return a bit, Billy reveled in his ability to command a private plane to take him home. What he failed to see was that it wasn't personal power that accomplished it, rather it was his open-ended American Express Card that facilitated the very costly flight.

A practically swaggering Billy entered Sconset House just after nine thirty. Maeve looked up from her podium and exclaimed, "Billy! You're the last person I thought I would see cross the threshold this evening."

"What kind of greeting is that?" asked Billy, leaning forward to catch her flowery scent.

"Oh, I'm just surprised a bit. Welcome home, Billy. And how is Camilla?"

"The same. There's nothing I can do for her there, so I came home where I can be useful. That's all."

"Well, this is a wonderful surprise." Maeve smiled up into Billy's eyes. For a moment she felt lost in those eyes, the color of the sky on a clear summer day. Breaking the spell, she looked down at the podium, a quick blush moving across her cheeks.

With a chuckle, Billy sauntered off in the direction of the cocktail lounge, nodding to familiar faces along the way. His usual crowd greeted him as he entered the lounge and Billy surrendered himself to the friendship and good time that awaited him.

As Billy smiled at his friends, he closed a door on Camilla in his mind that would never be fully reopened. Billy had made his choice, a choice it would take Camilla a long time to understand and accept. Never again would Billy allow himself to be so totally humiliated, especially by his wife. He decided to consult with his attorney as soon as possible as he accepted the jovial greetings of his fellows. Billy decided to completely distance himself from the low-life behavior he swore his wife preferred. Camilla had become a bad taste in his mouth in a very short span of time and in his self absorbed sphere of consciousness that disdain obliterated everything else she had been for him over the years. He could not risk any further embarrassment from Camilla and her consort and their illegitimate daughter.

Around eleven, Billy escorted his friends to the front door of Sconset House, and they finally departed, allowing Maeve to begin closing the restaurant for the night. Brian lingered near the front door speculating whether or not Billy needed an escort home. With a slap on the back and a wave motioning Brian out the door, Billy dismissed him with "See you tomorrow, old man. Care to tee off with me at ten?"

"Love to, Billy, but what about Camilla?" a puzzled Brian asked.

"She'll be just fine without me. Ten okay?"

"Sure," a tentative Brian answered, looking quizzically over his shoulder as he left for the evening.

Maeve finished locking up the kitchen and verandah doors, shutting off lights as she worked her way to the foyer. With just the dim podium light casting a glow over them, she finally made her way to an impatient Billy.

"What took you so long?"

"I'm not quite used to doing this, Billy. You didn't have to wait for me to finish. I'm sure you want to get home to call the hospital and see how Camilla…"

"I'm not in a rush to get home to call the hospital, Maeve. I've been waiting all night to be alone with you. I thought perhaps you'd like to join me at the house for a nightcap after your long, hard day."

"I don't think that would be wise," Maeve answered, nervously arranging her papers on the podium.

Reaching over to take her chin in his hand, Billy lifted her face and gazed into her eyes saying, "Come home with me, Maeve. I need you tonight."

Unable to think of anything to say, Maeve allowed Billy to escort her out of the restaurant and waited at his side as he secured the front door. In silence she entered the rose colored Explorer and allowed herself to be taken home with Billy. Jared's warning echoed in her mind hollowly, but was silenced as she looked over at the tall, handsome man driving beside her, a man with impossibly blue eyes. With a sigh, Maeve threw all caution out the window and allowed her simmering desire for Billy to come to the surface. After all, she reasoned, Camilla had Jasmine's father.

—≍╫╪≍—

Yolanda suggested she and Lincoln find a quiet restaurant for a late dinner after it appeared that Lincoln planned to spend the entire night alternately pacing the room and surfing television channels. With a sigh, Lincoln agreed, and the two of them hopped a cab to the Sonesta, where they were told a late night "lite bite" was served. Looking for a table in the surprisingly crowded little bistro, Lincoln spied Anne sitting at a table for four reading a book, a half-eaten salad before her. With a nod in her direction, Lincoln led Yolanda to the table where Anne immediately offered them seats.

"This is my sister, Yolanda. Yo, this is Camilla's close friend, Anne."

"Are you the woman who…" Anne began.

"I'm afraid so," Yolanda interrupted. "I'm so sorry that happened. I was just trying to protect my daughter and my brother."

"Camilla is the last person in the world they need protection from, Yolanda. I hope you get to know her and see for yourself what a treasure she is and how lucky Jasmine and Lincoln are to have her in their lives."

With a rueful smile Yolanda replied, "I've been told that a few times lately. And after the earlier events tonight, I can see that Billy is the one they need protection from."

"Billy?" Anne exclaimed snapping her attention to Lincoln. "What did the Sconset playboy do now?"

Lincoln launched into a blow-by-blow account of Billy's behavior which was punctuated by gasps and 'My God's' from Anne.

By the time he got to Yolanda's part in the scene, Anne had her arm around Yolanda's shoulder, tears of laughter streaming down her face. The ice had been broken between the two women and Lincoln looked at the two hoping that friendship would bloom between them.

After the laughter died down, a more serious Anne noted, "Billy won't be able to handle this, Lincoln. You have no idea how limited he is. Camilla has shielded him from life's difficulties just as his mother did before her. I have a bad feeling about this."

"It sickens me to think that Camilla has been married to him all these years. What was she thinking?"

"Perhaps she was punishing herself," Yolanda offered.

"You might be right. He's an awful lot like her father and maybe in some complicated way she was making peace with him," Anne continued.

"And a man like that is safe," Yolanda added.

"Safe until something shakes him out of his dream world. He's like Rip van Winkle waking out of a thirty years long dream. What will he do?"

"I'll tell you something he *won't* do," Lincoln stated, pounding his fist on the table. "He won't threaten or upset my daughter or Camilla again. I'll see to that."

"Let's hope so," Anne concluded as the harried waiter approached the table to take their order.

Camilla tossed and turned in her bed, unable to find a comfortable position to ease the throbbing ache in her back. The medication she was on gave her intermittent periods of sleep, during which she found herself in the same nightmare over and over again. In the dream, she and Billy were out sailing on a fairly large boat. They were enjoying a sunny sail when suddenly, a storm hit and the boat was tossed from side to side. Billy was safe in the cockpit at the rear of the boat, but Camilla clung to the mast of the boat, thrown from side to side, waves splashing over her.

Desperately, Camilla screamed to Billy to help her. She pleaded for a rope to hold onto. Billy ignored her and became obsessed with the wheel and the sails. Just as a wave broke over her and swept her into the cold ocean, Camilla woke up from the nightmare.

The dream sequence repeated itself over and over during the night. Finally, sometime around midnight, a nurse happened in on Camilla's muffled screaming into her pillow. With lights flipped on, the nurse called in several others, who busily took Camilla's vital signs and had Dr. Franklin paged. On his orders, Camilla was quickly whisked into the brightly lit intensive care unit where she was poked, prodded and hooked up to a myriad of devices she was only dimly aware of. All she was thankful for was an end to the dreams. However, any hope of sleep was lost because of the measures she did not realize were being taken to save her life. Camilla spent the remainder of the night in a nebulous state somewhere between sleep and consciousness and just before dawn fell into a dreamless sleep.

⟩⟨⟩⟨

The phone in Lincoln's room rang at six in the morning as he was stepping out of the shower. Dr. Franklin's clipped tones reported that Camilla had taken an extreme turn for the worse during the night, perhaps as a result of her upsetting visit from her husband, and they would attempt the surgery as soon as Dr. James flew in from Hyannis, which they anticipated would be at eight o'clock.

Interrupting the smooth flow of information, Lincoln shouted, "*What* upsetting visit from her husband?"

"Well, Mr. Jones, I heard the shouting out in the hallway and when I entered the room Mr. Smith was ranting and raving at Mrs. Smith. She appeared to be sleeping, but in retrospect, I think that the agitation probably made her black out. She was in no way able to cope with anything upsetting at all. I left her friend Anne with her."

"That's funny. Anne didn't mention it to me last night."

"She happened in after the altercation and perhaps didn't want to worry you. In any case, your daughter will be undergoing her surgery rather soon and I was sure you'd want to see her. I have left permission for you and Mrs. Hunter to go up to her room."

"And permission to see Camilla?"

"Mrs. Smith is in intensive care, Mr. Jones. I'm afraid Mr. Smith is the only one who can see her and he's, well. . ."

"He's what?"

"He has returned to Nantucket and said he has no plans to return to Boston."

"You mean Camilla is facing this alone? Please, Dr. Franklin, I must see her. Just for a moment. I think it would be good for her if I could . . ."

"No need to explain further. On second thought, I agree with you. You will have permission to go in. Can you be there in half an hour?"

"I'm on my way. And thank you, Dr. Franklin."

In a state of panic, the usual slow-moving Lincoln quickly pulled on his khakis and polo shirt. Thanking his lucky stars that he had already showered and shaved, he dialed Yolanda, informed her of the situation, and arranged to meet her in the lobby immediately. As he was about to leave he realized that he should phone Anne, had a hurried conversation with her and arranged to meet her in the surgical waiting room as soon as she could get there.

As he dashed down the hallway to the lobby, Lincoln had the nagging sense that he had forgotten something, and stopping short just before reaching the lobby he asked God to be with Camilla and Jasmine. Knowing he had done everything he could, he took a seat and waited for his sister to arrive.

CHAPTER TWENTY-SEVEN

The phone ringing at five in the morning startled Billy out of a peaceful sleep. Coming to, he realized that Maeve was gone and must have left earlier to keep appearances up. Nodding his head appreciatively at her discretion, he reached over and answered the ringing telephone. Silently he listened to Dr. Franklin explain the surgery about to take place and when asked whether or not he was going to be at the hospital simply answered, "No."

Dr. Franklin replied, "Good, Mr. Smith. I think that your presence after surgery would probably set back her recovery in view of the scene I observed last night."

"My situation with Camilla is none of your business, Doctor," Billy answered and was about to hang up the phone when he heard Dr. Franklin continue: "I want you to know that if Mrs. Smith does not make it today, I am going to have the hospital authorities file a complaint with the Boston police against you. I believe you can be charged with manslaughter, as your wife's reaction to you last night caused her condition to worsen to the point where if we don't operate now, I don't think she'll live out the day."

"How can you do such a thing? I'll have you know I'm represented by Chad Whithers of Camden, Whithers and Johnson. He happens to be one of the finest attorneys in Boston and is a personal friend. He'll never let..."

"Mr. Smith, you'd better talk to your lawyer friend right away, because I find your behavior to be reckless as well as reprehensible. If we aren't successful here today, I'm going to push for a manslaughter charge against you and, by the way, Massachusetts General Hospital retains the law firm you are speaking of as general counsel. Good day, Mr. Smith."

Stunned, Billy sat in the bed staring at the receiver for a long pause before slamming it down on the cradle. In frustration, he jumped out of bed, pulled on a sweat suit and ran down the stairs to the kitchen where he clumsily proceeded to make himself a pot of coffee. Glancing at the clock as he waited for the pot to finish dripping, he calculated that seven was the earliest time he dared call Chad at his Boston home, and that was over an hour an a half away. He had no idea how he could wait that long, and as he poured his first cup of coffee over a generous splash of Bailey's, his mind cleared a bit and he decided to shower and go visit Chad's wife Milly, who was in residence in their Sconset home for the summer. The knowledge that Milly could get Chad out of bed to listen to the story calmed him down a bit.

Billy brought the steaming mug into the gray marble shower stall and sipped at it as he let his upset stream off his back with the warm, throbbing pulse of the shower massager. He decided to charge Lincoln Jones with whatever he and Chad could cook up. There had to be something the man was guilty of, Billy told himself. With a sigh, he relaxed and allowed himself to revel in the memory of the previous night with Maeve.

⟫⟪

Billy was about to leave through the kitchen door when he saw Jared moving along the hedge toward him. Realizing that Jared had seen him at the door, he knew there was no avoiding his unwanted guest and he simply waited for Jared's approach.

"How is Camilla?" Jared asked without greeting.

"The surgery is this morning. I suspect I'll hear something by noon."

"Aren't you going up there to be with her?"

"No," Billy replied, trying to edge his way past Jared.

Jared, not about to let Billy slink away from him, blocked the path and asked "Why not?"

"Because there's nothing I can do up there and I'm needed here."

"Bullshit!" Jared shouted in Billy's face. "Something's going on here. You're supposed to be at your wife's side at a time like this. I knew something was wrong when you made your surprise appearance last night."

"Nothing's going on, Jared, and if you'll please get out of my way, I have to meet someone."

"At six in the morning? I don't think so, Billy. Unless Maeve is making a quiet little breakfast for the two of you."

"I'm sure Maeve is sound asleep, Jared. Now let me get by you."

Standing squarely in front of Billy, Jared crossed his arms and stared at his adversary. Frantically, Billy attempted to shove Jared out of his way. With his hands strong from years of sewing hats and carrying heavy trays, Jared grabbed Billy by both wrists and held him firmly in place.

"I'm going to call Anne and find out what's really happening with Camilla and then I'll be on the next plane to Boston. I won't be back tonight and I'll inform you when I shall return. Camilla needs the people who love her at her side and I, for one, will not abandon her."

"You can't go, Jared," Billy commanded. "We have a restaurant to run."

"You have a restaurant to run. I have a friend to comfort. I'm sure Maeve will figure out how to operate without me tonight." With a final twist, Jared released Billy's wrists and headed out the prettily flowering path in front of Billy. Curiosity getting the better of him, Jared stopped in the road a couple of houses past Camilla's and watched to see where Billy was headed. He was puzzled to see Billy turn up the shelled walkway leading to Chad Whithers' estate a bit further up Baxter Road in the opposite direction. Why was Billy so intent on seeing his lawyer so early in the morning Jared wondered as he picked up his pace and quickly made his way through Sconset Village in the soft morning light and on down to Low Beach.

⇌⇋

Jared reached Anne's room just as she was about to hurry over to the hospital. She quickly repeated the story she had heard from Lincoln about Camilla's condition, and how it had been worsened by Billy's visit. In the midst of their fears for Camilla they chuckled at Lincon's tussle with Billy and then quickly became serious again, thinking of the gravity of Camilla's plight. Jared assured Anne that he would be at her side to keep vigil as soon as possible and mentioned that Billy was speaking to his attorney as they spoke.

A puzzled Anne said, "That's pretty strange, don't you think?"

"It had to be serious for Billy to be willing to get the Whithers out of bed at the crack of dawn."

"Do you suppose the doctor has threatened Billy over his episode with Camilla? Lincoln did say that Camilla was moved to intensive care after Billy's visit."

"Possibly. Anyway, the old boy was intent on getting there. I thought he had a breakfast date with Maeve when I met up with him at the kitchen door."

"Maeve? Don't tell me…"

"Maeve is taking over Camilla's place, it seems, in just about every way. I warned her, but I guess she…"

"The snake. The weak-willed, slimy snake. I could just wring his neck!" Anne shouted into the phone.

"I know exactly how you feel. In fact I came close to doing the deed myself a few minutes ago. See you soon, lovey."

"Thank God."

⇒‡‡⇐

Milly Whithers surprised Billy by appearing at the door dressed in her tennis outfit, racquet in hand. "Billy," the sturdily build gray haired older woman exclaimed. "Is everything okay? I heard about Camilla. I'm so sorry you have to go through this."

"Thank you, Milly. I was wondering if you could get Chad on the telephone for me. Something has come up and I desperately need to speak with him."

"Certainly. I got off the phone with him a few moments ago. He should be sitting down with his morning cup just about now."

Milly graciously led Billy into Chad's study, dialed him up and discreetly left the room, closing the door behind her. Billy took the receiver from Milly and, settling back into Chad's deep maroon leather chair, began to tell the story. Chad interrupted Billy to warn him that he had to keep to the facts and not embellish the story with his personal frustrations. With a sigh, Billy gave the man a brief outline and when he was finished, sat forward waiting for Chad's response.

"Well, Billy, first of all let's pray that your lovely wife makes it this morning. I think you made a big mistake at the hospital. As you know, I represent Mass General and over the past few years, they have taken a number of abusive friends and relatives of patients to court. Even if Camilla comes through with flying colors they might want to lodge a formal complaint against you. For the life of me, Billy, I can't imagine what you were thinking. Tell me the truth now. Were you drinking?"

"Well, yes, Chad. I had a couple at the Hingham house before I went into the hospital. I really don't think the alcohol had anything to do with it, though."

"I think it did. I'm sure that if the hospital takes action against you, at the minimum, they will get an alcoholic treatment verdict against you. As you probably know, my hands are tied. I can't represent you in this matter, so I suggest you call Dave Bosworth over at Bosworth and Kennedy. You know Dave, don't you?"

"Yes, of course. I was out sailing with him just last week."

"Okay then, call him and alert him to the possibility of a suit."

"Off the record, what can I get that black bastard on, Chad?"

"From what I can ascertain, nothing. And off the record, Billy, I'm a very big fan of his work. We have a large piece of his in our solarium on Beacon Hill that we treasure. My suggestion is to lay low and leave him alone."

"Thanks, Chad." Billy concluded, slamming down the phone. *"I'm a very big fan of his work,"* Billy mimicked sarcastically as he stormed out of the Whithers' house and headed for home.

⚊⚊

Fear mixed with rage in Billy's gut as he hurried home. Never in his life had he felt so out of control, so vulnerable to danger. All he could think about was his own situation and how he could get out of trouble. Any concern he might have felt for Camilla was permanently dislodged from his mind by his hatred of Lincoln Jones and his fear for his own safety. Unaccustomed to dealing with anything more stressful than a delivery of restaurant provisions delayed by a canceled ferry, Billy graduated from Bailey's in coffee to cognac as soon as he arrived home. And then the phone started ringing.

Keeping up the pretense of being a concerned husband to the constant barrage of friends who called about Camilla further taxed Billy to the point where he felt as if he was losing his mind. When he finally got Dave Bosworth on the phone he babbled on to the lawyer incoherently, completely confusing his friend.

After piecing together the story as best he could, Dave recommended that Billy go about business as usual at the restaurant and under no circumstances, go to the hospital in Boston. With that recommendation in mind, Billy tidied up the kitchen and made the quick trip to Sconset House, where Chef Brandon was already preparing the exquisitely rendered sauces for which the restaurant was famous. The aroma of the bubbling pots and pans had a calming effect on Billy, and for the first time since the call from the hospital that morning, Billy began to feel like his usual self. Food orders needed his attention and the depleted bar stocks needed to be filled, all of which absorbed his thoughts for the remainder of the morning.

CHAPTER TWENTY-EIGHT

Lincoln was thankful Yolanda was with him on this most difficult of mornings. They decided to split up with Yolanda proceeding straight to Jasmine's room as Lincoln followed directions to the Intensive Care Unit. His heart dropped to his knees when he had finally passed through the red tape and was brought to Camilla's bedside. Everything about the woman he loved seemed diminished with only her wavy mahogany locks spread out on the white pillow full of life. Lincoln feared she had begun to depart from this world and he clutched her hand desperately.

"Don't leave me, Camilla," he whispered. "Take my strength and fight. Fight to live for us, my love. Please."

"I will, Lincoln. I'm doing the best I can, but I keep slipping into a bad dream. I'm falling off a boat. The water keeps surging in, trying to pull me away. Make it stop. Please make it stop."

"Okay, okay, now listen to me." Lincoln leaned forward earnestly. "Picture yourself with me in my old studio at the school. Picture yourself painting the beautiful scene of the parks across the street. See me by your side sculpting your face. I'm sculpting you happy, healthy, full of life. Smell the paints, my love. Listen to the chipping sounds my chisel makes. Are you there with me?"

"Yes. My feet are on the hard concrete floor. The sun is streaming in the window in rays of golden light. You look so happy, so…" Camilla dropped back into sleep, but now a small smile lit up her pale countenance just a bit and that bit of life on her face gave Lincoln hope.

He sat holding her hand until Dr. Franklin stepped to the bed and motioned Lincoln to follow him over to a small reception room on the side. "Well, Mr. Jones, you can see for yourself how far she slipped last night. Ordinarily, we would not attempt this procedure with her in such a tenuous state. However, without the surgery, I don't feel she would make it through the day. Do you have any questions?"

"What are her chances?"

"Not great. We will put her under and begin the procedure and see how she withstands the anesthesia before we begin on your daughter. If Mrs. Smith fails, there's no sense in opening Miss Hunter. If Mrs. Smith holds on, we have a team of top people ready to move as swiftly as possible. Your daughter will be in recovery fairly soon with Mrs. Smith following. That's about it for now. You can wait in the operating pavilion lounge. There is a chapel attached if you feel so moved."

With that, Dr. Franklin left Lincoln, who was then directed to Jasmine's room by a nursing assistant. He arrived to see a very groggy Jasmine being wheeled out of her room.

"I'll be fine, Daddy," she croaked in a dry whisper as she sped by him.

"Love you, baby," Lincoln called after her.

"Love you, too," Lincoln heard faintly from down the hall.

Yolanda took her bewildered-looking brother by the arm and together they followed directions to the lounge. "Let's call Mom and Pops," Yolanda suggested. "We want the power of their prayers now."

"Right."

⊶⊷

Shortly after calling their parents, Yolanda and Lincoln settled into a cluster of surprisingly comfortable overstuffed chairs in the far corner of the lounge. Everything in the room, from the soft mauve walls to the understated soft watercolor landscapes, seemed designed to soothe the nerves. The peace of the room was interrupted by Anne bustling toward them, her peach scarf billowing out behind her, concern etched into her usually happy features.

Lincoln and Yolanda filled her in on the condition of the two patients and Anne herself settled in for the long haul. But she couldn't sit still long and walked restlessly around the room, straightening paintings and putting magazines into neat piles.

Moving back to her group, she said "I just remembered Jared mentioned something curious this morning after he paid Billy a visit. Apparently, Billy was hell bent on paying his attorney a visit just up the road from his house at six this morning. What do you think?"

"I think Billy has lost it," Lincoln proclaimed. "He's the type of man who appears to be perfectly capable, but relies totally on a wife, a mother, or a girlfriend to make all his decisions for him."

"Just say it, Lincoln. The man can't tell his ass from his elbow without directions from his wife," filled in Yolanda.

"True, Yo, but it's even more than that. He has believed in Camilla so totally over the years that finding out about Jazzie and me has caused him to totally lose faith in the person he thought was infallible, a person who always put him first. And now she's too sick to be concerned with him to boot and he feels like he's lost his identity, I think. He feels empty and he's furious with her over it. The man has no character reserves to draw on, and he's literally lashing out."

"And listen to this," Anne interrupted. "According to Jared he's treating Maeve, the woman Camilla asked to take her place, as if she actually is Camilla. You add his need for a strong female to his drinking, and I think he's either having or about to have an affair with Maeve while Camilla is literally fighting for her life!"

"The man is out of control, as I said. He attacked his wife and me. He's either visiting his lawyer to set up protection for himself or he's trying to find something to pin on me." Lincoln paused. "I wasn't going to file a complaint about him trying to attack me in my room, but I just might go and visit the police after Camilla and Jazzie are out of the woods. Yes, I think I'll do just that. Start to dish out what the man deserves. Can you believe what he did to Camilla? I hope the hospital lets him have it."

The minutes crept by at a snail's pace. Anne, unable to sit still, appointed herself food runner and made several trips to the near-by cafeteria, bringing back cups of steaming coffee, more coffee, flaky croissants, and warm muffins. On her third trip from the food lines she bumped into Jared heading for the lounge. His overnight bag was hanging loosely from his shoulder, his hair was in tousled disarray and his shirt tail was hanging out the back of his pants, all revealing his desperate state of mind. Anne simply put her carry-out tray on the floor and took him in her arms.

"Any word yet?" Jared whispered in her ear.

"No, not a peep. Whether or not Jasmine has been operated on will tell the tale. If they haven't operated on her when she comes out, then the worst has happened."

"It's that bad?" Jared gasped, pushing Anne back and looking into her eyes.

"That bad. Dr. Franklin told Lincoln her chances are not good and if she can't withstand the early part of the surgery, then. . ."

"You mean if she dies in the early part."

"Yes."

Apparently she barely made it through the night after Billy accosted her. Thank God for the nurse who heard her moaning in her pillow. Isn't that just like Camilla, moaning into the pillow to avoid a fuss."

"Protecting Billy to the end. Will she ever realize what a cad he is?"

"I think there's a good chance, especially since she now has Lincoln back to compare him to. He's really a wonderful man."

"I agree."

"Lincoln's sister Yolanda is here, Jared. I know she sent Camilla out into the night, but I think she was only trying to protect her daughter and brother. Camilla was nothing to her and, well, I can see where she was coming from at the time. I think she's shifted her position and I've gotten to know her a bit. What I'm trying to say is that I like her and I hope that doesn't sound like a betrayal of Camilla."

"And you know I'd fight to the death to protect Camilla, so I'll take what you've said into consideration and make my own judgment. Agreed?"

"Agreed. And you'll get your chance right away. She's waiting with us in the lounge Let's go see if there's any news."

The two friends plodded along, Jared with his shoulder bag and Anne with a tray of more coffee and tea. When they reached the lounge, Lincoln and Yolanda were nowhere to be seen. Looking at each other, they silently took their seats, staring in unison at the doorway leading to the recovery rooms.

Ten minutes, seeming more like ten hours, dragged on until Lincoln emerged from the automatic door, a small smile brightening his face. "Jazzie has been operated on and is still

unconscious, but in recovery. Yolanda is with her. Camilla is receiving the kidney as we speak," Lincoln reported, wringing his
hands. "I guess this means our girl's still alive," he continued,
sitting down in a chair across from Jared and Anne, silently weeping into his hands.

Anne bolted over to comfort him and Jared stood by them,
awkwardly shifting from foot to foot, wiping tears away and smiling at the same time. Lincoln looked up and excused himself to
go back to his daughter with the promise that he would return
to them with news about Camilla as soon as he knew anything
at all.

Anne and Jared moved back to their seats and toasted first
Jasmine and then Camilla with cups of coffee. "What is going to
happen to Camilla when she regains her health?" Anne mused.

"I'm afraid to say that her life will be turned upside-down.
Sconset House will never be the same, I suppose, and while I know
that the restaurant and her marriage truly held her back, I've loved
the magic she created there with all my heart. Prescott, too."

"In all of this I've forgotten about Prescott."

"He arrives in New York tonight and I've left a message for him
to join me here in Boston tomorrow morning. I really need him
about now. How are you holding up without John?"

"It's hard, but he's put his work to one side and is running the
gallery for me and a small show at the Artists'Association. He's a
gem. I've asked him to go out to the restaurant and have a drink
with Billy tonight. Poke around a bit. Maybe after a few cocktails,
Billy will loosen up and spill the beans. I'm hoping John can remind him just how devoted Camilla has been to him all these years
and that he should be there for her, or something."

"If you don't mind my saying so, I think it's a waste of time.
Billy is not capable of supporting anyone, not even himself. He
needs help with simply that and he's getting what he needs from
Maeve. You didn't see the expression on his face this morning,

Annie. It was like looking into the eyes of a stranger. He has serious problems and, for Camilla's sake in her recovery, it would be best if he stayed away. Far away."

"I assume she'll want to recover at her parents' home. When we know she'll be okay, I'm going to have a private duty nurse set up to stay with her there until she can decide what her next step will be."

"I'm going to resign my spot at the restaurant immediately and stay with her. I'll move my hatting supplies with me and probably Prescott. We won't leave her side."

"It's going to be hard for Camilla to come to terms with all that's happened. She's such a perfectionist. Her standards for herself have been so high these past years, especially since her parents died. It will be great for her to have you and Prescott at her side."

"My goal will be to make her smile. A lot."

CHAPTER TWENTY-NINE

The waiting stretched on, minutes ticking by sluggishly when suddenly, Lincoln burst through the door and time speeded up to reckless proportions. Anne and Jared jumped to their feet, dashing forward to meet the frantic-looking Lincoln.

"She's out of surgery. She made it. The next twenty-four hours will be critical and if she makes it until tomorrow and if the anti-rejection drugs work, then…"

"We'll be bringing her home," Anne finished.

"Yes. But where will home be? I certainly hope she won't be going home to Billy's care," Lincoln said.

"She'll be going to her parents' home in Hingham," Anne filled in. "Jared and his partner Prescott, who arrives tomorrow, will stay with her there and we'll have a nurse hired to oversee her recovery. She's not going anywhere near Billy."

"I wonder what he'll say about that?"

"Probably heave a sigh of relief," Jared surmised. "Can we see her for a moment?"

"Yes. Dr. Franklin told me to get you. He's on the phone with Billy right now. Come on."

The three companions whisked through the doors, which had been such a terrible barrier just moments before. They found Camilla in a corner cubicle seeming to be hooked up to every monitor known to man. She was conscious and even managed a small smile as her friends gently hugged her, promising to take care of her. Dr. Franklin appeared at the edge of the curtained off cubicle and motioned for them to follow him to a consulting room down the hall.

"First of all, she got through the surgery by the skin of her teeth. But she made it and her vital signs are holding. We think the kidney will be accepted by her as it was practically a perfect match, thanks to Miss Hunter. At this point, we're guardedly optimistic."

"Thank God," Jared spoke for all of them.

"I am concerned about Mr. Smith, however. He seemed disinterested, at best, and if I'm right, his speech was a bit slurred. I think he was drunk."

"Not surprising," Jared spoke.

"I hope she's not going to be released into his care."

"No. She's going to her family home in Hingham and I will be staying with her throughout her recovery. And she will have a fulltime nurse," Jared informed the doctor. "When do you think she'll be released?"

"Two to three weeks, if all goes well. I'm going to ask all of you to leave now, except for Mr. Jones. You may come back to see her tomorrow when she's in her own room. I'm sure Mr. Jones will keep you posted on her condition." With that, Dr. Franklin ushered Anne and Jared out of the recovery area, where they bumped into Yolanda.

Anne hurried to her and quickly filled her in on Camilla's condition. With a sigh of relief, Yolanda embraced Anne and said,

"Jasmine's already being moved to her room. The girl's as strong as an ox. Says she's ready to go home tomorrow."

"Tomorrow?" Anne asked.

"She'll be in for a while, but certainly not as long as Camilla. I'll be taking her home, though, as soon as she's ready. I don't believe we've formally met," Yolanda said turning to Jared.

"I'm Jared Miles, a close friend. I'll be staying with Camilla during her recovery." Jared said coolly.

"I hope we can learn to be friends," Yolanda continued. "Camilla means the world to my daughter and my brother and I hope to get to know her as well." Yolanda looked down to the floor for a moment in embarrassment, not knowing what to say next. Jared let the awkward moment stretch on a bit before saying, "I'm sure our girl will welcome your friendship." With a huge smile lighting up her smooth features, Yolanda looked up and took Jared's hand. He smiled.

"Now tell me Yolanda, do you wear hats? I have some ideas I'd like to try out on you. When I get back to the city, care to be my model?"

"Absolutely."

⊱✦⊰

The first two weeks of Camilla's recovery moved along at a snail's pace. Billy remained ensconced at the restaurant, ignoring Camilla and focusing on his outings at the golf course, running the restaurant and Maeve. Camilla's feelings were hurt by his lack of concern, but the constant ministrations of Lincoln, Anne, Jared and Prescott more than made up for Billy's limitations.

Camilla made slow, but steady progress toward a full recovery. Jasmine was ready for release several days following the surgery, and the two spent many hours together during the last two days of her stay, Camilla in her bed with Jasmine in a wheelchair at her side. In those precious moments Camilla and Jasmine formed a bond that would never be broken. Although they did not have a past to share, they did have their professional interests to discuss. Gradually, Camilla led the conversations to her relationship with Lincoln so long ago and told her the whole story, leaving nothing out.

"You think Daddy is the love of your life?" Jasmine asked her on the morning of her release. Yolanda and Lincoln were in the admissions office filling out the paperwork and the two had a few moments before Jasmine and her family were to fly to New York.

"Yes," Camilla replied without hesitation.

"So will you continue your relationship with him when you are released?"

"I plan to after I clear up my situation with Billy. I can't go on with your father with so many loose ends dangling around me. I'm afraid it might be a bit ugly and I want you to promise to keep your father out of it. Please."

"I'll do my best, but that might be difficult. Daddy's frightened he'll lose you again. He's told me that over and over. Promise me you won't break his heart, Camilla."

"I promise, my dear. But he's going to have to be patient with me. I have over thirty years of my life to think about and bring to a conclusion. And right now, all I want to do is sleep. Do you think I'll ever get past the need for four naps a day?"

With a laugh, Jasmine kissed her mother and said, "Sleep while you can. I'm sure Daddy has plans for you, if you know what I mean."

"Jasmine, are you going to let Brian visit you in New York? I have to tell you it's all he talks about when he calls me daily."

"He calls me daily also and, yes, we have plans for the weekend after Labor Day. He'll be staying at Daddy's place and I'm going to show him the city. He's been so sweet. I can't believe he's for real."

"Trust me, Brian is exactly who you think he is. He's been like a son to Billy and me for many years. I have a feeling this is a very tough situation for him. I'm sure you have been the bright spot in his summer and I hope you and he can develop a relationship. Nothing would make me happier. So, what are your plans?"

"I'm spending the month of July, which is about to begin, you know, with Mom and Pops. I'm sure my grandparents will be in and out of the house daily. Then Daddy and I are going on a car tour of Italy for the month of August. We've always wanted to take the trip and I can't believe we're actually going to do it. I'm so eager to just be in Florence. I go back to work the day after Labor Day and then Brian is coming, so I have a lot to look forward to."

"I can't believe it's almost July. I'm going to be released July third and Jared has moved the location of Jessica and Jeremy's wedding to the Hingham house. He's there now working on the final arrangements with Prescott. He says all I have to do is show up. I'm glad I bought my outfit the day I got sick. The ceremony will be July Fourth, a day the restaurant is closed in deference to the fireworks at Jetties Beach. I promised I'd be there and, God willing and thanks to you, I will."

"You don't ever have to thank me again, Camilla. I had an ulterior motive, like having my mother around for awhile. I love you, Camilla."

"I love you too, Jasmine," Camilla whispered, wiping away a tear.

"And I'm terribly glad you've accepted Mom's apology. She's like a lioness when it comes to protecting her family. Unfortunately, Daddy kept you a secret for so long that when the truth came out we were all in shock."

"I admire Yolanda, Jasmine. She provided a wonderful home for you and has had a fabulous career at the same time. I hope we can be friends as time goes on."

Soon after Jasmine left to gather her belongings in her room Lincoln stepped quietly into Camilla's room and, finding her eyes closed, tapped gently on the door to see if she might stir. "I'd know your tap anywhere, Linc," Camilla smiled, lazily opening her eyes. "Come."

Lincoln materialized at Camilla's side, wordlessly taking her in his arms. They remained like that for a long moment neither wished to end. "My favorite place in the world," Camilla whispered in his ear.

"Where you belong," Lincoln whispered back. Standing up and moving into the bedside chair, Lincoln sighed, "I'm going to miss being able to see you, my love. I plan to visit you in Hingham July tenth and again on July twentieth. You know I have a large show mounted now and several small shows in the Hamptons in July. I have to be there."

"Linc, I understand. It's probably best to see each other sporadically while I'm sorting out my life and all. I would be tempted to just run away with you and leave things up in the air, and that situation could never make us happy."

"You're right, of course. I'm just having déjà vu flashbacks and then I feel the panic rise and I…"

"Don't call it déjà vu, Linc. We're not repeating our past. We're launching into our future."

"I'm going to begin construction of studio space for you in the apartment space I just bought for you upstairs over mine. It will be connected by stairs and we'll…"

"You bought me a place, Linc?"

"Came on the market yesterday and I grabbed it up. The view of Central Park is simply marvelous and I'll be right downstairs. I know what you need for painting and I've already designed the cabinets and I have a great idea for an easel with adjustable heights and a chair attached so you can sit if you need to."

"I don't know when I'll be able to come to New York, Lincoln. It might be awhile."

"I know. Whenever you're ready. It's a great space, Camilla."

"I'm sure it is. I just know I'll love it."

Another rap on the door announced Yolanda. Moving to the bedside she took Camilla's hand and gave it a firm squeeze. "You get better now, Camilla. You've got a very impatient family waiting for you."

"I'll do my best," Camilla smiled, returning the squeeze. "You take care of our girl now, and keep an eye on this handsome man for me."

"Sure will," Yolanda said, motioning for Lincoln to follow her out the door.

"Got to go," he said following his sister. "Love you."

"Love you too."

"*A family*," Camilla mused as she heard Lincoln's footsteps echo down the hall. "I actually have a family."

CHAPTER THIRTY

"Prescott, come here," Jared called from the flagstoned patio behind the Hingham house. "I need help hanging this basket."

"I don't know why you think I can help you," Prescott called, never-the-less moving out of the French doors leading to the patio. "Look at me."

Jared looked down on his diminutive lover of fifteen years from his perch on the stepladder where he was preparing to hang baskets of vivid pink and purple petunias from the intricate trellis-work extending along the side of the patio. "Just hand the baskets up to me one by one as I move along. Won't this be gorgeous in the noon light as they say, 'I do'?"

"It really will," Prescott agreed, handing a basket up to Jared. "I still think the impatiens would be better, but the petunias are nice."

"I'm sick of impatiens. Every other windowbox on Nantucket overflows with them. I've always been partial to petunias."

"I know. Your mother grew them and if your mother had them so should we."

"Right," Jared laughed, stepping from the ladder to move it a few feet farther along the patio edge. "My mother was always right."

"Could we hurry this along? I'm in the middle of my curry sauce for the salmon and I want it perfect for Camilla's first home cooked dinner."

"Five minutes. That's all I need. Camilla's limo won't be here for another hour. Anne said she'd call on her cell phone when they get off the highway so we can be at the door to greet her."

"Any word from Billy?"

"He called while you were marketing to say that he'll be attending the wedding tomorrow. He's leading the staff in a caravan from Hyannis. This should be very interesting."

"To say the least. I love this spot, Jared. I always dreamed of living in a big colonial mansion like this one with formal gardens in the back. It's picture perfect."

"Camilla was lucky to grow up in a house like this. I'm going to ask her if we could all spend Christmas here. Can't you just picture the tree in the formal living room?"

"Resplendent with my collection of German glass ornaments and crystal icicles. Yes, let's plan for it."

"Get me that basket, lovey. This angle kills my lower back."

"You'll be happy to know I brought our massage oils. I'll fix your back after you soak in the tub tonight."

"Your hands are magic, Pres."

"What do you think will become of Camilla and Billy?"

"I think their marriage, such as it has become, is over. It's been one-sided for the ten years I've known them and it was probably that way from the start. Personally, my take on Camilla is that she had a breakdown of sorts after she gave birth to Jasmine and when she recovered all she wanted was safety. Billy was safe. She knew she could control him and her emotional distance from him gave her space to have her world of art and her memories of Lincoln Jones. Guilt at her inability to have a child and her lie about it has been the glue that kept them together. Sconset House has been her refuge and albatross at the same time."

"Sorry, love, I don't see what you mean."

"Well, think of all the fun we've had with Camilla over the years. Except for Anne, all of her closest friends work for her. It's like a summer camp. The price she pays, however, is her art. She never touches a brush from the time we arrive until we all leave. I believe that's torture for her. That's why I think it's both a haven and an albatross for her."

"My God, and they say gay men are complicated? What do you think she'll do next?"

"Personally, I think she'll fight Billy for control of the restaurant. I can see her moving upstairs and painting in the living room. The view's positively inspirational. For her sake, though, I hope she lets go of Sconset House."

"And moves to New York to be with the love of her life. It would make a nice movie, but life isn't like that. I think Billy is going to try to grind her into the ground and after this illness, I don't think she'll be able to fight her way around her guilt."

"He has been positively diabolical since she had her crisis. Jessica says he's been spreading the story from table to table about his conniving wife and her sordid past. Of course he's half in the bag most of the time, and it takes Brian and Maeve to get him home at night. The rumor is that Maeve stays the night with him; however, she's always back home by the time Dottie gets up at six."

"If anyone can get to the bottom of the story, it's Dottie," laughed Prescott. "I can't wait to see her."

"Tomorrow's on our doorstep. There's the phone. Can you get it for me Pres?"

Nodding his head and saying, "We'll be there." Prescott disconnected the call and scrambled down the ladder grabbing Jared by the arm. "They're early. Let's get to the front door. Just let me turn off the sauce." Prescott said, hurrying into the kitchen.

⊷⊶

Camilla was actually happy to see her childhood home loom into view. For so many years she had hated to step foot into the house that had become her prison after Jasmine was born. For the moment those painful memories slipped to the side to make room for happier recollections from her childhood.

"I'd forgotten just how gorgeous this place is," Anne marveled as they pulled into the driveway.

"I'm kind of glad I decided not to sell it when they died. And Daddy's firm says they'll not schedule any functions here until I've left."

"That's the least they can do, seeing that you own it and let them use it."

"True, but they pay for all the upkeep for the use of it. I've been happy with the situation."

"Jared says he's made the den off the living room into a recovery room for you, complete with hospital bed and wheelchair. He didn't want you to feel trapped on the second floor."

"The den is great. It opens onto the backyard patio. I'll be able to wheel myself out there at will. Oh, Annie, I'm so tired. I hope the guys don't expect much of me tonight."

"I'm sure they don't. Look, there they are," Anne smiled, pointing to the two men frantically waving from the front door. "And here they come."

Jared and Prescott ran to the limo and simultaneously reached into the spacious back seat to hug Camilla and help her out of the car. "I'm so glad to see you both," Camilla enthused, trying to hug

207

both of them at the same time. The driver went to the trunk and quickly pulled out the wheelchair, to which the two men guided Camilla to in a smooth motion.

Within moments, Camilla was ensconced in her bed with the French door curtains pulled back so that she could see the spot for the wedding set up on the patio. After Camilla raved about how beautiful everything looked in the secluded area with its surrounding formal gardens, Prescott brought in a dinner tray with his salmon creation and a glass of champagne for Camilla. The others bustled into the kitchen and soon returned with their meals and champagne.

"To Camilla, the love of our lives," Jared toasted as the four leaned together to clink their glasses.

"You are all so wonderful." Camilla exclaimed. "You've been the light at the end of the tunnel for me."

"And a long dark tunnel it's been," Prescott included.

"Dr. Franklin says one more week in the wheelchair and I can begin walking around a bit. He thinks by September I'll be ready to begin painting. Right now, I can't see it, but he says I'm regaining my strength daily."

"Are you still on anti-rejection drugs?" Jared asked.

"Yes. I don't know if I'll ever be truly free of them. I guess they have tests to determine that sort of thing. Anyhow, it worked. All I have to do is rest and enjoy your company."

"About tomorrow," Jared began. "We are going to make certain you don't overdo it. So I'm telling you now that there will be no arguing with us when we send you to bed if we think you need a nap."

"Yes sir," Camilla laughed. "What else are you trying to avoid saying?"

"Billy's coming."

"Good. I had hoped he'd show his face," Camilla said grimly. "He never called me once to see how I was doing. It has been hard to realize that…"

"Don't torture yourself," Anne recommended. "He's finally revealed his true colors and that should make it easier for you to divorce the son of a bitch."

"Yes. I spoke to Daddy's partner about it and he's in contact with our, I mean Billy's lawyer Chad Whithers. It looks like Billy wants everything. He's hoping to name Lincoln as co-respondent or something stupid like that and prove that I deserve nothing. Of course, all Lincoln did was save my life. How could we have carried on an affair when I had one foot in the grave? It's preposterous, but apparently Billy has hired a detective to go over my phone records for the past I don't know how many years in an attempt to prove that I've been carrying on with Linc all this time. The only New York calls he'll find are to your place, Jared, and Jasmine's last winter when I was interviewing her. Tomorrow should be very interesting."

"It certainly should," Prescott spoke for them all.

"Your nurse, Katie Johnson, also comes tomorrow. I think you'll like her. She's young and perky, just like you will be again soon," Jared announced.

"I think my perky days have come and gone," Camilla smiled. "I'd be happy for middle-aged and plodding."

Anne said, "When I go home on Sunday I plan to have your painting supplies packed and shipped up here. I think you could work beautifully right in this room, and painting might just be the best medicine for you."

"That's a good idea, Annie, but the best medicine is the three of you. I'm so happy to have you here. I couldn't wait to get out of the hospital. I feel better already."

───※───

A short time later, Jared and Prescott left Anne with Camilla to help her get ready for bed. By seven-thirty Camilla was alone with her thoughts, trying to fall asleep. Her mind kept gravitating toward Lincoln and the new studio space he had acquired for her. With all her heart she wished she could just turn her back on her marriage and run into his arms, but knowing that she could never leave things unfinished, she forced herself to face her next step with Billy.

Both hospitals had approached her to push charges against Yolanda and Billy. Both times she'd said no, but while Cape Cod Hospital took no for an answer, Mass General decided to bring suit against Billy without her blessing. Camilla assumed that the hospital's counsel had contacted Billy and she anticipated that he was probably furious about the situation. And to add insult to injury, Lincoln had filed a formal complaint against Billy for assault, and Billy had already been issued a warning to stay away from him. The statement was clear that if he violated the terms, Lincoln could have him arrested. Lincoln had shown the document to Camilla.

Camilla could only imagine how humiliating this all was for Billy. She was fairly certain that no one from his family knew what was going on. They stayed out of the way during high season, and Camilla was pretty confident that he would not confide in either his parents or his brothers about this. It would be too embarrassing. Knowing that Billy never took responsibility for anything, Camilla knew that she was blamed by him not only for her past but for forcing him to behave so badly as well. He was probably even blaming her for his drinking, she thought with a grim smile.

Apparently, he was spending a lot of time with Maeve these days, and she would not put it past him to flaunt their relationship before her very eyes. Brian, never one to dissemble when it came to the truth, told her the speculation about Billy and Maeve so that she would be prepared if they came to the wedding. She could understand why he would go to Maeve. After all, she herself had relied on Maeve over the years to take over competently for her when needed. Maeve was the perfect replacement for her, she realized with a pull in her heart. "Damn you, Billy," Camilla murmured to herself. "You were not supposed to hurt me."

Camilla knew that she had to face the fact that she was the one who, in fact, had caused the biggest hurt and she knew she would have to deal with that fact for the rest of her life. It was almost easier to live with the loss of Lincoln and Jasmine than to come to terms with her own culpability in the injury department. Almost.

"Oh well," Camilla said to herself, rolling on her side to ease the back pain, "at least I'll look good tomorrow." Her new outfit hung outside the closet door waiting for her. She hoped Anne could manage something with her unruly hair, which really needed a trim. Trying to decide how to roll it tomorrow, Camilla drifted off into a deep sleep in the home of her childhood.

CHAPTER THIRTY-ONE

The morning of July Fourth dawned crisp and clear. Alarm clocks began ringing at Surf and Turf at six, with a bustle of activity as the staff of Sconset House prepared to journey to Hingham for Jessica and Jeremy's wedding. Jeremy nervously called his daughter Kim and son John to make certain they had the directions to Camilla's house. After being reassured for the fourth time that they were about to depart and knew where they were going, he went downstairs to make coffee for everyone, which he served outside on the Surf deck with pastries Chef Brandon had whipped up for the occasion.

Jessica refused to allow Jeremy to see her in her bridal ensemble and chose to travel in casual clothes. Everyone else, however, left Nantucket dressed for the occasion. Four rental cars waited for them at Hyannis Airport when they arrived at ten thirty. With Billy's car in the lead, the convoy made its way surprisingly quickly to Camilla's new residence in Hingham.

Jared and Prescott busily supervised the catered foods, which had been shipped over from Twenty-One Federal Street's talented chef. Waiters and a bartender had been hired in Hingham and they were following Jared's instructions to a tee. At twelve on the dot, the cars began to arrive and the women bustled Jessica into Camilla's room to help get her ready. Amid squeals and hugs, everyone, including Maeve, greeted Camilla and managed to get Jessica dressed at the same time. The men on the patio thoroughly enjoyed listening to the merriment coming from behind the curtained door. Every man that is, except Billy, who stood off to one side, sipping steadily at his Hennessey and looking around as if planning his escape.

At twelve thirty the women took their places, Camilla in her wheelchair up front as matron of honor and Jeremy's son John as best man next to his father. The justice of the peace motioned for Jessica to enter and amid sighs and muffled sobs, Jessica made her way to the front and in a matter of minutes was married to Jeremy. The onlookers barely gave Jeremy time for a quick kiss before descending on the happy couple with glasses of champagne for the toast. Jared turned up the light jazz which drifted over the assemblage gently, lending a soft touch to the event. Food was passed by the waiters and everyone except Billy seemed ready to put the tension of the past month to one side and enjoy themselves.

Jared noticed that after about an hour Camilla began to look worn out, with the telltale red blotches on her cheeks beginning to flare. He quietly wheeled her into her room, helped her into her bed, and promised to make her rest for only half an hour. Billy took her departure as a chance to speak to her alone, and as soon as Jared rejoined the festivities he slipped into the house and, without knocking entered Camilla's room.

"I expected you to follow me in," Camilla said, adjusting her bed to a more upright position. "We certainly need to talk."

"You seem to be making a good recovery," Billy said, taking a seat in the overstuffed chair next to Camilla's bed.

"Yes, I am. But I'm certain you didn't come in to check on my recovery. So what do you have to say?"

"I have to appear in court on August 15th at the request of Mass General. I hope that you are not part of this abomination, Camilla."

"I asked the hospital not to press charges, but Dr. Franklin wouldn't relent. I will not attend the hearing. I suspect it will be a slap on the wrist."

"We'll see. As you know, our attorneys have been speaking and I want you to know that I expect to keep all of our property, since you were the one at fault. I think you deserve nothing but your personal belongings, and that's what I am pushing for."

"I have nothing to say about that. My attorney has my best interests at heart and I trust him to proceed on my behalf. I do want you to allow Anne to supervise the packing of my things when she returns home. That will include all of my studio supplies as well as any of my artwork on the property. I want everything here, and I believe she'll be in touch with you in the next few days about it, or you could talk to her about it here. Now I really need to sleep for a while, so if you don't have anything else to say, I'd appreciate it if you would leave me alone."

"I do have more to say. I believe you were carrying on with that man behind my back all these years. I intend to prove you were and that information will solidify my claim that I was wronged by you."

"Billy, look all you want. It's your prerogative. You won't find anything. I can assure you of that. But, of course, you don't believe me, so do what you have to do. Have yourself a ball. Just let me sleep now," Camilla finished turning her back to Billy.

"Aren't you even going to say you're sorry?"

"No. I might have a month ago, but your recent behavior leaves you as the one to say you're sorry. And speaking of carrying on, from what I've heard, you're the one who's guilty. Perhaps I deserve everything we own since I have never once committed an adulterous act. Can you say the same thing?"

Billy abruptly turned and slammed the door, heading straight for the bar he ordered a tumbler of cognac and allowed the magical gold to take him to a safer place. As the liquor soothed him, the old Billy began to surface, and soon he was back to the lighthearted antics he was known for.

The festivities lasted until about four o'clock, when everyone had agreed to begin the trek home. As quickly as the party had arrived, everyone was suddenly gone, with Camilla still sound asleep in her room. Anne and Jared had taken turns checking in on her and at four-thirty she was awakened to take her medication. Shocked at how late it was, Camilla asked to be wheeled back to the party, but was told everyone had left.

"Jared," she began. "You promised."

"You wouldn't wake up, would she, Annie?"

"Cammie, you were out like a light. I'm sorry, sweetheart, but you needed the sleep. Here, let me introduce you to Katie, your nurse."

"Hello, Katie," Camilla smiled at the young blonde woman.

"Hello Mrs. Smith. I'd like..."

"Please call me Camilla. The Mrs. Smith thing turns my stomach these days."

"Okay, Camilla. I want to take your blood pressure and pulse. Go ahead talking. I'll try to be out of the way over here."

"I'm dying to hear what Billy had to say," Anne began and looking over at Katie, decided to wait until she was done. Katie quickly took the blood pressure and noted out loud that it was rather low. Jotting down the results, she quickly left the room to Camilla, Jared, Anne, and Prescott.

"Well, he said he has to go to court on August 15th to face Mass General. I assured him I was not personally pressing charges. Then he told me he intends to get everything in the divorce and that he is trying to prove that I've been having an affair all these years with Lincoln. Of course we knew that's what he'd claim and of course he'll find nothing. But he thinks he's right and that he'll prove that I deserve nothing. I flat out told him that I had never committed an adulterous act, I think I called it, and that I wondered if he could claim the same thing. I suggested that perhaps I deserved to get everything."

"You said that to him?" Anne squealed in delight. "I'm so proud of you!"

"That must have been when he slammed out of the room." Prescott noted.

"And proceeded to drink out the bar with a vengeance. We had to insist that Brandon drive his rental car back home." Jared finished.

"Kind of proves his guilt," Camilla said sadly. "I had truly hoped that nothing was going on with Maeve, but…"

"Don't think about it, Cammie. And why would it bother you, anyway?"

"He's making a fool of himself, Annie. It's not being with Maeve that gets to me so much, it's how openly he's showed all his weaknesses to the staff. His drinking is on display as is his abandoning me while I was so sick. And now Maeve. How can anyone respect him with all that going on?"

"I think everyone has known that you have made him respectable all these years. No one is surprised at what he's doing." Jared said, trying to soothe Camilla.

"I feel very badly about it, none-the-less. Very badly."

"Well, I say we wheel the old girl on out to the patio and have a bite to eat before the waitstaff comes back to take everything away," Prescott suggested.

"Great idea," Camilla smiled. "I'm pretty hungry after my long nap."

"After that interaction with Billy, I would think you'd be exhausted, lovey." Jared said as he helped her out of bed.

⊯⊯⊱

After Camilla had been tucked in for the night Anne, Jared and Prescott settled themselves on the patio in the comfortably overstuffed wicker lounges and prepared to enjoy the warm summer evening. Fireworks from Hingham Harbor glittered over the trees, imbuing the scene with their magic.

Jared broke the silence with a contented sigh. "I think the day went off beautifully."

"Splendid," Prescott agreed. "And your flower baskets were stunning in the mid-day sun. I think the two J's were thrilled."

"I'm sure they were. Camilla booked them a room tonight at the Four Chimneys. She made sure it would be one of those romantic rooms with a big fluffy canopied bed and a view of the harbor. They sure looked happy."

"What were you talking to Billy about? It looked serious," Jared asked.

"I arranged to begin packing Camilla's things to be shipped. I'm going to be pressed for time when I get back because John has to take a business trip day after tomorrow and I need to get back to the gallery. So I got permission from him to allow Mrs. Carter and Diana to do the actual work under my direction. He was fine about everything and we figure that the job should take about five days. What we were arguing about was the statues in the gardens. Billy thinks they are joint property and should be sold with the profits split. Camilla says they are hers and she wants the small ones shipped to Lincoln. *Rapture* is to be shipped to Jasmine as a surprise."

"Pretty big surprise," Prescott noted.

"Sure is. Lincoln will be at her place when it arrives to supervise its placement. Apparently, he had always planned to give it to Jasmine and then it sold. So Camilla means to send it where it belongs. Billy is very upset and I'm not certain how to handle this."

"I think you should have a mover come and cart them away one evening while Billy's tied up at the restaurant. And you should do it soon. If I know Billy, he'll have those pieces sold in a flash. A lot of Sconset people collect Lincoln's work, and I'm sure he could make a tidy sum on the sale," Jared surmised.

"As a matter of fact, I think you should have them moved tomorrow night. Jared's right. Billy's going to act fast on this and the sculptures will be gone for good," Prescott added.

"But what if he goes to the police and charges me with theft?" Anne asked.

"We'll threaten him. You're not going to *believe* what Dottie told me. She said that a couple of days ago she went into Camilla's office to get some tape for the credit card machine and guess what? She found Maeve and Billy doing the deed on Camilla's desk in the middle of the afternoon. Dottie's certain they didn't see her. Apparently she only got the door open a crack, but that crack was enough. She says the situation disgusts her and I'm certain she would make a formal statement to Camilla's lawyer if we needed it," Jared said.

"We could write a letter to Billy and leave it in the kitchen, threatening him with it if he goes to the police. I think that would work. Billy certainly wouldn't want Camilla to have that kind of ammunition especially after the threat she made this afternoon," Anne suggested.

"Great. Let's call the mover in the morning and write the letter before you leave. Do you think you can handle this alone, lovey?" Jared asked.

"I think so. I'll have John go with me. I'll call you as soon as the truck rolls away. I feel like Nancy Drew."

"And we're the Hardy Boys!" Jared laughed.

CHAPTER THIRTY-TWO

Anne sent John to Sconset House at eight o'clock to have a drink with Billy on the verandah. She knew her nerves couldn't take the stress of wondering if Billy would intrude on her caper, as she referred to the removal of the sculptures from Camilla's gardens, and John was the perfection diversion. Because there were a number of sculptors on Nantucket, Anne knew who to call for professional removal of the works, which would be followed by packing and shipment from the firm's warehouse near Steamboat Wharf.

John assured Anne that he would monopolize Billy for the hour and a half the movers estimated the removal would take. All she had to worry about was neighborly curiosity about the truck and she crossed her fingers that once it was backed into the driveway, the hedges and approaching dusk would camouflage the clandestine activity. As soon as the truck was in its place and the team of five men began working quickly and quietly to remove the sculptures from their bases and load them onto the truck, Anne called Jared from her cell phone and kept the line open, keeping him updated on the progress.

The small sculptures were easily removed and the caper took less than an hour. Camilla had *Rapture* attached to a rolling base so that it could be easily wheeled into the studio for safekeeping during the harsh winter weather. "I didn't know she had *Rapture* on wheels," Anne exclaimed into the phone. "All they had to do was pull out the stakes holding it in place and the piece rolled over to the truck, easy as pie."

"So everything's done already?" Jared responded.

"They're rolling out of the driveway as we speak. I'm going to put the letter on the kitchen counter now and follow the truck down to the warehouse. I want to oversee the packing. It will go out on the ten thirty freight boat in a small truck that will drive directly to Manhattan. They plan to meet Lincoln at six in the morning."

"So, with any luck, the pieces will be on the boat by the time Billy gets home."

"Right. Put Camilla on the phone."

"Hey, Annie, I'm thrilled," Camilla said. "Are you okay?"

"Just a little shaky. I'm glad I don't do this for a living. Never thought I'd be pulling a caper at my age!"

"Did you give them the check?"

"Of course I did, silly. Gotta go."

In a matter of minutes Anne had placed the threatening letter in the kitchen and was easing her Range Rover down Baxter Road heading for downtown. Her racing heart slowed down a bit as she wove along the Polpis Road in the early evening stillness.

The Hingham trio waited for a call from Billy and were not disappointed. At eleven-thirty the shrill sound startled them for a moment, and they let the phone ring three times before Jared answered with a calm, "Good evening, Billy."

"Who the hell do you think you are, stealing my possessions? I had a buyer set up for that stuff. Do you know how much money you just cost me?"

"I'm sure it was a tidy sum, Billy, but not nearly as much as all your Sconset property would add up to if you lost it to Camilla. As you probably read in the letter, Dottie saw you in a very compromising position. I'm surprised at you, Billy. Sex in the afternoon on your wife's desk? How upper crust of you."

"Go to hell, fairy. Put my wife on the phone."

"Absolutely not. Sleep tight, Billy. And give Maeve a kiss good night for us."

With extreme delight, Jared hung up the receiver and the three burst into peals of laughter. "You were brilliant, lovey," Prescott boomed. " 'How upper crust of you'" he mimicked.

"Jasmine is finally going to get the sculpture she always deserved."

"And Billy will have to eat crow on his big deal. I can see him cracking open a fresh bottle of Hennessey right now," Jared smiled.

"I hope he doesn't decide to go for a drive," Camilla murmured.

"You have to stop worrying about the man, Camilla. He certainly hasn't been worried about you as you held onto life. He tried to push you over the edge, for God's sake, girl!" Jared snapped.

"You're right, of course. It's just hard to stop being his wife. I never thought it would come to this."

"Well, it has. How about three cups of Sleepytime, Prescott, for the Three Musketeers?"

"Coming right up," Prescott said, rising to his feet.

Billy raged around the house, bellowing insults first at Camilla, then at Jared, and finally at Lincoln, and when he had exhausted his repertoire of grievances decided to have another look at the report on Lincoln Jones that Billy had hired a private investigator to prepare. Even though he had been assured there was nothing in the file worth mentioning, Billy sat in his favorite leather chair in the living room with the file in his lap. He needed something significant that would point to the fact that Camilla had been involved with an unseemly character prior to his marriage to her. His lawyer had pointed out to him repeatedly that Lincoln's race could not be used in court against Camilla which was why Billy had hired the investigator.

He must have been a Black Panther or something like that, Billy mused as he shuffled through the thin pile of papers. But what he found was a man totally immersed in his art. Lincoln had absolute no political affiliations and was, in fact, registered as an independent voter. "Totally boring," Billy sighed, tossing the file onto the marble inlaid coffee table in front of him.

A light knock on the kitchen door brought Billy out of his reverie. Moving quickly to the kitchen, he ushered in Maeve who stood outside the door holding a covered tray in her hands.

"What do you have there, my sweet little one?" Billy smiled as Maeve entered the room.

"I know how much you like sushi, so I ordered some from the Japanese restaurant in town and had it delivered to the restaurant. It came complete with chopsticks," she grinned, pulling the sticks out of her blazer pocket.

"This is the best thing that's happened today," enthused Billy, making a mental note that Camilla had never once brought him sushi. Logging up another black mark against his wife, he continued, "You're not going to believe what happened here tonight."

"What, sweetheart?" Maeve asked.

"Camilla had someone come here and steal the statues out of the gardens. I'd had it all set up with Bron Cavendish to buy them. I won't even tell you how much this has cost me, Maeve."

"But Billy, I remember when Camilla bought the large one. She was very excited when she saw it in the Jones Catalog and paid for it with the proceeds from a special show she had mounted at the end of the season. It cost a lot of money. You know it belonged to Camilla, Billy."

"Whose side are you on?" Bill pouted, pulling the wrapper off his chopsticks.

"It's not about sides, Billy. This is about right and wrong. You've been telling me you want all the property and I personally think that's unfair, but I haven't said a thing to you about it. And now you're fussing about Camilla's personal possessions. What's happening to you?"

"What are you talking about?" Billy snapped after swallowing his first piece of sushi. Wiping his mouth with a napkin, he leaned forward, looking into Maeve's concerned eyes.

"I don't suppose you know that Camilla took a lot of criticism from her friends for putting you first all the time. And she was still putting your needs before hers until the day she told you about Jasmine and all. Her first thought when she took sick was how to make things better for you. You've turned on her, Billy, over something that happened before she even met you. It makes me wonder what will have you turning on me."

"I won't turn on you, darling," Billy murmured, his blue eyes earnest.

"I'm sure you would have said the same thing to Camilla in May, but here it is July and you're willing to turn her out with only her clothing. Maybe you really are the spoiled person everyone says you are behind your back," Maeve countered as she rose to her feet and moved toward the door.

"No, don't leave me!" Billy shouted, stumbling to his feet to block her exit. "I need you, Maeve. What can I do to prove my loyalty?"

"God only knows, Billy. I truly care about you, but I can't abide your behavior towards Camilla. She's given me a lot and I'm starting to feel a mite badly about going behind her back."

"She knows, Maeve."

"Saints alive," murmured Maeve. "How?"

"Dottie saw us that afternoon in the office and she went ahead and blabbed it to Jared, who of course told Camilla. They've made threats if I do anything about the statues."

"What kind of threats?" Maeve asked as she raised her trembling hands to her flushed cheeks.

"They'll name you as co-respondent in adultery. Jared says Camilla will try to take everything. She claims she never committed adultery."

"Of course she didn't, Billy."

"That's why I'm trying to find some dirt on old Lincoln, but he's as untarnished as a choirboy."

"Let the statues go, Billy, and try to remember what Camilla has meant to you all these past years."

"Look, Maeve, my social standing is the most important thing in the world to me. I have a long family tradition to uphold here. Camilla has become a threat to everything my family stands for and I see that as betrayal. Her betrayal outweighs everything she did for me. Everything!"

"That's pretty callous."

"Camilla knew what my family stood for when she married me. Her family was in the same position and I can only guess how her parents must have reacted to her situation with Lincoln Jones. She is not what she wanted me to think she was and that means our marriage is over."

"I don't come from a family of social standing, as you call it. And I'm an Irish Catholic. I bet your family hates the Kennedys. So what does that mean for us?"

"That means that you come from a background we can invent. We can say your family is anything we need it to be and no one will ever know the difference. As long as you have no illegitimate children in the closet, we can make our future."

"Are you serious?" Maeve fairly shouted.

"Absolutely. You don't have any children back home, do you?"

"Of course not!"

"And you don't have any man in your life to get his pride bent out of shape."

"There's nothing about to jump out of my closet at you, Billy. Unless it upsets you that in the art circles I'm considered Camilla's student."

"The painting is totally unimportant to me. What is important is holding my head up high in my community. Now let me tell you something exciting. There's a little shanty in the village that very quietly came on the market."

"Which one?" Maeve questioned, her eagerness spilling over.

"The Yellow Finch."

"I love that cottage, Billy. It's so charming with those creamy yellow windowboxes full of flowers and the little birdhouses hanging in the trees."

"I had a feeling you'd like it. It's ours as of next week. You can move right in and we'll have our own little love nest, Maeve, my love."

"I'm so excited, Billy, I'm about to burst!" Maeve exclaimed, twirling herself around the kitchen, totally forgetting her previous upset about Camilla. Landing back in her chair, she continued, "I've always been uncomfortable with you here in Camilla's house. Come, Billy, the sushi's waiting for you."

CHAPTER THIRTY-THREE

The morning after the removal of *Rapture* and the smaller pieces, Camilla awakened feeling light-hearted. Deciding to bypass her wheelchair, she ambled into the kitchen, stopping along the way to enjoy the sweet summer perfume of the roses Prescott had arranged in vases throughout the house. She could hear the stirrings of her early rising companion and decided to surprise Jared with a full breakfast. She was just taking her fluffy biscuits out of the oven when Jared rushed into the room.

"Lovey, what on earth are you doing? I couldn't imagine what the noise was!"

"I'm feeling so well this morning I decided to walk on my two feet into the land of the living," Camilla smiled, going over to give Jared a hug, noticing for the first time that she could stand up straight and easily reach her arms around his neck.

"I can feel your strength returning," Jared said. "But let me finish up. You sit down and tell me how you're feeling."

Realizing it was in her best interest for a peaceful breakfast to obey Jared, Camilla took a seat at the breakfast bar and began. "I've been feeling so bad. No, not bad. Guilty. It's as if I've deserved Billy's treatment. Getting those sculptures off the property and shipped to Lincoln and Jasmine unlocked my anger and it energized me somehow. I'm furious with Billy, and so happy to be alive at the same time."

"Annie always says that guilt will snuff out your spirit if you let it, lovey. This is good."

"Can you believe the way he treated me?" Camilla yelled, fairly rising up out of her chair.

"Or the way he's betraying you with Maeve?" Jared added.

"That doesn't bother me so much, I guess because of Linc. I've been pining away for him for an eon, it seems, and maybe Billy was a band aid on my wound, but I have been a good wife to him, always letting him have his freedom and running interference for him with his over achieving family. They're harsh on him, you know."

"Doesn't surprise me."

"So enough of feeling bad. I'm going to ask Annie to have all my painting things shipped over today. I want to set up the solarium off the living room as a temporary studio and then I'll send my things off to my new spot at Linc's." Camilla planned out loud.

"I'm so pleased we're going to have you in New York. The theatre openings, the gallery shows, the dining experiences – I'm tingling at the prospect."

"I have everything ready for omelets over there," Camilla said pointing to the counter. "I'm starved."

"Music to my ears," smiled Jared.

"What do you think will become of Billy and Maeve?" Camilla asked between sips of coffee.

"Maeve is smart. Don't you think she'll see that he's using her as a workhorse the same way he used you? Even though he might call it love, she should know better."

"But don't forget that she's always struggled monetarily. I'm sure Billy will buy her things, and that kind of security might mean more to her than being realistic about where she stands with him.

I remember it was a sacrifice for her to remain with me those two winters we painted together. She had to give up working in the pub her family owns back home and she wouldn't spend a penny on herself. If I wanted a bite to eat at The Brotherhood I had to either go alone or force her to let me treat her. Billy's wealth will mean the world to her."

"Great. I just hope…" Jared began.

"You hope what?"

"Nothing." Jared turned, overly busy at the stove, but to himself he fumed, "I hope she doesn't get pregnant, but I'll bet money she does." Turning to Camilla with two plates of fluffy yellow omelets and buttered biscuits in his hands, he grinned and said, "Let's start arranging the solarium for you right away."

"I have some ideas," Camilla smiled with the old glint in her eyes Jared had missed so much that summer. His heart hitched a beat as he realized that Camilla was really going to recover.

The month of July sped by. Sconset House limited its reservations to accommodate the diminished staff and its rating in the restaurant review section of the local paper slipped to three stars from its traditional four. The reviewer did note that the tragic illness of Camilla Smith had set the operation back and he, for one, eagerly awaited the return to impeccability she brought to the operation.

The review set Billy off on a two-day binge, during which time Brian and Maeve took turns keeping him at home out of harm's way. The newly married couple, Jeremy and Jessica, took over as the staff's moral support, handling high season stress and frayed nerves. But when all was said and done, Sconset was simply not the same without Camilla standing at the Sconset House podium.

Jasmine was thrilled to learn from her father that *Rapture* now stood beneath a skylight in her penthouse loft. She begged Yolanda to take her over to see it and danced with glee around the stunning statue when they arrived. Yolanda was so impressed with Jasmine's flexibility and energy that she relented to Jasmine's persistent demands that she be allowed to move home. The following day, they packed her belongings, most of which had been shipped from Surf by Dottie, and moved her home. Not willing to be left out, Milly made a detailed grocery list and had the kitchen stocked by the time they arrived.

The three opened windows to air out the city stuffiness while they enjoyed lunch on the rooftop garden.

"I sure do miss the fresh salt air," Jasmine sighed, settling back in her lounge chair. "If it weren't for Billy, I could have fallen in love with Nantucket."

"From what I've heard from your mother, you did manage to fall in love with a certain young man out there," Milly proclaimed.

"Not yet," Jasmine grinned slyly, "but I have plans for him. He'll be here in September. And don't get that shocked look on your face, Grandma. He's staying at Daddy's."

"Well," Milly humphed. "I don't care how old you are, granddaughter, you'll have a proper courtship."

"I'm sure he'll be calling on her with flowers in one hand and chocolates hidden behind his back in the other," Yolanda laughed. "Relax, Mommy, she's over thirty years old. And I will point out that I'm ready for grandchildren."

"You two," Jasmine said, shaking her head. "It will happen. But my first priority will be getting Camilla and Daddy back together. I won't relent until they're married."

"Married!" Milly fairly screamed. "After what she's put us all through? We're not going to even talk about dating until I meet this person."

"Mommy, I think she's good for Lincoln. They're on the same dreamy world kind of wavelength, and when she looks at him the love spills right out of her eyes," Yolanda noted.

"Are we forgetting that she already has a husband?" Milly asked, arms folded across her chest, her head tilted at an angle of challenge.

"You're not going to believe what Dottie told me. Apparently they're about to file for divorce and Billy is carrying on, not very discreetly, with one of his waitresses. Dottie actually saw them . . . well, let's just say, she was disgusted by what she saw."

"My son would never disrespect her like that."

"Lincoln would give her what she deserves after all she's been through," Yolanda stated.

"And I want them both happy," Jasmine proclaimed. Leaning forward, she continued: "And you know I get exactly what I want!"

"Look out," Yolanda laughed.

⬥

Overnight the solarium in the Hingham house became Camilla's new studio. Slowly but surely, Camilla organized her materials and sorted through photographs, choosing the first subjects she chose to paint. Jared, who had never seen Camilla at her easel in all the years he'd known her, was fascinated by the process. Day by day, his friend who he had always thought of as extremely organized and structured transformed into a distracted, daydreaming artist.

Over and over during the first few days, Jared would ask Camilla in alarm what she was staring at, only to be assured that she was arranging her next work in her mind. Prescott suggested that he and Jared back away and see where her muse took her. His suggestion was just what Camilla needed since for many years she had not had to cope with personal distractions while painting. Jared felt he had found a new friend, one who was fascinating in a manner he never could have imagined.

On a number of occasions during the day, Jared would stand at the solarium doorway and simply observe Camilla painting. He swore she was floating on air as she moved in and out from the canvas in rhythm to her brush strokes. Her concentrated effort caused her to totally lose track of time, and Jared and Prescott argued quite a bit those first few days about how long they would let her paint before suggesting she take a rest. The three finally came to an agreement that Jared would come in after two hours of work and make her sit down. After speaking to Lincoln on the phone, he purchased a stool level office chair which Camilla was able to sit in for painting as needed.

Camilla fussed about the chair but relented when Lincoln insisted she conserve her strength. After all, he reasoned, he had built an easel with a chair for her and he wanted her to be used to sitting as she painted before she moved to New York. In no time, Camilla had adapted to the chair and her first painting was emerging from the canvas. It was a scene set on a hilltop in Italy looking down into a picturesque village.

Jared was struck by the vivid colors Camilla was using. She was famous for her misty scenes and had perfected a glorious chiaroscuro, which was in demand by many of her collectors. But this little village had flashes of reds, yellows, and blues and the foliage sported vivid greens and deep browns. When Jared asked her about it, Camilla explained that back in her days with Lincoln, her work had been noted for its bright colors and she thought she'd experiment with colors mixed with an impressionistic overtone and see where it took her.

In private, Jared and Prescott were ecstatic about her work and thought her newfound happiness was going to lead her to even greater successes in the art world. The two times Lincoln visited in July, he agreed with the two friends that Camilla was on her way to further greatness.

Lincoln's first visit lasted only a few hours as he had to return to the gallery that was showing his newest pieces at a reception for the Ambassador from France, who was a collector of his work. The second visit Lincoln planned, though, was for two days, and Jared and Prescott went overnight to Boston to allow Camilla and Lincoln the privacy they had missed for so long.

Camilla nervously fluttered around the house, changing her outfit four times, pinning her hair up and letting it down so many times that she finally gave up and let the unruly mass of waves hang as it chose.

Lincoln, of course, didn't care how she wore her hair. He just wanted to be with her, to hear her voice, see her paintings, and hold her in his arms. Yolanda had warned him over and over not to overwhelm Camilla with his passion, so that by the time he arrived Lincoln sported an attitude of cool control, which evaporated when Camilla opened the door and dazzled him with her look of health and happiness.

Gone were the pasty white complexion, the dark circles beneath her eyes, and deep furrows across her brow. Gone were the bony shoulders hunched forward with clothes hanging awkwardly from her too-thin frame. Joyously, he beheld his Camilla standing radiantly upright with sparkling eyes, rosy cheeks, and luxuriously shiny hair. Lincoln's practiced restraint took flight as Camilla opened her arms to him, allowing an embrace in which he no longer feared to hurt her. The passion denied for so long flamed between them, and as their lips met, both knew the joy they would share with each other that day.

Drawing back and into the foyer, Camilla smiled into Lincoln's eyes. "I'm so deeply in love with you."

"Ah, Camilla, my love for you burns hot in my heart."

"My divorce papers were filed in court last week, Linc, and I was thinking that it means my marriage is over in spirit... and I was wondering if..."

"Whatever you feel is right. Of course I was hoping, but I didn't come here for that alone," Lincoln said, unsuccessfully trying to control his excitement.

"I don't want to wait a moment longer. I've learned that life is oh so short, and it should be shared with the one you love."

"Let me show you just how much you are loved," Lincoln whispered in Camilla's ear as he swept her off her feet and into his arms, making strides to her bedroom. And in lovemaking slower paced but no less passionate than over thirty years before, Lincoln and Camilla became lovers again.

⇥⊹⊹⇤

A glorious moment in time later, the two emerged from the bedroom and enjoyed the leisurely dinner of cold salads, crusty bread, and crisp wine Camilla had prepared beforehand. Long, comfortable moments stretched between them as they gazed into each other's eyes in a state of bliss too exquisite to speak of.

When the meal was finished, Lincoln suggested they take a peek at Camilla's new work in the solarium. As the carefully arranged lighting was switched on, the dark space flashed alive with the new paintings. Lincoln slowly cast his gaze on each of the works in progress, and after what seemed an eternity turned with a smile lighting his dark eyes.

"I don't know what to say. I've become so used to the muted dreams you made that it's as if they'd been done by a whole new painter. And yet they take me back to the bright kaleidoscopes you used to experiment with. Remember the sunset refracted through a prism?"

"Yes," Camilla laughed. "It was so raw, so unrefined."

"Well this is that same energy harnessed by a master. The impressionistic touch brings in your dreamlike stamp but the vibrancy speaks of an aliveness I haven't seen in your work since . . . well, since… "

"Since I had you in my life. The light left when you and Jasmine disappeared. You're right. I've been muted. But now I have my life back in spirit and in truth. I'm adoring the process of creating in a way I didn't dream possible. The desperate need to disappear in my work is gone, and now I only want to celebrate what I have. Does that make sense?"

"Perfect sense." Lincoln turned and took Camilla's hands in his own. "I asked you to marry me once and you accepted. I hope the answer hasn't changed, my love."

"It hasn't changed. I will marry you, Linc, for now and forever."

CHAPTER THIRTY-FOUR

Camilla sank into her painting like a tired body finding relief in a soft bed. Each day as she worked, her energy increased and her enthusiasm for where life would take her intensified. Jared and Prescott were thrilled and told Dr. Franklin that the painting was therapeutic. Camilla would simply have said she was doing what she loved most.

One morning as Camilla appraised a work in progress, deciding what detail to add next, she realized she was relieved to be free of Sconset House. The thought astounded her; as she had told herself year after year that she could not live without her restaurant. But here she was, working in her parents' solarium, birds chirping outside the open French doors, and she was happier than she thought possible. The pressure of pleasing Sconset Houses's demanding clientele had slipped from her shoulders and Camilla had to admit to herself that she truly didn't care if she saw any of the customers ever again. For years, her summers had focused around seating the Madisons at the correct table, having two perfectly chilled martinis waiting at the Millers' favorite spot, eliminating all garlic from Mr. Hunter's menu. And the list went on and on, a mind-boggling summer of the special touches she was famous for. Her new-found freedom brought tears of joy to her eyes.

She did have to admit that she missed the camaraderie of her staff, but they called her often and she had her beloved Jared and Prescott at her side. And best of all, her daughter waited in the wings for her move to New York, where she would finally unite with Lincoln. The only sticky area for her was the property she owned with Billy. And she was having a difficult time accepting her lawyer's recommendations.

She had reluctantly allowed her father's firm to file for complete ownership of the Baxter Avenue house and a fifty percent amount of the proceeds of Sconset House and the cottages, if Billy decided to sell them. In her heart, Camilla wanted to let Billy have everything because, contrary to what the lawyers had predicted, Camilla knew she would never live in Sconset again, and for this reason, she was negotiating permanent access to her family home in Hingham.

Camilla's legal counsel had argued back and forth with her about taking a portion of the yearly Sconset House profits, their argument being that she was, in fact, responsible for the restaurant's reputation. Staunchly saying that the place was Billy's inheritance, she stood her ground, only half-heartedly agreeing to the possible sale proceeds with the knowledge Billy would never sell Sconset House. He might decide to lease it, but he would never sell the property.

Sitting down to enjoy a sip of coffee, Camilla continued to hash over her present state of affairs and came up short when her thoughts drifted to Yolanda. She had no idea why the woman had made such an abrupt turnaround in her attitude. She could certainly understand why Yolanda had attacked her that night in the hospital and, to a large degree, Camilla agreed with her reasons.

The more she thought about it, the more confused she became. With a perplexed strain creasing her brow, Camilla reached for the phone and dialed The Hitchcock Gallery.

Following a rundown from Anne on what had sold and possible future commissions, Camilla was able to wedge in her question about Yolanda.

"From my lofty point of view, and it is lofty," Anne joked, "there are two reasons. First of all, according to Jasmine, Lincoln threatened to never speak to Yolanda again if she continued to treat you badly. And I have a feeling Jasmine let her know that you would never take her place as the mother who brought her up from infancy. You can imagine how Yolanda must have felt. She must have been scared she would lose Jasmine to you."

"Okay. So she's being civil now in order to protect her position. Right?"

"Well, I suppose so, but I don't think it's as callous or calculating as you're making it sound. And another thing to consider is Billy's performance that night in Lincoln's room."

"Yes?"

"Yolanda saw the tail end of it and she told me she felt great empathy for you when she realized what a weak man you had married in the wake of your heartbreak with Lincoln. She knew Billy was no match for a man like Lincoln, and since Lincoln was hell-bent on winning you back, she decided to support him."

"Anne, is Billy really that shallow, or am I making up a case against him to alleviate my guilt?"

"He wasn't that bad with you forming his very existence, Cammie. But when you were gone, the real Billy surfaced and despite his outward handsome appearance, he's pretty ugly."

"Being responsible for some else's behavior is a heavy burden to bear, Annie. I don't know how to hold that, you know?"

"Let Billy grow up, Cammie."

"I hope I didn't make him into the child I lost."

"So what if you did? Billy let you do it, which to me means that he wanted it that way. You met each other's needs, so to speak."

"I'm happy now, Annie."

"Great! That's the best news I've heard in a long time."

"When are you coming to see me?" Camilla smiled, leaning back in her chair, the worry creases a thing of the past. "I want you to see my new stuff."

"Are you serious? You've got canvasses ready to look at?" Anne squealed.

"Yup. So when will you be here?"

"Is tonight soon enough?"

"Dinner's at seven."

"See you then."

<hr>

Camilla was thrilled her dear friend had arrived so quickly. A knock on the door announced Anne's arrival at five and after receiving Anne's stamp of approval on her weight gain and healthy coloring, Camilla ushered her into the solarium where she left her at the doorway and went to the kitchen to join Jared and Prescott who were creating a wonderfully fragrant paella. Nervously, Camilla paced around the kitchen adjusting the plants and decorative pieces. When she knocked over a basket of letters, Jared turned to her and said, "Relax, honey. It's only Annie."

"But she's my toughest critic. She knows what the people like and this is my only means of support now, so you know…"

"The paintings are wonderful," Prescott pronounced, walking to Camilla and wrapping her in a gentle hug.

Long moments passed. Jared and Prescott happily scrubbed the shellfish for the final touches of the dish while Camilla sat at the breakfast bar nervously tapping a pencil on the surface. When she finally heard Anne's footsteps, she sprang to her feet and eagerly awaited the verdict.

"I feel as if I'm watching Picasso enter a new period. Should we call this orange?"

"Call it whatever you like. The paintings. What about the paintings?"

"I love them, Cammie. They're so full of life. Can I take the finished piece to the gallery?"

"No. I'm not ready for that. These are for next year. And they're only a start. I'm going somewhere with these colors, but I don't know where. I want to show the whole journey from the first piece. Does that make sense?"

"Of course it does. But you know me, always eager to show off your latest. I would like to take a photo of it, though, to send along to the Tate in preparation for your show next fall."

"Hmmm. I forgot all about that show. So it would be a year from this September?"

"Exactly. It's a big step, Cammie."

"It's a step I'll take," Camilla smiled, walking over to embrace her friend. "As long as you think my work's okay."

"Of course it's okay. I bet you showed it to Lincoln when he was here. What did he think?"

"I think he's a little biased, but he said it reminded him of my very early paintings."

"He loved them," Jared broke in. "For God's sake, lovey, you're considered to be one of the finest painters in the country. Accept that fact and go where you have to with your style."

"Nicely put," Anne nodded. "So what are you two dishing up over there?"

CHAPTER THIRTY-FIVE

S torm after storm blew in off the Atlantic during August, causing a generally testy environment to prevail in Sconset with
cocktail party after cocktail party forced inside to avoid the cold
spattering rains driven by gusty winds in over the cliffs. Business
at Sconset House prospered, however. Once the diminished staff
had made adjustments and added two extra servers, the season
moved toward its conclusion fairly smoothly, with capacity crowds
seeking inside entertainment.

Maeve and Billy became fairly open about their relationship,
with Maeve moving into the Yellow Finch and Billy spending most
nights there with her. The eyebrows that had been raised at the
start of the summer concerning their relationship were soon lowered as the topic ebbed to the background while the Sconset crowd
pursued its fun with a vengeance, squeezing in golf, beach, and
boating when the weather permitted and lounging in front of a
crackling fire with open book when forced inside.

Billy kept up his usual banter with his regular customers,
seeming to enjoy every moment he had at the restaurant. His

usual booming laugh burst forth from the cocktail lounge as in years gone by, and his late-night port and cigar ritual continued. Everyone missed Camilla, however, and as the season progressed and the late summer regulars arrived on-island, Maeve, who stood at the podium again, was forced to repeat the story of Camilla's illness over and over, her sense of hypocrisy mounting with each telling of the tale. She had no one to share her growing tension with, because everyone she knew sided with Camilla. In fact, Maeve's only remaining close relationship was with Billy, and while she reveled in their shared moments, her overall sense of isolation made her days almost unbearable. Consequently, she couldn't wait to get back to Ireland, her family, her paint brushes. Adding to her distress, she was late for her period, telling herself over and over that she couldn't possibly be pregnant, as Billy's lack of children meant he was probably sterile. Her morning queasiness didn't help her case of nerves at all.

Billy planned to close Sconset House on Labor Day, a full month early. The staff had mixed feelings about the early close and in response he decided to let them stay at Surf and Turf until Columbus Day if they wished, at which point the unheated cottages would be closed down and prepared for winter. Several decided to take him up on his offer, as they were assured of picking up end-of-the-season jobs at any of the many restaurants dotting Nantucket.

No one, not even Maeve, knew about Billy's upcoming court appearance, scheduled September tenth. His lawyer was working on an out-of-court settlement and Billy had high hopes the judge would laugh the whole thing off. But as the end of August came into sight, Billy was informed that things did not look great for him, and in response his drinking increased. It broke Maeve's heart to watch him damage himself, and she and Brian began looking out for him as a natural course of events. The drinking baffled Maeve. She thought they were happy together, but his wild consumption of alcohol had her doubting their love. Sometimes she wished she had never heard of Nantucket.

⊷⊱⊰⊶

Jasmine and Lincoln left for Florence on August third. Their motor trip through Italy was an excursion they had planned for years, and Jasmine was thrilled that her doctor had given her final clearance for the trip. Lincoln was considerably less enthused, since his worry over Camilla's health put a damper on the trip, and he left with a schedule of phone times every other day at which hour Camilla promised to be waiting for his call. Coupled with his natural dislike of disruption, Lincoln's worry felt like a black cloud hanging over their trip but he ultimately forced himself to appear to enjoy himself for Jasmine's sake.

Camilla secretly relished Lincoln's commitment to her. She wasn't used to anyone looking out for her particular needs, and Lincoln's concern along with Jared and Prescott's total devotion to her recovery touched her deeply, underscoring how much she had sacrificed emotionally in her marriage to Billy. Over the summer Jared, Prescott, Lincoln, Jasmine, and even Yolanda had spent hours with one another on the phone, all establishing a friendship Camilla hoped would continue when she moved to New York.

Camilla decided she wanted to do something special for Jared. After long whispered conversations with Prescott, she decided to buy Jared a little store for his hat business. Prescott had his eye on a quaint little spot on West Eighth Street that he had heard a while back was going to come on the market. It was operating as a little breakfast and lunch place, which Prescott felt, could be modified to include a hat showroom in the front. Both of them thought it would be perfect for Jared, and after numerous phone calls and clandestine faxing, Camilla purchased the spot for Jared in mid-August.

The day the keys arrived at the Hingham house, Prescott planned a lobster feast which he spent all afternoon preparing while Camilla occupied Jared in the solarium planning which pieces of furniture she would need shipped from the Baxter Road house to her new studio in New York.

At six o'clock Prescott called them to the dining room, where the table was set. Two shiny new keys had been placed on Jared's plate. When the news was out of the bag Jared was, for once, speechless. Following an expectant silence, his teary thanks filled the room and a whole new barrage of planning ensued. By midnight he had decided to return to New York with Prescott on Labor Day weekend to begin renovations at his shop, which he decided to call "Camilla's." Opening day was planned for October fifteenth, a date by which Camilla hoped she would be living in New York. The restaurant aspect of the shop would become a cozy nook in which customers could enjoy specialty teas and coffee concoctions along with breakfast and tea-time pastries while trying on hats or just relaxing. Little did they know that in a very short time the shop would become one of the trendiest spots in an already trendy neighborhood, with Jared holding court daily.

⇌

Camilla painted. A crate of the custom made canvasses she used arrived early in August, and by mid-month she had six paintings in various stages. The photographs Camilla used as reference pieces took on added meaning for her since Billy had carefully chosen her shots over the years on his treks. She meant to keep good thoughts about him in her heart as she looked over the boxes of pictures, some dating back twenty years, from which she composed her current paintings.

The Tate Gallery phoned with enthusiastic praise for her new painting and set a deadline of the following June for six pieces which would create the show's brochure and promotional materials.

Camilla was happy. Sometimes she felt her feet barely touched the floor as she moved around the home of her childhood, from her beloved studio in the solarium, to the telephone table in her room for her calls from Lincoln and Jasmine, to the eat-in kitchen that had become the heart of the home into which Jared and Prescott had breathed life after it had been virtually vacant for so long.

"Everything is perfect," Camilla sighed. The feeling lasted until September tenth.

On the morning of September tenth Billy made excuses to Maeve, who was left alone in the middle of the Sconset House closing and made the lonely trip to Boston for his court date, promising to take Maeve to a party at the Joslins' later that night. Meeting in the conference room held aside for lawyers and their clients, Billy was advised to accept a suspended sentence with two hundred hours of community service which his lawyer had set up to be served at Our Island Home, Nantucket's only nursing home.

Appalled, Billy asked for a few minutes alone with his lawyer, Dave Bosworth, and fumed, "I can't do that. Get me off the hook completely."

"Look, Billy, I've worked them down from jail time to alcohol rehab to this. Dr. Franklin holds a very prestigious position at Mass General and he was unwilling to move from his position that you jeopardized his patient's life while she was in the hospital. It's your final offer, and I suggest you take it. The hospital almost never loses and you're looking at hard time if we take it to trial."

"But community service at that skeevy place. My God, if this ever gets out…"

"You'll do the time in the off-season when your friends have long gone home. We'll keep it very discreet. No one will find out. And who knows? You might actually like it."

"Unlikely," Billy muttered as he signed his name to the papers and quickly left the building, not even bothering to shake Dave Bosworth's hand.

The flight home did nothing to settle Billy's nerves, and he stopped for a few drinks at the Faregrounds before driving home to Sconset. His wheels crunched over Sconset Houses's shelled driveway just as the cool fingers of an early fall fog took Sconset in its grip. Finding the front door locked, Billy walked the short distance to the Yellow Finch and found Maeve in her favorite overstuffed chair, her feet propped up on the matching ottoman.

"Why aren't you ready for the party?" Billy smiled with false enthusiasm, leaning down to kiss her.

"Billy, sit here with me," Maeve suggested, motioning him to the ottoman. "I have something to tell you."

"What is it, pumpkin? You look all tuckered out."

"I went to see Dr. Carver today and she confirmed my suspicions. We're due to be havin' a baby this coming March, Billy."

Billy jumped to his feet, causing the little shanty to shake with his force. "A baby, Maeve? I'm going to be a father?"

"You certainly are," Maeve smiled up at him warily.

"This is the best news I've ever had, Maevie-cakes!" Grabbing her by the hands, he dragged her to him and danced her around the tiny living room, her feet flying out in the air.

"Put me down, Billy. You'll be getting me sick again," Maeve wailed.

"Oh," Billy said, gently easing Maeve back into her chair. "So, the divorce will be final in October and we'll get married right away. Shall we do it in Ireland, my love?"

"That would make me so happy," Maeve smiled, wiping away tears of joy. "I wasn't sure how you'd react."

"I've been waiting for this for, oh, so long, Maeve. I'm going to be the best father you can imagine."

"I'm sure you will."

"Now, go get dressed. We're due at the Joslins in thirty minutes. And let's keep our news to ourselves until we're properly married. Okay?"

"You took the words from my lips, my love," Maeve said, rising from her chair. "I've laid out some things I thought you might like to wear."

"'Now this is the woman for me,' a very self-satisfied Billy thought to himself as he followed Maeve to their bedroom.

Billy's heart was so full of joy that night, he virtually forgot his earlier woes. The Joslins lived in a remote spot on Nantucket called Pocomo, a long winding trek from Sconset that seemed all the more circuitous because fog was obscuring the many curves along the way. Right at the Wauwinet turn-off a deer bounded in front of the car, scaring both of them as Billy had to veer sharply off the road to avoid hitting the animal.

Maeve breathed a sigh of relief when they entered the long drive and squeezed Billy's tiny MG between two oversized Range Rovers. "Thank God we're here," she murmured.

"I won't let anything happen to our little mother," Billy assured her as they moved to the house dimly aglow in the deepening mists. The evening's festivities were the traditional last hurrah for Billy's set. A few couples would return on Columbus Day, but tonight was the final event of a long list of summer parties. As such, the liquor flowed a bit more freely and the hors d'oeurves being passed around seemed all the more delectable. Around ten o'clock Billy, swaying a bit from the repeated toasts for a quick winter, found Maeve sitting by the French doors, gazing out at the Japanese lanterns bobbing around the patio in the mist. "A lovely theme for a painting," she whispered, looking up at Billy.

"I think you need rest, my love. Let's go."

With a grateful smile, Maeve joined Billy in bidding everyone farewell and they emerged from the sprawling summer home.

"The fog is pea soup," Maeve noticed.

"I've been driving in it all my life. Don't worry," Billy assured her, his speech slightly slurred.

"Let me drive home tonight," Maeve urged, trying to take the keys from Billy's hands.

"Absolutely not," Billy returned, holding the keys behind his back. "I'll get us home in a jiffy."

The little roadster made its way out of Pocomo and just as they were about to turn onto the Polpis Road, at the same spot where the deer had jumped in front of them earlier, a huge Expedition careened out of control around the corner, and in an effort to avoid the huge on-coming vehicle, Billy slammed full force into a telephone pole. Maeve hurtled out of the car where she slammed into a boulder. Billy went through the windshield. Miraculously, the falling electric wires missed both of the unconscious victims.

The occupants of the Expedition called 911 on their cell phone and within fifteen minutes Billy and Maeve were aboard separate ambulances racing to Nantucket Cottage Hospital. The EMTs phoned ahead and the two were immediately placed, side by side, in the med flight helicopter for transport to Boston.

CHAPTER THIRTY-SIX

The long summer of change finally drew to a close for Camilla. September tenth found her alone in her parents' rambling colonial mansion for the first time since the beginning of her recuperation. She relaxed in her favorite overstuffed rose dotted chintz chair at her phone table, luxuriating in a long mid-evening call from Lincoln. The abbreviated chats originating in Europe had given way to calls measured in hours since Lincoln's arrival home three days earlier.

Lincoln had filled Camilla in on all he knew about Brian's upcoming stay with him to visit Jasmine. Since Brian had never been to Manhattan, Jasmine planned to spend their first day visiting all the usual tourist spots, culminating with dinner at Tavern on the Green, the penultimate tourist eatery diagonally across the street from Lincoln's home. Sunday would include a picnic lunch in Central Park's Sheep Pasture and a Broadway show opening they would attend with Prescott and Jared in the evening. Since Brian had not planned a departure date, the rest of their time together would be a question mark.

Brian had been calling Camilla daily, with questions ranging from wardrobe choices to which flowers and gifts to bring for Jasmine. Both Lincoln and Camilla were delighted with the blossoming relationship between Jasmine and Brian and on the spur of the moment, Camilla decided to travel to New York with Brian.

Lincoln was ecstatic with the idea, and after repeatedly confirming that Camilla was well enough for the trip, they settled into their own plans, which consisted of hours of un-interrupted intimacy.

Camilla reveled in the moment, a satisfied smile on her lips following their conversation. The phone's ring interrupted her reverie and assuming it was Lincoln, she answered with, "Yes, my love."

"Hello? Hello? Is this Mrs. Smith?" an official sounding male voice asked.

Coming to attention, Camilla sat bolt upright and answered, "Yes, it is. And who are you?"

"I'm sorry to be bothering you so late at night, Mrs. Smith. I'm Dr. Anderson. Your husband was in an automobile accident earlier this evening on Nantucket and he and his passenger, a Maeve O'Connor, were airlifted to Mass General a short time ago."

"My God, Dr. Anderson. Is Billy okay?"

"No, he's not. He sustained a major head trauma and is in a coma. He did begin to come to on the airlift and called your name. You are Camilla, aren't you?"

"Yes. Is he going to regain consciousness?"

"Hopefully, Mrs. Smith. However, his high blood level of alcohol is not helping us at all. Does he have a drinking problem?"

"Yes, he does," Camilla sighed. "And Maeve?"

"Also in a coma. She was sent over to Brigham and Women's to stabilize the cranial swelling. Fortunately, she had not been drinking, but her physical injuries were more extensive. She was thrown out of the vehicle."

"Good heavens," Camilla murmured, now pacing as far as the phone cord allowed.

"I suggest you come in immediately. I surmise from the phone number I got from your answering machine in Nantucket that you're in my hometown, Hingham."

"Yes. I'll come right in. I'll call a cab directly."

"Come to emergency ICU, Mrs. Smith. Please hurry. We need a detailed medical history for Mr. Smith."

Camilla stood in shocked silence, the receiver still in her hand. A chill ran up her spine, leaving her trembling. With unsteady fingers Camilla dialed Lincoln's number and hurriedly filled him in. All Lincoln could do was take a deep breath and wish her well. All his fears of losing Camilla again flooded through him, constricting his throat, barely allowing him to utter his few words.

Feeling disconnected, Camilla hung up the phone, called a cab, and quickly pulled on jeans and a silk blouse. A buff colored blazer completed her ensemble, and grabbing her purse, she ran to the kitchen to retrieve the keys Jared had left hanging beside the patio door. With shaking fingers, Camilla fumbled with the locks, set the alarm system, and emerged to the front entranceway, where she sat on one of the two benches flanking the front door to wait for her cab.

⚔

Camilla's trembling subsided slightly as the cab whisked her into Boston and slowly the enormity of what had happened began to sink in along with the realization that Billy had gone to court earlier that day. Her lawyer had tried unsuccessfully to persuade her to attend the hearing, but she had firmly held her position that it was the hospital bringing charges against Billy, not her. How ironic that Billy would need the hospital just a few hours later.

Camilla knew that the accident, coupled with the alcohol, had not happened as a coincidence on the day Billy went to court. She wondered if Maeve had accompanied him, as she knew the situation would have been almost impossible for Billy to deal with alone. Camilla began to blame herself for his accident as she drew nearer to the hospital. She knew she should have pushed for dismissal of the charges.

The hospital's particular smell brought back Camilla's feelings of sickness and suffering. The mingled scents wafting through the emergency room had clung to her during her long stay there, blanketing her like a thick Sconset fog, blocking all other scents as fog blocks sight. Only recently had she completely banished the unpleasant sensation from her nostrils. And now, here it was again.

In a few short moments, Camilla found herself at Billy's side. Only his familiar shape beneath the covers and his large golden haired hands singled him out as someone she knew. Thick bandages swathed his entire head and there were tubes leading to monitors Camilla could not identify.

But he was alive. The steady beeps emanating from the heart monitor indicated that and Dr. Anderson and the nurses were guardedly optimistic about his chances for recovery.

After giving Dr. Anderson a history of every illness and injury Billy had suffered in the years of their marriage, Camilla was left alone at his bedside, the over thirty years of their relationship vibrating in the space between them. Unbidden memories darted through Camilla's mind. A young Billy gesturing toward the area they would make the cocktail lounge. An older, softer Billy bursting into their kitchen to share a golf triumph. Billy sighing with satisfaction after his first sip of coffee in the morning. Tears filling his sky blue eyes when another pregnancy hope turned to ashes.

Disgust freezing his features when she told him of Jasmine and Lincoln. Camilla sat staring at his inert shape, allowing the panorama of their relationship to play before her eyes.

Her heart warmed at the good memories and she cried anew at the painful. But nowhere could she find the thrill of passion she felt for Lincoln. One moment with him held more than all her years with Billy combined, and the realization saddened her. For the millionth time she wished she had sought Lincoln all those years ago and claimed him as her family. Idly, she wondered if Billy had found passion with Maeve.

But he had called her name. Camilla. The wife who, she felt, had driven him to drink too much. What was he trying to tell her she wondered as she flipped through her address book for his brother Jonathan's phone number.

Jonathan's voice, thick with sleep, greeted Camilla from his home in Greenwich, Connecticut. A Type-A personality, Jonathan pretty much ran the family's brokerage firm on Wall Street, coached his son's soccer team, took tango lessons with his wife and carried a low golf handicap. Concern sharpened his voice as Camilla's news sank in.

As it turned out, Billy's parents were at a financial summit in Singapore and had brought their other son Dan and his wife along with them. Jonathan and Camilla decided to keep the situation to themselves for the time being, and after jotting down Jonathan's cell phone and office numbers, Camilla clicked off, sighing to herself, 'As usual, it's all left to me.'

Billy's lifestyle, dominated by his decision to not work for the family's firm, disappointed his family, and while they all loved him, he was detached from their mainstream and would go for months without speaking to them. Judging from Jonathan's usual cordiality, Camilla assumed that Billy had not mentioned their marital situation to his family.

It was now two in the morning and Camilla settled back in her chair, alternately praying for Billy and Maeve's recovery and dozing off into the panoply of her marriage to Billy. At six the nurses led her to a lounge, where she freshened up and found hot coffee and bagels waiting for the anxious families of the ICU victims. It was strange to be on the other side of the bed, so to speak.

With a sigh, Camilla took her steaming coffee back to Billy's bedside and began her day long vigil.

At nine o'clock Anne called Camilla's cell phone. Lincoln had called several times and, checking the caller id and not knowing what to say to him she had not answered the phone. After three rings she clicked onto Anne's frantic questions. After filling her in on Billy's condition, Anne asked the obvious question, "Why are you there? And why aren't you answering Lincoln's calls?"

"Billy asked for me, Annie, on the med flight. And I feel responsible for this."

"How could you possibly be responsible for Billy's drunken accident? You weren't even there!"

"Yesterday was his court appearance, Annie."

"And?"

"It's my fault he had to go to court. I think I could have tried harder to stop the proceedings."

"Look, Cammie, Mass General wanted to make a point in its case against Billy. Their outrage was justified and by taking a member of the so-called elite to court, they appeared to be very, how would you say, egalitarian in their across the board stand against in-hospital harassment. There was no way they were going to drop their charges. There was simply nothing you could have done."

"But still, the whole situation Billy was in this summer was my fault, Annie."

"Absolutely not, Camilla. It was simply life unfolding. And be honest, Billy didn't waste any time finding his own happiness with Maeve. All of Sconset was buzzing about them shacking up together in Yellow Finch."

"I suppose, but.... "

"But nothing! Don't indulge yourself in this foolishness, Cammie. Lincoln's wild with worry. You won't answer his calls and he knows you're doing it deliberately. Don't hurt him over Billy just because he called out your name in a drunken coma. He probably wanted you to do something for him."

"You don't hold anything back, do you."

"That's what best friends are for, Cammie. You know I love you like a sister, and I don't want to see you squander your happiness on Billy Smith."

"Okay. Look, I'm going to stay the day and go home to Hingham this evening. Tell Lincoln I'll call him when I get in. I just have to see this through. It's as if I'm ending a long chapter in my life and I want to end it properly."

"I can see that. Just be careful, Cammie, and don't blame yourself. Understand?"

"Yes," Camilla sighed, clicking off and settling back to watch Billy's vitals signs glow and beep in his little cubicle.

CHAPTER THIRTY-SEVEN

F ollowing his call to Anne, Lincoln decided to take her advice and trust in Camilla. After all, he reasoned, if he could wait thirty years, another couple of days wouldn't make any difference. But what seemed reasonable in his mind was at extreme odds with his heart, which was clutched tight in his chest, a hard fist of fear waiting to open up and spread throughout his being. The sense of impending doom was familiar to Lincoln, and he coped with it as he always had by immersing himself in his sculpting.

And so he entered his studio, blasted a tape of his favorite Rachmaninoff, and worked on his latest piece, a sculpture of Zeus he had been commissioned to produce for the Greek Consulate. The towering figure had been roughed out and standing on an elaborate staging built with shelving to hold his tools, Lincoln began modeling the right arm complete with the traditional thunderbolt. Hoping to absorb some of the god's strength as he sculpted, Lincoln lost himself to the grandeur of the music filling the vaulted room and the powerful sinews his hands were bringing forth out of the marble.

Yolanda's voice startled him out of his muse and looking around bewildered, he found her standing at the base of the staging, hands on her hips, foot tapping impatiently.

Lincoln motioned her to turn down the music as he slowly climbed down to the floor level. "I wasn't expecting you," Lincoln began when the Russian master was silenced.

"I have news," Yolanda beamed, "and when you didn't answer the door, I let myself in with the key you insisted I keep in my purse. What's wrong with you?" she continued, focusing in on the grim set of Lincoln's features.

"Something's going on with Camilla. I'm probably overreacting, but I'm worried I'm going to lose her again."

"Okay, okay. Let's go make a pot of coffee. You look as if you need a cup and you tell me your story while I get the brew going."

"Good idea," Lincoln muttered as he followed his sister out of the studio and into the kitchen. Perched on a stool at the breakfast bar, Lincoln began as Yolanda puttered around assembling the coffee supplies and fishing in the refrigerator for eggs and bread. "Last night, right after Camilla and I made plans for her to come into the city with Brian this weekend, she got a call from a Boston hospital saying that Billy and his girlfriend Maeve had been in a bad accident on Nantucket and had been flown in. Supposedly, Billy came out of his coma for a moment on the flight and called for Camilla. She dropped everything, called me to say what had happened, and rushed to his side. And now all morning, she won't answer my calls to her cell phone."

"She's probably either sleeping or in some kind of crisis with her husband, Lincoln. She's still married to him. She's still obligated to be with him, brother. Get a grip. Camilla's doing the right thing."

"I don't care if it's the right thing. I don't want her with that man even if he's in a coma. Yesterday was Billy's court date and Camilla thinks he got drunk following it and feels responsible for him drinking too much and smashing up his car. I'm afraid her old sense of being responsible for every aspect of the man's life is kicking in and I feel threatened by it. What if he needs her to nurse him for months and months? I don't think I could take it, Yo."

"Okay. Number one: The man is from a wealthy family and I'd guess Camilla has already contacted them. I bet when they arrive on the scene she'll hand Billy over to them and walk away. They're able to pay for any care the man will need. Number two: the Irish girlfriend was in the crash with him. Further writing on the wall that their marriage is over. Number three: he's used to Camilla taking care of him like a child, so of course he'd call out to her. I can't think of number four, but I'm sure it will come to me."

"So you think I'm over reacting?"

"Yes, I do."

"You have a lot of faith in her, Yolanda. How did that come about?"

"Since I'm doing so well numbering, let me start with number one. Both you and Jasmine want her to be part of our family and you know family harmony is my first priority, so I had to make myself accept that. When you threatened to never speak to me again I realized I had to make a serious attitude adjustment. Number two, when she looks at you she brims up with love and it just spills out all over the place. What sister wouldn't want that for her lovelorn little brother? And three, I see a lot of her in Jasmine. In fact, some of Jazzie's greatest strengths are a mirror of Camilla. There's a lot to be said for genetics here, but my point is, seeing so much of my baby girl in her, I have to like he."

"You should tell her that."

"She already knows, but you're right, I should say something officially. And I have a fourth reason. She brought Jared and

Prescott into my life and something big is about to happen because of them."

"Is this the news you came over here to tell me?" Lincoln smiled; leaning forward as his sister placed two sunny-side-up eggs, toast, and coffee in front of him.

"I'm getting tired of all the travel involved with Celebrate! I've been training my assistant Georgina to handle my role on the road and I'm going to stay at home to handle the business side of the company. You know I'll make a few appearances at our big events like the national meeting of NAACP, but I'm basically going to stay home."

"If that's what you want to do, go for it, girl. But what does that have to do with Jared and Prescott?"

"You know Desmond Phillips?"

"The piano player?"

"Yeah. We've been friends since grammar school back in Brooklyn. We've been working on a CD for about a year and we finished the studio work last spring. The finished product is all original work Desmond composed with my lyrics. It's kind of jazzy and full of soul. So, I got the first discs last week and on a whim I took one to Jared and Prescott to listen to while they're busy getting Jared's new place ready to open. Well they had called me back about it before I even got home. They want to book us for opening night and any other dates we can give them. Isn't that great?"

"I'm so proud of you, darling," Lincoln beamed. "And I assume your usual recording company will produce the new CD."

"Right. *Dizzy and Yo* will be on the stands by Christmas, and who knows where it will lead?"

"Did you bring me a copy?"

"Of course. Here, I'll pop it in your player now." Pulling the CD out of her purse, Yolanda walked over to the sound system in the kitchen that controlled music throughout the massive condo and popped it in. In a moment the sultry strains of *Love Me Only* filled the kitchen, with Yolanda's deep, seductive voice perfectly accompanied by Desmond's light touch on the keyboard.

Lincoln leaned back, savoring the strong coffee and the mesmerizing sound of his sister's voice. "Beautiful, baby," was all he could say.

Leaning over to whisper in his ear, Yolanda continued, "And number five, Camilla is good luck."

"Yeah, my girl's good luck. What do you think, Yo?"

"I think that if she gets stuck with that loser, she's going to get a visit from your big sister. Don't worry, Lincoln. We're not going to lose her this time."

"I hope not," Lincoln sighed clutching his sister's hand.

⟞⟝

Lincoln was about to finish cleaning up the kitchen after Yolanda's departure when the phone rang. Hoping it was Camilla, he grabbed it on the first ring, not even waiting for the caller ID to pop up. It was Anne, calling to give him Camilla's message.

"So, she'll call me tonight?" Lincoln confirmed.

"That's what she said. She's in contact with Billy's brother and I assume he'll make an appearance soon. She's really wiped out, Lincoln. It sounds like she was up all night, so don't expect too much from her tonight."

"That's a tough one. She's got me kind of worried. I guess I'm just going to have to deal with it."

"You will, Lincoln. Let her make her final peace with Billy. Then she'll be absolutely free."

"Yeah. Thanks for getting back to me, Anne. You're the best."

"You're not so bad yourself. Talk to you soon. Bye."

Lincoln took Yolanda's CD out of the kitchen player and made his way with it into the studio after hanging up the phone.

Popping it in the studio sound system, he carefully adjusted the sound level and mounted Zeus's staging. Taking his tools in his hands, Lincoln returned to refining the god's strong arm to the strains of his sister's music.

CHAPTER THIRTY-EIGHT

D r. Anderson found Camilla napping in her chair at Billy's
side when he made his two o'clock visit. Nudging her shoulder gently, the doctor awakened Camilla to give her his news.
Groggily, she focused on him and, with fear widening her eyes
asked, "Is he okay?"

"Now that the alcohol has been flushed out of his system with
intravenous fluids, his reflexes have sharpened and his brain activity shows he's really just sleeping now. We think he's coming out
of the coma."

"That's great. When will he wake up?"

"Hard to tell, Mrs. Smith, but I have a suggestion to make. Why
don't you go home to Nantucket and pack up his pajamas, robe,
toiletries, you know, and bring them back to him tomorrow. He'll
be needing his things soon and I'm sure you need a good sleep in
your own bed. Okay?"

"Yes. I was going to return to Hingham tonight, but Nantucket
will be fine. I guess I'll cab out to the airport now and catch a
plane to the island."

"Great idea. I've been trying to place you, Mrs. Smith, and it just came to me. You own Sconset House, don't you?"

"Yes, my husband and I do."

"What a lovely spot. We were there last year for the Carpenter wedding."

"That was such a beautiful event. Everyone was so happy. Didn't they have fireworks off a barge after the ceremony on the verandah under the stars?"

"It was so sweet. Brought a tear to my eye, I must admit. It's a magical place, Mrs. Smith."

"I know," Camilla smiled through the wistful tears in her eyes. "So I'll see you tomorrow."

"Great. Check in with my service if you have any concerns."

With a final pat on Billy's hand, Camilla gathered her blazer and purse and departed the hospital for the cab ride to the airport. Fortunately, traffic was moving quickly and Camilla easily made the three o'clock flight on Cape Air to Nantucket. Her heart was beating in nervous anticipation as the little plane touched down at Nantucket Memorial Airport. Hoping no one would recognize her, Camilla hurried through the lobby and took the first cab in line. It was one of those golden early fall days on Nantucket, her favorite time of the year. The autumn angle of the sun hitting the water made the island actually glow with its golden light, attracting many artists and photographers eager to capture Nantucket's unique beauty. Ten minutes later, Camilla was on the front steps of Sconset House inserting her key into the lock of the restaurant.

Looking around her, Camilla was surprised to see a few people wandering around the tiny village center. Usually, Sconset was pretty much deserted in September except on the weekends. She surmised that more and more people were discovering Nantucket's glorious fall weather. The usually sticky lock gave Camilla trouble, and she was about to try the verandah door when the key finally turned and she entered the foyer where she had spent so many hours of her life greeting the Sconset House clientele.

Camilla slowly stepped into the main dining room, flipping on lights as she moved deeper into the restaurant. Everything seemed in order. The tables were stripped as they should have been and all the vases had been emptied and polished, waiting for next year's parade of flowers. Camilla didn't know exactly what she'd expected to find, but assumed she'd see some evidence of things left undone in her absence. Instead, everything was as she would have left it for the long winter. The realization that Sconset House had operated successfully without her tugged at her heart. She had put so much of herself into running the restaurant, she supposed her departure would have changed things somehow. But everything was perfectly in order and Camilla began to feel foolish about her secret pride that no one could run the place as she did. 'Perhaps Annie was right.'she mused as she made her way through the Lily and Rose Rooms to gaze out at her beloved view from the verandah. The click of the front screen door closing jolted Camilla out of her reverie and she turned to see Dottie at the doorway, blinking to see who was in the restaurant.

"It's me Dottie," Camilla called out.

"Camilla? Is it really you?" Dottie called out as she ran through the restaurant and caught Camilla in an exuberant embrace. "I saw the front door open and I thought I should check it out."

"I'm so glad to see you," Camilla hugged her back. "I thought you'd be long gone home to Maine."

"Billy let us stay at Surf and Turf for the month of September if we wanted to. He felt bad closing a month early and so Jessica, Jeremy, Dave, and I took him up on his offer. We're all at Twenty One Federal for the month. You know how it is out here in September. Everyone's looking for help. You look great, Camilla."

"I'm feeling like my old self, Dottie. I see you're just as pretty as ever. Any new romance in your life?"

"Well, actually yes." Flashing up her left hand, Dottie waved her engagement ring before Camilla's eyes. "I'm getting married. Can you believe it?"

"I'm thrilled," Camilla exclaimed. "Who's the lucky guy?"

"It's Dave."

"Dave? The playboy of Nantucket?"

"Not any more. One night he told me he was sick of watching me throw myself at, well, you know how many dates I have in a summer. And I told him I was sick of making excuses for him to the parade of girls out here looking for him all season. It started out as a fight and just as I was about to really let him have it, all of a sudden, I was in his arms and he was kissing me as if I was the only girl in the world. And it was as if he was the only guy in the world."

"I'm not that surprised. You two always did keep a close eye on each other."

"And we talked a lot on the phone last winter. It's kind of like that movie *When Harry met Sally*. We were best friends.

And now we're going to get married. He's already met my daughter and he bought a little pub up in Camden. So he'll be running the pub while I make my pottery. We haven't decided whether or not we'll return to Sconset House next year. Maybe we'll just stay up in Maine. The wedding will be in Camden on Thanksgiving weekend. Please say you'll come, Camilla."

"Of course I'll be there. I wouldn't miss it for the world. I'll bring Jared and Prescott with me."

"Fabulous! We only set the date last week. I'm kind of in shock. I never thought I could have this kind of happiness. You know?"

"I know exactly," Camilla smiled, hugging Dottie again.

"I've got to get into town for work," Dottie pouted. "You here for awhile?"

"Just til tomorrow morning. I have to bring Billy some things in the hospital."

"Right. How's he doing?"

"They think he's going to wake up soon, so I came to get him his things."

"I heard that Maeve's parents flew in from Ireland this morning. They say she'll live, but she's going to have a long recovery. I have to say that the whole staff was loyal to you, Camilla. We pretty much shut Maeve out after it was clear she was sleeping with Billy. And Billy. What he really needs is rehab, Camilla. He smells of booze all the time. Everyone, especially Brian, protected him all summer. It was like a family secret or something."

"Hmm," Camilla answered. "Tell the others I love them and I'll see them all at your wedding. Give Dave a kiss for me, Dottie."

"I will. I'm so happy you're well, Camilla. I just would have died if you hadn't made it."

"I'm a tough old bird. See you."

As quickly as she had appeared, Dottie was gone out the door, leaving a smile on Camilla's face. With barely a glance back, she followed Dottie's path and left the restaurant, closing the front door with a resounding slam. She would never return to Sconset House and over the years her regrets would fade into simply fond memories of her time there.

⋙⋘

The rose colored Explorer sat in the parking lot, and finding the correct key on her ring, Camilla started it up and made the short drive to her home on Baxter Road. As she wove through the narrow lane she slowed as she passed Yellow Finch. It was a cute little place and Camilla noticed new curtains in the windows. The window boxes overflowed with yellow and orange nasturtiums and more birdhouses than ever hung from the branches of the trees. The spot looked happy. Camilla gunned her vehicle and left the home of her husband's newfound happiness behind. She didn't know whether to be happy for him or angry with him.

Her undecided feeling continued until she was in the kitchen of her home. It was her space and always had been. It was obvious that Billy had not spent much time in the house, but had kept the cleaning service going. It felt as if she had never left. Wandering through, she slowly made her way to her studio and spent a bit of time inventorying her painting supplies left behind, making plans for the moving day soon to come. But what would she do with the house? The final divorce agreement awarded it to her, and now as she stood looking out to sea she knew that was the proper thing. She was the one who had lived in it year round all those years. Everything in the house had been selected by her. Her very thoughts, her dreams, her joys were imprinted on the walls. She loved the house, and for now would simply keep it.

As she gazed out over the ocean, she picked up the studio phone and dialed Lincoln. He picked up on the first ring as though he was waiting for her.

"I just came out of the studio," he said guardedly.

"I'm on Nantucket," Camilla answered. "I came to get Billy some things to bring back to him tomorrow."

"And then what are you going to do?" Lincoln asked.

"I don't know. I just don't know what to do next, Linc."

"Look, it's only Tuesday. Still plan to come to me on Saturday. Please."

"I'll try, my love, but I can't make a promise. I'm going through something very important here and I have to see it through. I truly love this house. I wish you could be standing next to me watching the golden sun shimmer on the ocean. Maybe I'll just keep it for visits. Or maybe I'll rent it out."

"I don't want to be in a house you shared with Billy," Lincoln announced. "Do you understand?"

"Yes, I do. But all those years without you, this was my refuge. This spot kept me sane."

"I can appreciate that, but we have to move forward. Don't turn back, Camilla."

"I'm not, Lincoln. But I have to gather the bits of myself that are here. I must."

"Just don't dwell on it. You sound tired. Anne told me not to demand too much of you so I'll say goodbye."

"Okay, Linc. I'll call you in the morning. I love you."

"I love you too," Lincoln murmured as he hung up his phone.

Camilla stood for a few more moments at the window, and on an impulse ran upstairs to don a sweat suit and sneakers. Soon she was trotting down the stairs to her beloved beach, which was shrouded in shadows with the sun hitting only the spots down near the watermark. A large crop of red rose hips dotted the embankment, a fond reminder of the early summer beach roses called Rosa Rugosa which cover the cliffs with pink blossoms. In years past Camilla gathered the hips and boiled them down with honey and white wine to make the most delicious pancake syrup. She had to force herself not to start picking.

Instead, she wandered out to her favorite big boulder, glowing in the sun near the water line. Climbing onto the big rock, she laid down on its sun-warmed surface and let the late afternoon sun soothe her. She let her mind wander from speculation about Billy and Maeve, to Dottie and Dave, to Jasmine and Brian, and finally to her beloved Lincoln. Just seeing him in her mind's eye made her tingle with love and passion for him. She hated that he sounded morose, and yet she felt unable to ease his mind while she had so many of her own loose ends to consider.

A familiar voice from the past softly called her name, and she sat up to find her mother's best friend and summer Sconset resident, Peggy Henderson, at the base of the boulder. Peggy's crown of white hair gleamed in the lowering sunlight and burnished her long, athletic build, which was always such a contrast to her mother's petite, almost featherlike appearance.

"Aunt Peggy. How nice to see you," Camilla exclaimed, jumping down from the rock and embracing the woman, who stood as tall as she did. "I heard you weren't on-island this summer."

"That's true, Camilla dear. Ward's mother had a hip replacement, so we spent the summer on the Vineyard at her place helping her get on her feet."

"Is she okay now?"

"Yes, she's the healthiest ninety-five-year-old woman I've ever known. Love the old girl dearly, but I had to get away for a bit of Sconset before the northeast wind takes over. Well, Camilla, I might have not been here, but the Sconset rumor mill kept me posted on your, how should I call it…"

"My situation?"

"Yes, your situation. But first off, how is your health? You know, I always told your mother that kidney situation when you gave birth was more than a chance occurrence. Of course you had kidney disease. What's the matter with doctors, anyway?"

"You ought to know, Aunt Peggy, being married to one all these years," Camilla laughed.

"True. True. I was planning to take a trip up to Hingham to see you, Camilla. Now, if what I hear is true about you and your long lost love, I have something I've waited a long time to tell you. It's about your mother."

"Oh my. Okay. Well, I guess it's been a day for revelations, so why don't we go up to the house. I'm sure I can find some crackers and those smoked mussels you love so much. I bet there's even some sherry in the pantry. And you can tell me your story."

"It's a long saga, so we best get moving,." Peggy said as the two women moved towards the stairs. "You look great, dear. I was expecting to see the worst, but you're glowing."

"Thanks, Aunt Peggy."

CHAPTER THIRTY-NINE

I t didn't take Camilla and Peggy long to get settled in the living
room, where they sat across from each other on the sofa and
loveseat with a smoked mussels and sherry snack before them on
the coffee table. Easing back into the overstuffed, pillowed sofa
Peggy began.

"I know a lot more about you than you might think," she said.
"Bear in mind that your mother and I were the closest of friends,
and when you had your baby and your father behaved so abysmally,
I was the only confidant your mother had as she endured her own
agony over the situation."

"Excuse me, Aunt Peggy, but my mother never lifted a finger to
support me then. She stood by my father as if his actions were her
plan all along."

"I know it looked like that, but she was truly in pieces over the
situation and, perhaps you aren't aware of it, but it threw an irrevo-
cable wedge between your parents that was never healed. It was at
that point that your mother moved into the guest room and barred
your father from her bed for the rest of their lives."

"Really? I hated them both so much at that point, I guess their own problems went right over my head."

"Understandably, dear. But, to understand your mother's situation, I must go back to our days as roommates at Columbia. It was the year after the war ended and we had become the closest of friends. Both of us studied journalism, although your mother was the most remarkable poetess. The Columbia publication printed her work continuously, and when her first book of verse was published, she gave a number of readings. It was at a poetry reading that she met your father.

"Hal was fresh out of law school, working in the district attorney's office in Manhattan. He fell for Dorothy on the spot and, I have to say, was rather obsessed about her. She was a dream, really. She was so petite and sweet with a crown of fluffy golden curls that she never tried to corral into one of the elaborate hair designs so prevalent at that time. She was a beautiful free spirit and, I believe, had a future as a great poetess."

"I'm sorry to disagree, but my mother was the most rigid woman I ever knew. It's hard for me to picture her as a free spirit. In fact, we looked so little alike that I had a childhood fantasy I had been adopted so I wouldn't grow up to be uptight like she was."

"You certainly do favor Hal, don't you? But you did get her curls and her artistic temperament. Well, you'll have to trust me on this, she was a happy free spirit before Hal. One day I was asked to write a bio for the campus newspaper on Filmore LaPierre, a jazz pianist of some note. He was playing at a little jazz club in the Village and, of course, I asked Dorothy to accompany me on the interview."

"Excuse me, but when my parents died I found a carton filled with Filmore LaPierre's albums hidden in the attic. I believe the box was marked 'Christmas decorations'."

"I'm not surprised. So, on a snowy New York winter night your mother and I sat in a smoky little jazz spot feeling so avant garde, watching Fil play. Your mother was mesmerized by him. He was, shall we say, of mixed blood. Perhaps you could have called him a Creole. Your mother couldn't take her eyes off his beautifully expressive hands teasing music out of the piano. When he had finished his set he joined us for the interview and while he cordially answered my questions, he couldn't take his eyes off your mother. They were positively enthralled with each other."

"This is shocking, Aunt Peggy!"

"I knew it would be. I went through a lot of soul searching as I made my decision to tell you this. But I do believe that children can be the vessels of their parents' lost dreams. I know that is true with my son, and I and I think it was true of you and your mother. Well, we went back to that smoky little club many times to watch Fil play. He and your mother became closer and closer, holding hands under the table and that sort of thing.

"Unfortunately, your lovesick father had to be lied to over and over on the nights we went to see Fil. I don't know exactly what your mother told him, but he apparently didn't believe her. And you must know, I don't think she cared all that much about Hal except that he was a good catch and would make her family happy. But love and passion? I've always felt your mother saved those things in her heart for Filmore LaPierre. Anyway, one night Hal followed us to the club, hiding in the shadows, and when Fil took Dorothy's hand during the intermission and she smiled up into his eyes, your father ran forward and grabbed your mother's hand right out of Fil's. Now remember, this was 1946. Fil stood back and watched your father hustle his love right out of the club. I ran along after them, but your father pushed me out of the way and sped off in his car with Dorothy."

"And then what happened?"

"Your mother was never too clear about the details, but apparently, Hal went to your grandfather and told him what your mother was doing. He offered to save her reputation by marrying her, and the following Monday Dorothy was wearing an engagement ring. She dropped out of school and was married within the month."

"And what about Filmore?"

"I don't know. Of course he went on to become a great jazz musician, but I don't think your mother ever saw him again. And, I want you to know that as far as I know, she never saw Fil other than when I was with her at the club. But I could be mistaken. Frankly, I hope I am."

"So mother really didn't have a leg to stand on against my father when I became pregnant."

"No, she didn't. I did hear them argue at a party they were giving once. I think your father had had too much to drink and said that if he hadn't saved her respectability, that you might have been almost as dark as Lincoln. He hated your lover with all the venom he had stored up against Filmore LaPierre. Your relationship with Lincoln was his worst nightmare come true. While it was all happening, he said you were just like your mother and he meant it in the worst possible way.

"Your father broke your mother's spirit and took all the joy and lightness out of her life. Her greatest joy was your artistic talent. Remember, she found the best instructors for you and went to great length to nurture your talent."

"She did do that, Aunt Peggy. And she must have suffered as I did."

"Yes. I'll bet you didn't know your mother was a poetess. I'll send you a copy of her book and some of the unpublished pieces. You'll get to know a woman you would have loved dearly," Peggy concluded, wiping a tear from her eye.

"Thank you for telling me all this. It makes my parents more human in my eyes and more deserving of my forgiveness."

"Your father was married to a woman he loved desperately but who never truly returned that love. It turned him into a bitterly driven man. And your mother pined away for her beloved pianist. Now, Camilla, I've told you all of this for a reason. Don't repeat your mother's history any longer. Let the break with Billy be clean and final. Go to Lincoln. Do it for your dear mother, my sister at heart. I only wish I had told you this story years ago."

"You couldn't have while they were alive."

"True. But I could have told you five years ago when they died. You could have had five more years."

"But I have the future, Aunt Peggy. And I can let go of the anger and resentment I've held in my heart against them. It's truly an American tragedy."

"Yes," Peggy agreed, rising to her feet in preparation for departure. "Don't ever neglect the compass of your heart. It will lead you to your destiny."

⋟⊢⊣⋞

The sun was setting as Peggy made her way up Baxter Avenue to her Sconset home. Camilla felt as if she had been slammed into by a truck. She sat for a long moment in numbed shock, slowly sipping her sherry. With a huge sigh she curled into the soft loveseat and pulled an afghan over her. She slept there in a dreamless deep sleep until awakening at five in the morning with a plan of action for the day in her mind.

Camilla quickly packed Billy's things, and after rummaging in the back of her closet found a linen suit that wasn't terribly baggy on her. After showering and donning the outfit, she cleaned up the snack remains of the night before, called a cab and was at the airport for the six thirty plane to Boston.

She wanted to complete her mission to bring Billy his belongings before calling Lincoln. And she wanted to get that obligation out of the way as soon as possible. She only wished he would wake up and tell her why he'd called out her name. In her scheme of ending things cleanly, that fact was leaving her open to questioning her motives and the situation made her terribly uncomfortable.

Without looking back, Camilla left Sconset.

CHAPTER FORTY

Camilla's plane was delayed when the ever present, fact-of-life, fall fog clung to the Nantucket Memorial Airport longer than was expected. At eight-thirty her plane was finally called and, jittery from too many cups of coffee at Hutch's, Camilla stepped into the tiny aircraft. As the plane lifted off the runway the fog followed suit, leaving behind another golden fall day. All Camilla wanted to do was get to the hospital and leave Billy's clothes for him. "And then what?" she kept asking herself.

An hour and a half after her takeoff, Camilla entered the surreal ICU ward and checked in with the nurses at the desk. With sparkling smiles they informed her that Dr. Anderson was with Billy and that she would be happy with his news. Leaving Billy's belongings at the desk on the nurses' suggestion, Camilla followed her usual route to Billy's cubicle. The curtains were drawn and Camilla stood outside the perimeter. To her surprise she heard Billy saying, "You mean Camilla has been here with me?"

"Of course," Dr. Anderson replied. "I sent her home to gather some bed clothes and toiletries for you yesterday. She should be back soon."

"But I don't understand. Our divorce is about to be final."

"I had no idea. We called her when the paramedic said you'd called her name out during the med flight. Sorry."

"I don't know why I did that. Do you know how Maeve O'Connor is? Please let her doctors know that she's pregnant. We were celebrating our news the night of the accident. I guess I celebrated a bit too much. It's my first child."

"Miss O'Connor is doing fine. Miraculously, the baby is also fine. She's facing quite a bit of physical therapy, but nothing that can't be healed."

"Thank God," Billy said.

Camilla felt the blood rush out of her, causing her hands and feet to tingle. She ran to the adjoining chapel which she had sat in several times and found a seat as faintness threatened to steal her consciousness. Bowing her head between her knees, she took deep breaths and felt stable enough to raise her head. Once the initial shock of the information she'd heard sank in, Camilla felt her heart open up like a brilliant red rose. He was going to have a child. The child she couldn't give him. "Oh, thank God,'" she murmured. And he was drunk with joy over the child.

"What am I doing here?" Camilla asked herself, and with a shout of joy jumped to her feet. At the desk she asked the nurses to call her a cab and, with an expression of pure relief on her face, she stood outside the hospital waiting to be taken to her home in Hingham.

"Isn't it a glorious day?" she asked the cab driver as she entered the vehicle.

"It would be a lot more glorious if those Fenway bums had won last night. Two games out in the middle of September. The story of my life," the cab driver replied.

With a giggle, Camilla gave the driver directions to her home and settled back to enjoy the scenery. As soon as she entered the Hingham House she checked her messages and found that Lincoln had called twice and Anne once. Getting out her address book Camilla looked up Yolanda's number and was lucky to reach her at home.

"Hello, Camilla," Yolanda cautiously returned Camilla's greeting. "What's happening?"

"I've made a decision and I need your help," Camilla began. "I'm coming into New York as soon as I can pack and get to the airport. I suspect I'll be at LaGuardia around two. Will you please make sure Lincoln is home? It's a surprise visit and I just want to make sure he's there."

"Is this a good surprise?"

"I hope he thinks so. I'm going to his place to stay, Yolanda. That is, if he'll have me."

"Thank God, girl. I don't know how much longer my brother could stay in the limbo you put him in. I'll make sure he's home. When you know your arrival time call me. I'll get Jasmine and we'll pick you up at the gate. We're going to have some celebrating to do with my brother tonight."

"Absolutely. I'll call you as soon as I have a flight."

"I'm going to get our girl now so we'll be back when you call us."

"Great!" Camilla fairly shouted into the phone as she slammed it on the hook.

Her next call was to Anne. "Annie, you won't believe what I overheard Billy say to his doctor."

"Don't keep me waiting," Anne eagerly answered.

"He was worried about Maeve because she's pregnant."

"Jared was right about that," Anne interrupted.

"Jared has a crystal ball now?"

"He said Maeve would get pregnant to snag Billy for good. Well, good luck to them. Right?"

"Right. They were out celebrating her news the night of the accident. It wasn't my fault, Annie. I'm not to blame."

"Of course you're not to blame. So now that you're off the hook, what are you going to do?"

"I'm flying in to New York to be with my Lincoln, of course. It's a surprise, so don't call him or anything."

"I won't. What else, honey pie. I can feel there's more."

"I got the Baxter Avenue house in the divorce, which will be final quite soon. I want you to call Lily Parker and have her put it on the market. I'll be calling the movers to go in and pack up everything except Billy's stuff, which I think he must have mostly moved to Yellow Finch. Then I'll have everything brought to New York. I hope the place sells fast."

"Are you sure you want to sell it, Cammie? You love that house."

"I certainly do. But Lincoln won't have anything to do with it and it will always remind me of Billy. It was my place of lonely winter longing for my lost true love, and I want to put that feeling way behind me. So please call Lily for me and wish me luck."

"Luck, lovey! Does this mean I'm going to have to open a gallery in Manhattan?"

"It certainly does. What do you think?"

"Start looking. I can see the logo now. Hitchcock Galleries, Nantucket and New York. Has a nice ring, doesn't it?"

"Sure does. I have to go, Annie. All I can say is you were right, as usual. And when we have a moment, I have a story to tell you about my parents. Aunt Peggy paid me a visit last night. You won't believe it."

"How about I come to New York next week? I have to meet with the Channing anyway."

"Perfect. I'll call you tomorrow. Oh, I left the house keys in the Explorer's glove compartment. Let Lily have them."

"Get going. Love you, Cammie."

"Love you too, Annie."

⚒

It didn't take Camilla long to pack and once again she found herself riding in a cab to Boston, this time to the airport. The shuttles ran fairly frequently to New York and she booked space on the two thirty flight to LaGuardia. After checking her bag Camilla pulled her cell phone out of her purse and dialed Yolanda. Jasmine answered on the first ring. "Camilla? Is it really you?"

"Yes, Jasmine."

"And are you really coming to New York?"

"I just checked my bags. I'm due at LaGuardia at three fifteen. Can you and your mother pick me up then?"

"Of course. Oh, Camilla, I'm so excited! Daddy's going to just die of happiness when he sees you at the door."

"And so will I."

"Do you have a minute?"

"They haven't called the flight yet."

"I wanted to ask you something. You know I call Yolanda Mommy. It dates back to when I was a little girl and so I'll always call her Mommy. But you're really my mother, so I was wondering, and I spoke to Mommy about it, I was wondering..."

"Would you like to call me Mother, Jasmine?"

"Yes. I had a hard time getting that out, didn't I?"

"Did you think I'd refuse you?"

"Well, I thought you'd like it, but I wasn't exactly sure."

"I guess we'll have to spend some serious time getting to know each other then because you need to know without question that your calling me Mother will make me about the happiest woman on earth," Camilla smiled through her tears.

"Great. So we have to get on the road if we're going to get to the airport on time."

"Don't rush. If you're not there I'll simply wait for you. Let's make sure we have a lot of fun today."

"Sounds good. See you soon... Mother."

"See you soon."

There was an unusual amount of turbulence on the flight to New York and Camilla, a reluctant traveler at best, was fairly woozy when they finally landed. She began to feel a bit better by the time she retrieved her bags. The fresh air outside the terminal helped a lot, so that by the time Yolanda and Jasmine arrived in the *Celebrate!* van, Camilla actually felt ready to ride into the city.

Jasmine chattered the whole way in about her upcoming weekend with Brian and her new interns at work. Camilla looked forward to seeing the restoration operation her beautiful daughter supervised. Suddenly Camilla's broad smile froze and she seemed to stiffen all over. Yolanda saw the change in the rear view mirror and quietly asked, "What's happening, Camilla?"

"I don't know, Yolanda. I'm scared to death all of a sudden. It's as if a cold wind passed by and sent chills up my spine. I'm just so..."

"Afraid of being happy?" Yolanda finished.

"Afraid that when I'm happiest, I lose it all. I've been in a forced state of... I don't know, I guess maybe calm... for so many years, I don't know if I can let myself feel true happiness."

"You're not alone, Camilla. I happen to know a man who also lost his happiness just when he was filled with joy. He too created a world for himself that protected him from feeling anything other than a controlled range of emotions. He's frightened, too."

"Can two people live happily ever after, Yolanda? I believed in it a long time ago, but then I decided it didn't really exist. The world makes up the fairy tale and then takes the dream away. I want to live happily ever after with Lincoln and I just don't know …"

"All you can do is take the risk. Look at the risks our Jasmine was willing to take to find happiness with you. She suffered and even went through major surgery to put that contented smile on her beautiful lips. I've never seen my girl so strong and confident. Right baby?"

"Totally," Jasmine nodded. "As soon as I knew about you, Mother, I knew I'd never be truly happy until I found you. I had to buck heads with my whole family to get to you. I had to keep my secret to myself when every moment I wanted to shout to the world that you were my mother. I had to risk your rejection to get to the happiness I feel now. Maybe you just had more steps to go through to reach out and grab the love of your life back. To claim what is yours."

"You're very wise, Jasmine. Both of you. So like my Annie. Well, I'm just going to have to…" Camilla faltered.

"Walk into my brother's life and live your love," Yolanda concluded.

"Live my love. Okay."

"And you'd better get ready because that's his building over there," Yolanda said pointing to a tall granite structure with broad panes of glass on each floor overlooking Central Park. "I'm just going to pull into the underground parking and let you out. We called the doorman and told him to let you go right up to Lincoln's floor. So, out you go. We're going to park and walk around the block before we come up. Go for it, Camilla."

"Please, Mother," Jasmine added.

Slowly, Camilla got out of the car and entered the pulsing bustle of Manhattan. It felt like a rush of energy surrounding her, giving her the strength to walk toward the entrance even though her tingling legs wanted to crumble beneath her weight. She turned back to see Yolanda and Jasmine giving her thumbs-up and wide smiles. *My family*, Camilla mused, a slow smile forming. *I have a family.* With that thought firmly in her mind, she identified herself with the doorman and was ushered through the richly paneled mahogany foyer, past tall beveled mirrors with elaborate floral arrangements on sideboards in front of them, to a large old elevator with the same rich mahogany on the doors. Knowing it was the only door on the floor, Camilla pushed the seven and glided up to Lincoln's place. When the elevator opened, a small hallway led to his door.

She slowly walked the short space in the quiet, dimly lit vestibule and pushed the button next to the door. She could hear a series of deep chimes echo throughout Lincoln's home and she waited. She waited for what seemed an eternity and was just about to ring the chimes again when the door opened with Lincoln's voice behind it saying, "Did you forget your key again, Jazzie?"

"I don't have a key yet," Camilla said and that brought Lincoln out from behind the door, where he stood in his dusty sculpting sweats, a bewildered expression on his face. Slowly, his eyes softened and the silly grin he always wore when he was with Camilla began to shape his lips. "Camilla," he murmured, reaching to take her in his arms. Camilla felt the old rush of heat he brought to her when they were close suffuse her, driving the quivering fears away forever. And when his lips met hers and his strong arms held her so tenderly, she knew she had finally come home. "Oh Lincoln, I love you so," was all she could think of saying.

"My love. My only love. You're home now. Come to me."

"Forever?"

"Yes, forever."

Made in the USA
Middletown, DE
08 July 2016